Sleep Like a Baby

ALSO BY CHARLAINE HARRIS

AURORA TEAGARDEN MYSTERIES

All the Little Liars
Poppy Done to Death
Last Scene Alive
A Fool and His Honey
Dead Over Heels
The Julius House
Three Bedrooms, One Corpse
A Bone to Pick
Real Murders

LILY BARD MYSTERIES

Shakespeare's Counselor
Shakespeare's Trollop
Shakespeare's Christmas
Shakespeare's Champion
Shakespeare's Landlord

SOOKIE STACKHOUSE / TRUE BLOOD NOVELS

After Dead
Dead Ever After
Deadlocked
Dead Reckoning
Dead in the Family
Dead and Gone
From Dead to Worse
All Together Dead
Definitely Dead
Dead as a Doornail
Dead to the World
Club Dead
Living Dead in Dallas
Dead Until Dark

HARPER CONNELLY MYSTERIES

Grave Secret
An Ice Cold Grave
Grave Surprise
Grave Sight

CEMETERY GIRL TRILOGY (WITH CHRISTOPHER GOLDEN)

Inheritance
The Pretenders

MIDNIGHT, TEXAS NOVELS

Night Shift
Day Shift
Midnight Crossroad

Sleep Like a Baby

CHARLAINE HARRIS

Minotaur Books
New York

This is a work of fiction. All of the characters, organizations, and events portrayed in this novel are either products of the author's imagination or are used fictitiously.

 For information, address St. Martin's Press, 175 Fifth Avenue, New York, N.Y. 10010.

www.minotaurbooks.com

Designed by Omar Chapa

Library of Congress Cataloging-in-Publication Data

Names: Harris, Charlaine, author.
Title: Sleep like a baby / Charlaine Harris.
Description: First edition. | New York: Minotaur Books, 2017.
Identifiers: LCCN 2017021226| ISBN 9781250090065 (hardcover) | ISBN 9781250090089 (ebook)
Subjects: LCSH: Teagarden, Aurora Roe (Fictitious character)—Fiction. | Murder—Investigation—Fiction. | GSAFD: Mystery fiction.
Classification: LCC PS3558.A6427 S58 2017 | DDC 813/.54—dc23
LC record available at https://lccn.loc.gov/2017021226

First Edition: September 2017

10 9 8 7 6 5 4 3 2 1

For Patrick, Timothy, and Julia, who provided the opportunities to educate me in how a new mother feels

Acknowledgments

My sincere thanks for the advice of Detective Robin Burcell, former police officer and current mystery writer. I'd also like to thank my beta readers, Dana Cameron and Toni L. P. Kelner (aka Leigh Perry), for their time and thoughts on how to improve this manuscript.

Sleep Like a Baby

Chapter One

I was standing at the backyard fence, watching the Herman twins (a) play with their dog, and (b) water their flowers. It was early in the morning, the only time of day it was tolerable for me to go outside in July in Georgia, since I was approximately as big as a rhinoceros.

"Are you past your due date, Roe?" Peggy called, as she tossed a ball for Chaka for at least the twentieth time.

I sighed. "Yes, three days." I'd put on my new cerise-framed glasses to cheer myself up. During my whole pregnancy, I hadn't cared which pair I wore, because I'd been so absorbed in my changing body. I'd pretty much gotten over that by now.

Lena turned the hose off and came over. (I had learned to identify them by their hair. Lena parted hers on the right.) Both the sisters were in great shape. They took turns walking the dog and they played tennis. Peggy and Lena were very self-sufficient in the household-repair department, too. I found them admirable and daunting.

"I was early with my twins," Lena said. "Three weeks. But they were fine."

"Where do they live now?" I knew they weren't local.

"Cindy lives in Maine, and Mindy is in Spartanburg."

"Peggy has a son, right?" I thought I'd met him once.

"Kevin. He's in Atlanta, but he's a doctor and a dad, so he doesn't have much spare time."

I nodded. It seemed like all I had now was time, but I could imagine being busy. Instead of waiting. And waiting. For the baby who would not arrive. I watched Peggy give Chaka a series of commands, all of which Chaka obeyed promptly.

"What kind of dog is he?" I said. He was clearly *something*. I'd never seen a dog like him.

"Rhodesian ridgeback." Lena smiled. "We got him from a rescue group. We couldn't have spent the money to buy a puppy. But he'd been . . ."

Suddenly, I felt a gush of warmth. *Oh my God,* I thought, embarrassed beyond belief. *I can't control my bladder. This is the rock bottom.*

"Well," Lena said calmly, her gaze following my own horrified stare. "This is the end of your wait, I think. Your water just broke."

For just one moment, I was the only adult in the room. In my arms was the most important person in the world, Sophie Abigail Crusoe, two hours old. *She's perfect,* I thought, marveling. *I'm the luckiest woman in the world.* My daughter had just been presented to me as a swaddled bundle. I'd barely caught a glimpse of her as she emerged from her nine-months residence. Yielding to an irresistible urge, I unwrapped her just to make sure every part of her was present and in order. She *was* perfect. And she didn't like being unwrapped. Sophie made her dissatisfaction known in no uncertain terms, and I hastily (and clumsily) re-swaddled her. I felt guilty. I'd made Sophie cry, for the first time.

My husband, Robin, stuck his head around the door and eased inside, as if he weren't sure he was welcome. "How are you?" he asked me for the twentieth time. "How is she?"

Robin might be feeling a little guilty, too, because I hadn't had the easiest labor. In our childbirth class I'd met a second-time mother who'd told me she didn't know what all the big fuss was about. She'd felt like she had indigestion for an hour; then her baby had popped out.

About midway during the twelve hours it had taken me to bring Sophie into the world—twelve *very long* hours—if that woman had walked in my room, and I'd had a gun, I'd have shot her dead.

But it had all been worth it.

"I'm fine," I said. "Just tired. And she's so great. All eight pounds." I held her out to him, smiling. "And she has red hair."

Red-haired Robin took Sophie as carefully as if she were an ancient Ming vase. He looked down at the tiny face, and my heart clenched at his expression. He was totally smitten. "Can I put in a moat around our house, and build a ten-foot wall?" he asked.

"I don't think the neighbors would approve," I said. "We'll just have to do the best we can to keep harm away from her." I tried to stifle a yawn, but I couldn't. "Honey, I'm going to sleep," I said. "You're on watch."

Even as a mother of two hours' experience, I was sure one of us should be on duty at all times.

As I drifted into sleep, feeling I deserved it for a job well done, I counted all the people who already loved Sophie: my mother, her husband, Robin's mother, Robin's siblings, my half brother, Phillip . . . and I felt so blessed that Sophie had been born into this protective circle.

Though the moat and fence seemed a wise precaution.

Chapter Two

Two months later, I had put that notion out of my head and was even able to laugh about it. A little. We'd resumed our lives, but with a huge difference. The central core of our existence was Sophie: her needs, her wants, her well-being. Though we were on the old side to be first-time parents (I was thirty-seven, Robin was forty), I felt we were coping like champions. On the whole.

Robin would get up with Sophie at night, bring her to our bed, where I would nurse her. I'd dive back into sleep while he changed her diaper and put her back in the crib. I would get up early in the morning, and take care of Sophie until noon or two, when Robin would have finished work. Then he'd give me a break for a few hours. Sometimes I took a nap during that time, sometimes I did a household chore. Sometimes I just read.

Phillip, who lived with us, donated the odd hour or two snatched from his busy high school schedule, so I could go to the grocery without taking the huge bag of necessities that a baby required. A couple of times, my mother came over when Robin had to speak at a luncheon or a signing.

By trial and error, we were able to provide full-time baby coverage without extreme exhaustion . . . up until the time Robin had to leave for Bouchercon, the world mystery convention.

I came in the front door carrying a package of diapers. I'd taken Robin's car. Our two-car garage was more like a one-and-three-quarters car garage, and it was so nerve-racking to park side by side that one of our vehicles was usually left in the driveway.

After depositing the diapers in Sophie's room, returning to the car for the other bags, and checking again that the baby was still asleep, I joined Robin in our bedroom, right across the hall from Sophie's. Robin was packing. He was so methodical and careful about the process that I enjoyed watching him. Also, I'd found something I wanted to show him.

"Look," I said. I flourished the bouquet of yellow roses.

"Who sent you flowers?" he asked, looking up from folding his shirts.

"The card was blank." I looked at it again, stuck on its plastic prong. No, I hadn't missed anything. "I checked it twice."

"What florist?" He stood back and looked down at the suitcase, frowning slightly. He was reviewing his mental list of the items he'd packed. I didn't talk until he gave a decisive nod.

"Blossom Betty's," I read. That was the logo on the card. "Where's that?"

He picked up his phone and did a quick search. "It's in Anders," he said.

"Huh. Weird." Anders was halfway to Atlanta. Lawrenceton had once been a small town some distance out of Atlanta, but the space in between the two on the map was rapidly filling up with bedroom communities. Anders was one of those.

"They're really pretty," I said. "You like roses, right? Especially yellow ones? You said that in an interview. So I'm guessing that someone meant to congratulate you on the nomination."

"By sending me flowers?" He looked doubtful. Then he shrugged and coiled up another belt to place carefully in the middle of the bag. "Okay, that's it except for my shaving kit," he muttered. He looked at me with a resigned face. "You have to quit reading my interviews. I've said some weird things when I felt under pressure."

I went to the kitchen to put the roses in a vase. While I arranged the flowers, I realized I was feeling a bit sluggish. Not quite ill, but not really well, either. I was glad when we turned in for the night and I could legitimately crawl under the sheet. I was restless all night, but toward dawn I fell into a heavy sleep.

When I woke, Robin was already shaved, and he'd combed his unruly red hair. I was startled that I'd slept so long. I scrambled out of bed, with a hazy feeling that I was starting the day off on the wrong foot. In honor of his departure, I went about toasting some English muffins and scrambling eggs.

I caught a glimpse of Phillip as he grabbed a muffin on his way out the door. His friends Josh and Jocelyn Finstermeyer were already parked outside.

Robin perched on a barstool, enjoying a cup of coffee and a hot breakfast. The hot breakfast was a little unusual, I admit. I feel I am doing well to even start the coffeepot, most mornings. I turned away from the plate I'd prepared and coughed into my elbow.

"You're sick," Robin said.

"Oh, maybe a little cold," I said.

Robin touched my forehead, and went into our bathroom, reappearing with a thermometer.

I had a low-grade temperature. "It's nothing," I said, with forced cheer.

Robin looked at me sharply. "I'll cancel my flight and my hotel." He meant what he said, but I could detect his disappointment. He had a panel this afternoon with some of his idols, and the awards banquet would be tomorrow night. Ever since the day he'd gotten the phone call from the nominating committee, Robin had been walking on air.

For the past twelve years, Robin's sales had gained momentum, but he'd never before been nominated for more than a minor award or two. This year, for the first time ever, Robin was on the highly prestigious Anthony ballot. Only my reluctance to take a small baby into such a public venue had kept me from traveling to Nashville with him. Robin's friend (and best man at our wedding) Jeff Abbott had promised me he'd film Robin's acceptance speech—if Robin got to make it.

After I'd read the other nominated novels, I thought *Panel of Experts* had a real shot at winning. It was Robin's best book to date; plus (and this never hurts), he was a popular and respected writer.

"You're going," I said firmly. I stared Robin down across his suitcase. He was getting on that plane.

To give him credit, Robin was still dubious. "I'm worried about you. I don't want you to get sicker. Maybe call the doctor and see if you should even be breast-feeding?"

I hadn't thought of that. Sophie and I were a package deal until I weaned her. She would not take a bottle, which made me curiously proud, but it was actually quite inconvenient.

Robin, who'd been looking at me with baffled concern, brightened. "Listen, you want me to call that woman your mom hired? Who came every day after Sophie was born?"

"Virginia," I said.

My mother had figured home help was the best assistance she could give me. Though I had initially resisted the idea of sharing my first few days with my baby, I'd given in when I realized how exhausted I was. Virginia had had the energy to put a meal on the table and do the laundry as well as take care of Sophie's diaper changes while I took a nap and Robin tried to catch up on his work.

At that time, Virginia had stayed from 8:00 A.M. to 5:00 P.M. for five days. I'd recovered from the birth as quickly as I had because Virginia picked up the slack. Though I'd appreciated all Virginia's help, I couldn't say I'd bonded with her.

This morning, I figured it would be better to hire Virginia and not really need her than to go without her (possibly essential) help. I didn't often get sick, but when I did, I did a good job of it. If I was even thinking of going back to bed when Robin left, I'd need Virginia.

Robin checked his Contacts list and called her on the spot. He liked to walk around while he talked on the phone. He wandered into Sophie's room to look at her sleeping, and then down the hall, all the while exchanging a quiet dialogue. When he came back into the bedroom, he was beaming. "Her last job just ended. And she's willing to stay nights instead of days. If you're getting sick, your temperature will be going up at night. I'll only be gone till Sunday afternoon." He was much happier now that he could leave with a clear conscience.

"Do we still have the bed she used?" My mother had loaned us a folding bed. Phillip had the second bedroom, and Sophie the third, so Virginia would have to share with Sophie, as she had before.

"Aida told me to keep it for a while, just in case. I'll get the foam slab," Robin said. We'd bought it to make the folding bed a bit more comfortable. "Won't take me a minute to set it up, and if you tell me where the sheets are, I'll put them on."

The plus side to owning an older home (and one of the reasons I'd bought this house) was that all the rooms—including the bedrooms—were really sizable. Virginia wouldn't be cheek by jowl with the crib.

"The sheets are in Sophie's closet on the second shelf," I told him. While Robin took care of the bed, I called my ob-gyn, Dr. Garrison. Her nurse relayed my questions and called me back in five minutes. We had a conversation about Sophie's risk in being close to me, and how I could minimize the chances of her getting whatever it was I was coming down with. I was punching the "end" icon when my husband reappeared.

"What did Dr. G say?" he asked.

"My milk is okay. I should wear a face mask when I'm holding her, wash my hands thoroughly and often, and minimize contact. So it's good Virginia's free."

"Do we have face masks?"

"You had some you wore when you mowed the yard. They're in the garage, third shelf, middle."

"Great!" He hustled out to bring them to me. "Anything else before I call Uber?"

"Can you check the mailbox? I forgot yesterday." Sophie was making her "eh, eh" noise, which meant I'd better get in there quickly or the dam would break. I pulled on a mask.

As I finished putting her sleeper back together, Robin was flipping through the catalogues and letters, putting most of them in a pile for the recycling bin.

"Polish rights," he said after a quick glance. "I'll take care of them when I get back."

He opened a large envelope, and shook out the contents. Several pieces of mail landed on the end of the table, all of them hand-addressed and battered-looking.

Fan mail.

From time to time, The Holderman Agency accumulated enough letters for Robin (sent by readers who were savvy enough to look up his representation) to throw them in an envelope and send it along. I counted five letters and a book. Robin opened the book first, read the inscription, put it down. "Self-pubbed," he said. "But I like the writer." Robin sorted the envelopes in quick succession, tossed two of them, and opened the remaining three. He smiled at the first letter, and the second letter was okay, too. But his face darkened as he opened a greeting card. "What is it?" I asked.

"Betty is thinking about me," he said dryly. "I have no idea who Betty is."

Every now and then, Robin got some fan attention that was a little too intense. "You're just so sexy," I said, and grinned at him. Sophie and I settled in the rocking chair in the corner to begin our ritual.

Robin grimaced before he tossed the card. He put aside the other two to answer.

Sophie was too absorbed in glugging my milk to note the mask.

Thirty minutes later, Robin's Uber ride arrived, and he left, blowing me a kiss from the doorway. I didn't blame him. I was toxic. Though I hadn't told my husband, because he was already worried, I was feeling worse by the hour.

The day dragged along. I got a couple of phone calls, one from my mother, who wanted to know how Sophie was, and one from the Friends of the Library asking me to donate something to the bake sale. I watched Sophie, read a little, and cleaned away the breakfast dishes. I felt useless. My energy level was at zero. I kept waiting to perk up, but I didn't.

Phillip got home at four. "Hey, Roe!" he yelled. "Where are you?"

"In the bedroom," I called back, and my voice came out scratchy. I'd made myself sort the laundry, but I was moving at a snail's pace.

Phillip stood in the doorway, looking at me critically. "What's up? Robin texted me and told me to come straight home after school. So I got Josh to drop me off. Though I was planning to go the library to study." A hint of accusation, there.

"Phillip," I said, "I'm going to be really frank. I need your help, and I'm going to need it until Robin gets back. I'm afraid I'm sick, and I'm getting worse. I can't take care of Sophie by myself. Virginia Mitchell is coming to stay at night, but please be here when you can."

This is one of the great things about my brother. He didn't whine or protest. "Sure. I love the munchkin," he said. "Except for my volunteer work, I had no plans for tomorrow."

He did love Sophie, though he was still nervous when he handled her. Now, he shifted from foot to foot. He was going to ask for something. "I do want to ask you if it's okay if Sarah comes over tomorrow night. She hasn't ever seen *Spy,* and since we Tivoed it, I thought . . ."

"Sure," I said. I added cautiously, "Unless something else happens in the meantime." I picked up a load of darks and carried it to the washer-and-dryer closet in the hall. Though Sophie was napping, the sound of the washer had never bothered her.

That task done, I lay down, which was very unusual for me. Being prone was such a relief, I realized I was beginning to feel very miserable indeed. I hovered between sleep and wakefulness for at least an hour. When I glanced at the clock, I knew Sophie would be stirring soon. I dragged myself to my feet. I had better get up and moving.

Robin should have had his panel by now. He would be sitting at the signing table. I hoped he had a long line. I wanted him to have a great time . . . and I wanted him to win. I asked myself if I regretted having sent him off to Bouchercon: surprisingly, no. Good for me! I gave myself a mental pat on the back.

While the dryer did its job, I put a pizza in the oven for Phillip and me; a one-step instant supper. He was in his room on his computer, but he'd left his door open, a great concession.

Then I heard Sophie crying. I plodded back to her room after washing my hands. And putting on a pair of the disposable plastic gloves I'd unearthed, the ones I used for icky housekeeping jobs. And pulling the mask over my nose and mouth. This time, Sophie howled at the sight of me. I lifted the mask and smiled; that calmed her down. But I had to put it back on, and my daughter was *not* happy with my odd look. I changed her diaper very slowly, and re-snapped her sleeper, which took twice as long as normal. She seemed to weigh five pounds more as I carried her over to the rocking chair in the corner and got ready to feed her. Midway through, I heard the timer go off for the pizza, and I called to Phillip to get it out of the oven.

"Go on and eat, if you want," I added. "I'm in the middle of feeding Sophie."

Another thing Sophie didn't like was me raising my voice while I was holding her, I now discovered. But after a minute or two, she quit fussing and latched back on to my breast. For the moment I was happy simply being in that rocking chair and looking down at our child.

Being a mother was still a miracle to me, and taking care of Sophie was nothing like I thought it would be. As an only child with few relations, I'd never been around babies much, but I'd learned a lot in our short time together. The cycle of caring for her was simple but taxing, as gazillions of women since the dawn of time had discovered.

Change her, feed her, burp her, put her down for her nap. Now that she was two months old, Sophie was often staying awake for a while between naps. She was looking around her with some purpose. It was wonderful to watch her arms and legs wiggle and thrash, or to see her attempt to reach up for her mobile or a toy.

Until this evening, watching her every move had been endlessly intriguing. But right now, I felt so listless and thickheaded I couldn't enjoy much of anything. I put her on a blanket on the floor and watched her flail around for maybe twenty minutes, talking to her in a nonstop stream so she would know I was close. I was hardly aware of what I was saying, to tell the truth.

I was about to call Phillip to lift her and lay her down in her crib—she was showing signs of getting tired—when I heard the front doorbell chime.

"I'll get it," Phillip called. I heard him talking. Then Virginia was looking at me from the doorway.

Virginia Mitchell, who'd told me she was twenty-three, was an African American woman with close-cut hair. Today she wore cropped running pants, an exercise bra under a complicated tank top, and a thin zip-up jacket, which she was removing. Virginia's narrow feet were tucked into high-end running shoes, and her glasses were clearly sports-friendly. She had a large bag slung over her shoulder. I remembered that: it was just as large as mine, and just as shapeless.

Virginia didn't look like a babysitter or household help. She looked as though she sold pricey athletic gear at lululemon. "Roe, you don't look too good," she said.

I had no doubt I looked as bad as I felt, but at the moment, I didn't care about anything but my increasing awareness that I was really ill. "Good to see you again. Thanks for helping us out in a crisis," I croaked. I began the laborious process of getting to my feet. "Sophie's fed, changed, and she's had some playtime. She should be tired in a minute."

"She's grown so much in two months! And she's sleeping through the night, your husband told me?" Virginia was already squatting down to smile at Sophie. Sophie looked interested.

"Sometimes six hours straight," I said, making an effort to keep on track. "I'll feed her one more time before I turn in for the night. If she wakes up, see if patting her doesn't put her out again. If it doesn't, bring her into my bedroom. I'll wear a mask. The doctor says it should be okay. The cat has her own door now, so she won't have to be let in or out." Moosie, my deceased sister-in-law's pet, was a sweet but timid creature that had never exactly become "our" cat. But she did live with us. Moosie came in and out of the cat door on her own schedule, emptied her bowl regularly, and every now and then demanded lap time.

"I think I remember you feed her in the morning?" Virginia said.

I nodded, feeling my head ache with every movement.

Virginia looked at me narrowly. "How's your mom? She been in to see you today?"

Not too surprisingly, my mother had been a frequent visitor right after Sophie had been born, and she'd also been responsible for hiring Virginia, on recommendation of a friend. "Mother's fine," I said faintly. "But she and John are at his family reunion in Savannah."

"She's not even in town? When do you think she'll be back?"

"Couple of days." At this point I hardly cared. I got the message; Virginia was anxious to identify an adult family member close at hand, in case I got much sicker. But she wisely let the subject drop.

"Do you want me to fix you some supper? Maybe a salad? Or some yogurt?" She was settled on the floor beside Sophie.

I had to repress a gag. "No, thanks. I heated up a pizza for Phillip and me, but I can't eat it. If you're hungry, half of it's yours." My bed was calling my name. "If you don't remember where something is, just ask me or Phillip. I'm going to lie down now."

"Anything in particular you want me to do while Sophie sleeps?"

"I am so glad you're here," I said sincerely. "I just need you to be in charge of the baby. And if Phillip doesn't put the pizza away . . . if there's any left . . . I'd appreciate it if you'd stick it in the refrigerator. And there are clothes in the dryer, but nothing that really needs folding. There's SmartWater in the pantry, and other drinks and snacks. Help yourself."

"If you need me, call me. The roses are so pretty."

"What?" I drew a blank for a second. "Oh, the yellow ones. Yeah, I don't know who left those."

"The florist didn't know?"

"Found 'em on the doorstep."

"If the florist didn't ring the doorbell, I guess they were hand-delivered by the sender," Virginia said sensibly.

I hardly cared who had sent the flowers or why they'd been abandoned on the doorstep. I just wanted her to leave me alone.

"I'm just going to rest a little, now that you're here," I said, trying to suppress the longing in my voice.

"You don't look like you feel very well at *all.*" Virginia was obviously anxious.

"I really don't," I said. "But I'll do my best not to give you any germs."

"Climb in bed and don't worry." She leaned over the baby, smiling. "I'll take care of Miss Sophie."

I could have kissed Virginia's feet, but instead I gave her a more socially acceptable grateful nod before I tottered across the hall. I had made the bed this morning, which seemed like a hundred years ago. I eyed it with almost indecent anticipation. As I pulled off my clothes and put them in the hamper, I realized I was shaking. I slipped into my favorite nightgown. Despite what I had told Virginia, I crawled between the sheets and was officially in bed.

I hadn't felt this ill in years. *You've got the flu,* I admitted. I wondered, in a dull, remote sort of way, how I was going to cope for the next few days, even with Virginia's help. I was shivering so much I pulled the covers up around my neck. I'd opened the book I'd left on my nightstand, and I planned on reading. But then I thought I'd just lay it down for a second. And I was out.

When I surfaced, Phillip was standing by the bed looking down at me.

"You look like one of the Walking Dead," he said, after a comprehensive scan of my face.

"Oh, thanks. That helps my morale."

"Maybe one of the fresher zombies from *FTWD,*" he conceded.

I blew my nose and tossed the tissue into the wastebasket I'd positioned beside the bed. "That's one of the things you don't say even if you think it, Bubba. Virginia and Sophie doing okay?"

"They're fine," he said. "Do you want me to stay home from the cleanup day? I'll only be gone from ten to two. But you look pretty feeble."

I'd completely forgotten that Phillip had promised to help at the park cleanup day tomorrow. Father Aubrey Scott had challenged our youth group to put in so many community volunteer hours a year. He'd pledged that our church would take a part in the "Clean the Park" program this Saturday, in anticipation of the Halloween celebration next month.

"You can't let Father Scott down," I croaked. "I can manage taking care of Sophie by myself for a few hours. Virginia's coming back tomorrow night."

"I'll come straight home from cleanup," he reassured me, looking a little self-sacrificing. It didn't take a detective to figure out he'd had more plans for Saturday afternoon. I rustled up enough energy to thank him appropriately. He patted me on the arm. "I'd hug you, but, germs," he said.

Virginia knocked on the doorframe awkwardly, because she had an armful of the world's most beautiful baby, who was making unhappy noises. "Someone's hungry," she said, smiling. "You ready?"

I sat up against the headboard and began to unbutton my nightgown. Phillip yelped "Hold off!" and exited the room as if he were on fire.

I had the mask and the gloves handy, and I pulled them on before I took the baby. Poor Sophie. She must have thought her mother was very odd. But since she was seriously hungry, she didn't object to the mask. I popped out my boob and got her situated on a pillow across my lap. As I looked down at her, I marveled at the reddish fuzz on her lovely round head, the curve of her plump cheek, the grip of her tiny hands.

Having her had been the worst physical experience of my life. When I remembered it, I shuddered. But as I looked down at the prize I had received for a few hours of suffering, I knew I would have gone through twice the pain to have my baby. Considering the ages of her mom and dad, Sophie might well be an only child, but I was not troubled by that. I was lucky to have a baby at all, because for years I'd believed I wasn't fertile and would never have a child. I was so in love with her.

Big love notwithstanding, by the time Sophie was through all I was able to feel was my own misery. She was full and wakeful and wet again. Virginia, who'd glanced in a couple of times, deftly scooped Sophie out of my arms. I stripped off the gloves and the mask with some relief, and rebuttoned my nightgown.

"After I burp her and change her, I'm going to put her under the activity station," Virginia said. "Let her enjoy some wiggle time. Can I bring you anything? Some fruit juice?"

I pictured a glass of apple juice. I didn't feel nauseated. "That sounds like a good idea," I said. "Thanks so much." I'd always heard nannies were just supposed to take care of the baby in their charge, not act as maids. When Virginia had shown herself willing to cycle the laundry through on her first stay with us, I'd been impressed.

"Your brother is a nice-looking boy. Polite." She had brought me a glass of juice. She stood in my doorway, looking across to Sophie's room to watch her having "awake" time.

"He is," I agreed. The cold fluid felt good on my throat, though I shivered even harder. I rearranged the pillows bolstering me up so I could lie flat, and pulled the covers up to my chin again. “We’re glad to have him here.” *Almost all the time,* I added silently. From being the parents of no one, we’d become in loco parentis for Phillip when he’d run away to live with us, and now we’d added our very own infant. From footloose and fancy-free, to moving in together, to adding Phillip to our family, to getting married. *And* having the baby. Within less than a year.

That was a lot of life.

I managed to stay awake to read, though I didn’t enjoy it much. I had to read through the same passage over and over to get the sense of it. What I needed was a book I’d read before. When I was ill, a familiar book was a better companion; but I didn’t have the energy to go to our home library, which lined the walls of Robin’s office. I turned on the television with the sound down low and closed captioning on, and watched a show about law enforcement in Alaska. I couldn’t have told you what had happened, when the closing credits ran.

Virginia came by the door a few times. I realized I could call her if I needed her, but she was here to take care of the baby, not me. It took me ten minutes to talk myself into crawling out of the bed and staggering into the bathroom, where I found some Tylenol and gulped the pills down with a mouthful of water.

I surfaced some time later to hear a voice rising and falling. I lay with my eyes closed, trying to figure out who was talking. Oh, Virginia. Since she could hardly be arguing with Phillip, especially with such vehemence, she must be on her cell. Her voice was suppressed, but angry. I started to call out to ask her if she was all right, but then I realized it was hardly my business.

Virginia’s agitation made me anxious. I was relieved she seemed calm when she brought Sophie to me a short time later.

I couldn't have told you what time it was, and we didn't speak. I nursed Sophie automatically. Afterward, Virginia, blessedly, swooped down to whisk Sophie away. I could hear her singing to the baby, in a very pretty voice, and then I was out again.

Chapter Three

When I woke up in the morning, the sun was shining through the blinds. I had to visit the bathroom in a very urgent way. To reach it, I had to hold on to the furniture. That scared me. It was after seven, and the monitor was on the bedside table, so Virginia had left.

At eight thirty, Phillip came in with a weeping Sophie. He was already dressed in jeans and an old T-shirt for his job on the cleanup crew. "I changed Sophie, and I walked around with her. But she keeps crying." He was clearly anxious.

"Okay, hand her over," I said, trying to sound like I was on top of the situation. Sophie, red in the face and screaming, was still beautiful, but maybe on a more primal level. I took my precautions with the gloves and the mask—again—and put her to the breast so quickly that Phillip didn't even have time to turn around. I flipped the sheet over her head so I wouldn't traumatize my brother.

There was instant silence, except for the adorable little noises Sophie made when she ate.

"Wow," Phillip said, with some relief, appreciating the quiet. "Um, Roe, you really don't look any better. Are you sure you'll be okay while I'm gone?"

"Just come home as soon as you can," I said. "I can handle her until then. Virginia will be back this evening. And before you go? If you can bring me some diapers and the box of wipes, I can change her in here."

"When do you think you'll be better?" Phillip actually sounded worried. "Should I call the doctor? Or take you to an emergency care place?"

"I'm sure I'll run some more fever later today, but right now I'm okay." That was *somewhat* true. "And you know, if I feel terrible, I can call . . . someone." I'd been about to say my mother, but she was gone.

He looked relieved. "So when does Robin get his award?"

"Oh, don't jinx him! Tonight, I hope. They'll announce the winners at a banquet."

"This is a big deal?"

"If you're a mystery fan, it's just about the *biggest* deal. It would make Robin so happy."

"You're really crazy about him, aren't you? I mean . . . you didn't get married because of Sophie being on the way."

On the one hand, this really wasn't Phillip's business. On the other hand, he seemed to need reassurance. "Never doubt that Robin and I are a real couple," I said gently.

He reddened. He kissed Sophie's head to give himself a moment. "Sorry," he said gruffly. "It's just, I would hate it if you two started fighting."

Phillip had seen and heard enough arguing between my father and his second wife, Phillip's mother. "We won't," I said firmly. "I can't say we won't ever disagree, because we do from time to time. But we'll never have screaming fights."

"Sure, good," he said, in the disbelieving and long-suffering way teenagers have. "Remember, Sarah's coming over this evening to help me babysit?"

Sarah Washington and Phillip started "talking" to each other, which was like an exploratory flirtation, late the year before. They'd moved on to the next stage. "If you don't get so involved with Sarah that you forget about Sophie," I said, because I couldn't think of any way to say that tactfully. "But also, Virginia will be here."

Phillip grinned. "Okay, Sis," he said. He was fully aware I'd rather he called me Roe.

"Have a good time at the park," I said. "Tell Josh I said hi." Josh, who had become Phillip's best friend instantly, was one of my favorite people. In addition to Josh picking Phillip up in the morning and bringing him home in the afternoon, Josh and Phillip ran track together.

"Are you really gonna be okay?" Phillip asked.

"Sure," I said, to reassure him . . . and myself.

But an hour later, as I heard the front door close behind Phillip, I felt unsure. Was I endangering Sophie by insisting I could care for her adequately?

I could only take the day one step at a time. If worse came to worst, I could call someone. The problem was, most of my friends had babies or toddlers and would not want to be in the same room with me. I could understand that.

I kept Sophie on the bed with me, carefully centered as far from the edge of the king bed as possible. Easing slowly to my feet, I staggered into the bathroom to brush my teeth and wash my face. I was scared to shower; I might not be able to hear her cry over the sound of the water.

Blessedly, Sophie slept for two hours. I didn't have the attention span to read, so I simply watched her for a while. She slept with such deep abandon, so relaxed and still, her arms thrown out. I actually laid my (gloved) hand on her chest to feel it rising and falling as she breathed. Robin had confessed he did this, too, so it didn't make me feel too creepy.

I turned on the television, again with closed captioning. I found a daytime channel that carried old movies. The women were all wearing hose and heels and hats. I really disliked wearing the three h's myself, but I had to admit they all looked terrific.

Toward the end of the movie, I began to shiver again, and I pulled the blanket up. I was running a fever again.

I'd turned down the ring volume on my cell so it wouldn't wake Sophie, and when I looked at my phone log, I found I'd missed a call from Robin. He'd also sent a few text messages I hadn't read. I discovered that Robin was worried about me, missed me and Sophie, and looked forward to coming home. (That was all reassuring, and I can't say I didn't enjoy the reassurance.)

I texted back to tell him Virginia had stayed the previous night and been a great help, and she was coming back tonight. Phillip was helping, too. I didn't mention the fever, or Phillip's absence. I wasn't trying to be a martyr; but I did want Robin to enjoy his big day. If I complained, he wouldn't. *V. pointed out flowers hand-delivered,* I added. *Can't think who by? By whom?*

If I got any worse, I'd have to call someone. I ran through names in my head, but I hesitated. It seemed very *needy,* calling someone on a Saturday. And exposing them to the flu. And asking them to change my baby's diapers.

While I was debating, I felt my phone vibrate. Robin was calling. "Hi, honey," I said, keeping my voice low.

"Is anyone there with you? I got worried when I didn't hear from you until now. How are you feeling? Running any fever?"

"Phillip's not here right now," I said. "Sophie's asleep."

"You didn't say how you're feeling."

"I'm definitely on the sick list," I said, trying to sound hearty. "But I'll be better soon." I hoped.

"How's the baby?"

"She's good. Not sick." Of course, he was afraid Sophie would catch a cold from me. I knew I had the flu, but I didn't bring up the "f" word to Robin. It would scare him. After all, I was being as careful as I could to prevent Sophie from catching it.

I remembered to ask him how his panel had gone, and he told me the moderator had run a tight ship. Robin approved of moderators who were on the ball. He'd had a good signing line, he said. His publisher was sponsoring a table at the banquet, and Robin would be sitting there with his editor and his agent. I closed my eyes while he talked, glad to hear his voice, but unable to work up much animation. *I'm sick as a dog,* I thought, and somehow it made me feel better to confess that, if only to myself.

"About the flowers," he said.

I was surprised he'd returned to that topic. "Yeah?"

"If anyone else leaves a present without you knowing . . . let me hear about it," he said. "I just don't like that."

Sophie wiggled and made a little noise. "Honey, I have to go," I said. "The baby's waking up." I glanced at the clock. I realized with dismay that I still had hours until Phillip got back. I heard a distant sound that I realized was someone knocking at the front door.

"And someone's at the door," I told Robin, trying to sound bright.

He said a hasty good-bye.

I was relieved to have gotten through the conversation.

I heard the front door open and close. I had not remembered to ask Phillip to lock it behind him. Oh my God. I tried to summon the energy to be frightened.

"Roe? Roe? It's Emily."

That was the last voice I expected to hear. I was relieved . . . and flabbergasted.

"Emily? I'm back here, last door on the left," I called back, alarmed at how weak and croaky my voice came out. I pulled on my mask because I could tell from the tickle in my throat I was going to have a coughing spell. And I was right; it racked me.

Emily Scott, our priest's wife, was in my bedroom doorway before I could finish the paroxysm. I was as amazed as if Mother Teresa had popped in . . . or I would have been, if I hadn't felt like death warmed over.

On her warmest days, Emily had never been more than polite to me, so I couldn't imagine why she was risking infection to visit this plague house.

"Oh, Roe," Emily said, when she got a good look at me. "I talked to Phillip when I dropped Liza off at the park. He says you're sick. I see he wasn't kidding. The flu is going around."

I nodded, since I was still coughing. After a moment, I was able to pull off the mask.

Emily was immaculate in a good pants-and-blouse outfit. Her hair and makeup were smooth and tasteful.

I felt even more disheveled and smelly.

Emily's gaze was caught by Sophie's hand waving. Thank God, the baby had woken up right on cue. She was adorable as she kicked her little legs and waved her little arms. She hadn't started fussing yet.

"Oh," Emily breathed. "She's so cute!"

My heart expanded to include Emily Scott. "Yes," I said modestly. "She's great."

"Can I pick her up?" Emily saw the diapers and wipes on the bed beside me. "Oh, Roe, you've been taking care of her yourself? While you're ill? Where is . . . oh, wait, this is the weekend for Robin's award thing, right?"

"I didn't want him to miss his big moment. At least, I hope it's his big moment," I said. "Virginia Mitchell is coming in at night."

"I heard she's pretty good. But you're on your own now? I'm glad I came by," Emily said. "I'll take care of Sophie for a while, okay? So you can shower and take care of yourself without worrying."

"Oh, Emily," I said, feeling a bloom of gratitude unfolding. I didn't bother to hide my relief. "That would be *wonderful*."

Sophie seemed to be content at the moment, so Emily carried her off to give her a bath and a wardrobe change. "Is the sink in the hall bathroom okay for a quick wash-off?" Emily called.

"Yes," I called back. I would have agreed to anything Emily proposed at that point. She was a baby-charmer; there wasn't a peep from Sophie.

Though I was reluctant to leave the warmth of the covers, this was a golden opportunity. I dragged myself out of the bed, and in so doing I discovered the sheets were wet with sweat. I laboriously stripped it. No matter how sick I felt (and that was *pretty damn sick*), I couldn't stand the idea of getting back between those sheets. Moving very slowly, I remade the bed and tossed the soiled ones into the hamper. My nightgown followed the sheets.

By the time I stepped into the shower, I was exhausted. But all my effort was worth the consequence. It was a wonderful shower, close to the top of the list of my all-time best. The hot water felt unbelievably good. Turning it off reluctantly, delighted to feel clean, I dried off as quickly as I could and used another towel on my hair.

I was freezing by then, my teeth chattering. I pulled on some pajamas Robin had given me, lightweight and cheerful and decorated with stars. No matter how debilitated I'd become, a clean body and clean sheets were real morale boosters.

By that time Emily was bringing the baby back, and Sophie too looked refreshed. She was wearing her pink sleeper with the bunnies all over it, my particular favorite. And now, she was hungry, as she made abundantly clear.

I didn't know how Emily would react to my breast-feeding, so I tried to be as discreet as I'd been when Phillip had been in the room. But (again to my surprise) Emily sat on the slipper chair and seemed prepared to chat.

"Is it really safe for you to breast-feed?" she asked. "Shouldn't I try to fix her a bottle?"

"I'd say yes in a heartbeat, but Sophie won't take a bottle. She just won't. Believe me, we tried, so we'd have an alternative, in case something came up . . . like me getting the flu," I said ruefully. "It's me, or nothing." I recounted my talk with Dr. Garrison. "That's why I look like a spacewoman."

Emily nodded and dropped the subject. "How is Phillip liking public school?" she asked.

Emily's daughter, Liza, had had a crush on Phillip, which he had good-naturedly tolerated. That's a pretty normal occurrence. But my brother and Liza had gone through a crisis together. Now they were friends, despite the difference in their ages. Not that the two hung out—teen society would hardly stand for that, and probably that was their own inclination, too. But when they saw each other, they had a conversation: not the norm between a sixteen-year-old boy and a twelve-year-old girl.

"Phillip really seems happy," I said. "And he says classes are not too easy, but not too hard."

"I remember he was in some kind of home-schooled network?"

"Yes. I didn't know those existed until Phillip came here. I had to learn a lot in a hurry." He'd landed in Lawrenceton right before his mid-semester exams. Many phone calls and e-mails had ensued.

"Do you think he'll stay here? Or go back to California?"

"We're happy to have him. He's happy to be here. My stepmother is off e-mail and the telephone in a commune in California, and my dad has so many financial problems that he isn't exactly anxious for Phillip to come home."

Emily shook her head. "They don't know what they've given up."

I was pleased that she shared my good opinion of my brother.

I switched Sophie to the other side. "How is Liza doing, in her new school?" I asked. After Liza had endured a year of bullying, the Scotts had withdrawn Liza from the local middle school and enrolled her in a Christian academy in the next town.

Emily smiled, and it made her whole face light up. "Her grades are great! She comes home from school with a smile on her face. She has new friends. I worried after the kidnapping. . . ."

Last year, Phillip and Liza had been abducted. I'd found them none too soon. "Does she have nightmares?" I asked. I looked down to see Sophie's eyes closed in concentration. She was so beautiful!

"She hasn't said so. But she can't forgive them."

"The kidnappers? Or the girls who were tormenting her?"

"All of them. That's quite a few people to hate."

I would not have thought of suggesting Liza forgive them, myself, but I was not as good a Christian as Emily. I hesitated before I spoke. "I think forgiveness doesn't happen overnight. I think it comes in increments. When someone has made your life hell, maybe you have to recover from the fear and anger first? Before you start working on the other thing."

Emily considered this idea. "Maybe that's true. Has Phillip talked about it?"

"Not a lot. But he's actually looking forward to the trial."

Emily looked surprised. "Really?"

I shrugged. "He wants them to pay for what they did."

"Hmmm. When she sees justice done, maybe that'll give Liza some kind of . . ."

Don't say it, I thought. Don't say it, don't say it . . .

". . . closure," Emily finished.

I sighed, I hoped not audibly. I realized closure was a necessary event, mentally and emotionally, but it seemed to me closure might gain traction as gradually as forgiveness did. These were not clear-cut stages with a beginning and a definite end. "We'll all feel better when it's over and done with," I said gently. Sophie had let go of my breast, and her eyelids were fluttering. "She's almost asleep," I said quietly.

"I'll burp her." Emily reached down for Sophie, and I handed her over along with a receiving blanket to drape Emily's shoulder. With a smile on her face, Emily patted Sophie gently.

"You really have to be forceful when you're burping her," I said. "And I warn you, she burps like a sailor."

Just then, a huge belch erupted from my little baby. Emily

laughed out loud. She continued patting Sophie, regularly, softly. Sophie's eyelids fluttered once, fluttered twice, and she was out.

Emily raised her eyebrows in query. *Her crib?* she mouthed.

I nodded. "Please."

When Emily returned, she seemed to have something on her mind. Maybe she'd had a goal all along.

"Thanks so much for dropping by in my hour of need," I said, to prime the pump.

"Need me to do anything else while I'm here? Start some laundry? Get out something for your lunch?"

"You've done so much already. I'm incredibly glad I got to take a shower without worrying about Sophie, and without carrying her."

"Then I'm glad I stopped by." She hesitated, then said abruptly, "I never gave you a chance to be my friend. I was jealous of your history with Aubrey."

"Aubrey and I had decided to call it quits before he even asked you out on a date," I began, not sure where this was heading.

She raised a hand to let me know she had more to say. "I'm sure he told you he couldn't be a father," she said, with startling frankness. "I know that's probably what sparked his interest in me, since I already had a child young enough to really bond with him. I like to think that I earned his love and trust for myself."

"Of course you did!" I said. "I can't imagine Aubrey with anyone else." Emily wasn't through, though.

"I hope your marriage is as happy as ours," she continued.

"We have every intention of making it that happy." I managed to smile at her.

This conversation was puzzling. And tiring.

"You've known Robin for a while, I think?" Emily said.

"We'd dated before he went to California to work on the script. After he left, I met Martin and got married. And Robin had other relationships. But once we saw each other again, it just felt right."

"Do you ever think about Martin?" Emily said.

That seemed to come out of the blue. "Yes, of course. You really can't not-think about your first husband. Don't you? Gosh, I don't even know the name of your first . . . ?"

"Connor," she said. She took a deep breath. "I do think about him, but not happily. He hit me."

I flinched. How could this woman, collected and Christian, have been subjected to such abuse? Not only was I angry on her behalf, I was a little dismayed to be the recipient of such a confidence.

"Why?" was all I could think of to say. "How could that happen?"

"Connor drank. When he was drinking, he was a horrible man. When he was sober, he was so sorry, always. He kept promising to change, to go into therapy. Especially after Liza came. But it would happen all over again. When he had the car accident, and they told me he was dead? The first feeling I had was relief."

"That's a horrible way to remember someone. I didn't say that well. I mean that he made himself so mean and weak that he lost all the respect you had for him." Now I understood Emily's reserve. If someone you loved treated you that way, it would be hard to open up again.

"I kind of wondered," Emily said, "if you had had the same experience?"

"No," I said thankfully. "Martin didn't drink much, and when he did, he got really affectionate." I had to smile, a little. "Martin really wanted to make me happy by giving me things

I'd like. He was thoughtful that way. He never raised a hand to me. I always felt . . ." I struggled to express it. "I felt he was wrapping me in cotton batting so I wouldn't get broken."

Emily nodded in understanding. "So he took almost too much care of you? You wondered if he thought you couldn't take care of yourself?"

"Exactly," I said, relieved. "I realize that I had it incredibly easy. He wanted me to be happy, and he wanted to be the one who made me happy. That's impossible to complain about, in view of your experience. He understood so much about me. But I *never* felt I knew everything about him."

And I hadn't, for sure. Gunrunning, shady semiofficial ops . . . I felt sad all over again, remembering my growing sense of unease as Martin's past began to unroll in front of me.

I had been head over heels in love with Martin from the moment I saw him. It had been a feverish, beautiful, terrible experience. I had no doubt he'd loved me, too. But there had been cracks in our marriage, issues we hadn't had time to settle before he'd died.

Emily shook herself. I watched her straighten and stiffen, become the Emily I recognized. "I hope I didn't impose on you. Today's the day Connor died. It makes me feel better to talk about it. I almost never speak his name. It's time to pick up Liza. I'd better go."

"I appreciate your sharing your story with me." And that was all I would ever say about her first husband, unless Emily brought it up. "Thanks so much for checking on me, and for being so helpful. You were a lifesaver."

"You sure you don't want me to fix you some lunch?"

"No, thanks. Oh, my gosh, you missed yours!" It was after one o'clock.

"I'll be on my way to the store before swinging by the park. If you need me again, give me a call."

"I'm grateful," I said with absolute sincerity.

I heard the front door shut behind her.

I lay back in bed and made an incredulous face, though there was no one to see it. Truly, you couldn't anticipate what was around the next corner . . . ever. The day before, I could not have imagined the conversation I'd just had, much less that I'd had it with Emily Scott.

I wiggled down in the bed, listening to Sophie's regular breathing over the baby monitor. I checked the clock. Phillip should be home in an hour, give or take a few minutes.

I didn't exactly go to sleep, but I lay curled up in a stupor, rising in and out of awareness. When I hit my next upswing, I had yet another surprise. My friend Angel Youngblood was standing by the bed. For a moment, I thought I was dreaming.

"Phillip let me in," Angel said.

"Good." I struggled to rouse myself.

"I heard you were sick. So I brought some soup and some bread."

"Oh, thank you. That's so nice! I'm really beholden."

"Bullshit. Like you didn't have a baby shower for me when I was expecting Lorna. Like you didn't bring three meals' worth of food to the house after I brought her home."

I didn't know what to say. That was what anyone would do. I was Angel's friend. Besides, this relationship ran two ways. I could have one-upped her by reminding her how she and her husband, Shelby, had done everything for me when I'd had to get Martin's body back to Lawrenceton, and people had been coming into town for the funeral, and my life had been chaos.

"Angel, I love you," I said.

She smiled, a fleeting grin that made me happy, too. "I'm going to have a word with Phillip before I go home. Shelby's watching Lorna. She's a terror. Got him wrapped around her finger. Good-bye. Get better." And she was gone, as abruptly as she'd appeared.

I heard her talking to Phillip. Angel was saying, "You make sure she takes some Tylenol every four hours." But I drifted off to sleep again.

Angel had put the fear of God into Phillip, who brought me a bowl of tomato soup and some crackers about thirty minutes later. They were on a bed tray, which I barely remembered having. "Sophie's in her swing," he said. "She's fine. Virginia should be here in an hour or less."

I made myself scooch up against the headboard so the tray could span my lap. The soup was redolent of red peppers and basil, and it tasted wonderful. This was the first food I'd enjoyed in what seemed like forever. I couldn't complete the bowl (or eat the crackers), but I felt better after I got something in my stomach.

Phillip even remembered to come back and get the tray without any prompting. I wondered what Angel had said to him; not that Phillip wasn't ordinarily thoughtful, but this evening he was extra careful with everything he did for me.

Whatever she'd told him, I liked the result.

Chapter Four

Virginia was right on time. I guess I was so miserable I thought I'd cornered the market, but I found out very quickly that I had been wrong. My babysitter/house help was in a sour mood. Though she was dressed in her usual exercise chic, her scowling face didn't match. Clearly, something had riled her: but just as clearly, she didn't want to talk about it. With no pleasantries and without uttering a single extra word, Virginia determined that Sophie did not need a bath, that she would want to be fed pretty soon, and that I had decided to live.

As I answered her questions, I never saw even the slightest smile. *But that's not a job requirement*, I reminded myself. She took excellent care of Sophie; that was the important thing. Despite Virginia's blend of unhappiness and anger, I felt a profound relief now that I had competent backup on-site.

Phillip drifted into my room an hour later. It was apparent he had showered and changed into a newer pair of jeans and a nicer shirt. It was also apparent he had something to tell me.

"Sarah's coming over tonight, remember?" He looked down at me doubtfully. "Is it okay if she comes in to say hello? She really likes you."

I thought there was a subtext here. Then I realized I must look like hell, and Phillip was hoping I would brush my hair (at least). "I showered," I protested. "But maybe I forgot to brush my hair while it dried." My hair had a mind of its own, and managed to be both curly *and* wavy. "Okay, I'll try to get neater. Sarah can stand in the doorway to speak. Bring me my brush."

Phillip looked relieved, and fetched it from the bathroom. "Okay, Sis."

"I'll be glad to see her," I lied. I felt marginally more human, but that wasn't going to last. Despite the Tylenol, my fever would go up. I could still feel it lurking, ready to pounce. And I'd used a whole box of Kleenex. After Phillip brought me a new one, he wandered away. I refluffed my pillows and lay back, enjoying a moment of comfort and content.

Inevitably, I thought about Robin. By now, he'd be at the cocktail hour before the banquet. It seemed unworthy to pray that he won, so I compromised by praying for his happiness. Surely that was okay? Then I discovered I had to look in a mirror to brush my hair. I made a trembly trip to the bathroom.

After I crawled back into bed, grateful to pull the covers up around me, I decided to read. But it was no good. No matter how many times I read a page, I couldn't retain the sense of it. With regret, I laid my book down and reached for the remote. I watched a couple look for a house in Guatemala, I watched Jeremy Wade try to land a giant killer fish, and I stared at a few minutes of an old sitcom. I was thinking about turning off the television and burrowing down in the bed when Virginia knocked perfunctorily on the doorframe. I smiled in what I hoped was a welcoming way, and she took a step in.

"Did you get up and clean your kitchen today?" she said, with stern disapproval.

"No, a friend came in," I said, wondering if it had been Emily or Angel who'd been so thoughtful. If I'd had the energy, I would have been a little piqued by Virginia's attitude.

"Because I would have done it. You don't need to be wasting your energy on something like that."

"I don't think I've actually been in the kitchen for a couple of days," I said, as mildly as I could. The realization was an unpleasant surprise.

"Those roses? They're looking like they're on their last legs." She'd taken it down a notch, herself.

"I'd forgotten all about them." It seemed like a month ago I'd found them on the doorstep. "Pitch them, please. By the way, Phillip's friend is coming over tonight." I assured Virginia she was welcome to go in and out of the living room/kitchen area as frequently as she liked while Phillip and Sarah watched the movie. It wasn't that I didn't trust Phillip; and after all, to a great extent, his dating life was his business. But at least while they were under my roof, I didn't want the two to get overwhelmed by a surge of teenage lust.

Then I felt terrible for even thinking of such a scenario. It showed a lack of reliance in Phillip's judgment, to say nothing of Sarah's.

But Virginia was smiling. Her face came to life. I felt I was seeing the real woman.

"I'll make sure to walk through every ten minutes or so," she said, and I felt reassured. And guilty. She was harder to get to know than most people.

I wondered if I was spoiled; most people warmed to me quickly. It was the first time I'd ever thought about it. But I didn't think about it long. I thought about sleep, and Tylenol, and Robin's big evening.

In a few minutes, it was time to feed the bottomless pit, otherwise known as Sophie. It was comforting to hold her, now I was secure in the knowledge that I could pass her off to Virginia right afterward and be sure Sophie my baby would be well taken care of.

I heard Sarah arrive right on time. Because she had good manners, and maybe because Phillip had glanced in to see I'd upped my game with the grooming, she came back to say hello. I'd been impressed with Sarah every time I'd talked to her, and tonight was no exception.

Sarah seemed sensible, smart, and articulate (on the character end), and on the physical end I thought she was very attractive, with a big smile, lots of curly hair, and caramel skin.

"I hope you don't get scared around babies," I said.

"I have two little brothers. I'm baby-proof." She grinned at me. "I hope you feel better. Phillip told me not to get close."

Phillip called, "Sarah, the movie is ready," from the living room. She gave me a little wave and vanished. I snuggled down in the bed, trying to persuade myself I felt better. But I felt hot again. It was good enough to simply lie there and feel no necessity to make a decision or make myself rally. I could hear the movie beginning, but the sound was distant enough not to bother me. Closer, I could hear Virginia talking to Sophie, who'd evidently decided to have a play period. Virginia began singing in a pretty soprano. I recognized the tune of a familiar hymn. Sophie must be enthralled; my own singing was pretty dreadful.

I lived my life at one remove that evening. I didn't sleep, but I was in a waking trance. From time to time, I could hear Phillip or Sarah laugh. The movie was funny; their date was going well. I roused myself a little when Virginia brought in Sophie about ten o'clock. As I fed her, I heard Virginia's voice again, but not raised in song. She was having a long conversation on her cell phone, and it was not a happy one. Again.

Obviously, something was wrong in Virginia's life. Should I ask her about it? I decided not to. Because (a) it wasn't any of my business, and (b) she'd shown no inclination to become my buddy, so she wouldn't appreciate me trying to dig into her troubles.

I glanced at the clock as I switched Sophie to the other side, prodding my slow brain into calculating what Robin was doing now, in the central time zone. I had dimly noted when the banquet started. I figured the awards ceremony would begin maybe an hour and half later. There were at least eight awards to be handed out, if I remembered correctly. Best Novel was the last category, of course.

After Virginia had come in to get Sophie, maintaining a tight-lipped silence, I struggled to stay awake. My eyelids closed without my volition. I jumped when my cell phone rang. "Robin?" I said, full of hope.

"I won!" Robin yelled. "Roe, I won!"

Faintly, I could hear the sound of many voices.

"Oh, honey, I'm so happy for you. You really deserve it. Where are you?" I began crying from sheer relief and weakness as I tried to shake the cobwebs from my head.

"I'm in the men's room," Robin said.

That was unexpected. "Is this a trend?"

"It's the quietest place I could find. I can't believe it!" Suddenly he went quiet and reflective. "I never thought *Panel of Experts* would win. After all, Lee had a book. And Sara. And Tim Hallinan." All three were writers Robin held in esteem.

"This is *huge*. I bet Harry was ecstatic." Harry Holderman, who'd become Robin's agent five years ago, had proved to be a powerhouse in Robin's career.

"You should have seen his face!" Robin was back to exclamation points.

"Was Jill just as excited?" Jill had been Robin's editor for his past three books.

"She called her boss as soon as we heard."

"I could not be more thrilled," I told him, trying very hard to sound it. "You earned that Anthony. But I'll bet a lot of people are waiting for you, honey. You need to go do a victory lap around the bar. I'll see you tomorrow afternoon." *Thank God.*

"Are you all right? Your voice sounds kind of scratchy. How's the cold?" Robin no longer sounded excited, but anxious.

"I'm fine, Sophie's fine, Phillip's fine," I said, lightly, doing my best to sound hale and hearty. "Safe trip home! And congratulations again, from the bottom of my heart. It *couldn't* have gone to anyone else."

"I love you," Robin said, suddenly and forcefully.

"I love you, too." I was so happy for him. After I ended the call, I wondered if it was time to take some more Tylenol, but when I figured up the hours, it wasn't. I slid down in the bed, the covers pulled up to my chin.

If Sarah came to tell me good-bye, I didn't know it. If Virginia came in to check on me, I didn't hear her. Now that I'd talked to Robin, and rejoiced for him, there was no reason for me to stay awake. I was so relieved to let go of the nagging worry that he might be disappointed. I got to relax in the knowledge Robin had gotten the reward he deserved.

I reached up to switch off my lamp. Descending immediately into crazy fever dreams, I woke just long enough to realize I was sweating. But the dreams pulled me under again.

Chapter Five

A baby was crying, but that must be another fiction of my fevered mind. When the crying continued, an alarm bell went off inside my head. *I had to wake up.*

I surfaced, gasping. Something was very wrong. Sophie was crying, for real, and she was very upset.

Why hadn't Virginia brought her in to me, if Sophie was hungry? That was why Virginia was here. How could she sleep through Sophie's piercing wails? I was really angry, almost as angry as Sophie. Weirdly, it sounded as though there were two Sophies.

Disoriented and upset, I managed to sit up. I *was* hearing Sophie cry in stereo. The baby monitor was on my bed table. That made no sense, either. Virginia should have it with her.

I didn't hear Phillip stirring—but in his deepest sleep, a tornado could touch down in the front yard, and he wouldn't know about it.

I struggled to throw off the covers and swing my legs out of the bed. A nasty clammy feeling overwhelmed me. My pajamas were wet with sweat. Ugh! But I couldn't take the time to change. I put on my glasses, grabbed my robe, and stepped into my slippers. I staggered across the hall. The little turtle night-light showed me Sophie was thrashing with agitation. Her face was scrunched up and red with the force of her protests (Robin called that her demon face).

She seemed so heavy when I lifted her out of the crib. I was alarmingly weak. I managed to get Sophie to the changing table, pull up her nightgown, and change her soaked diaper. The harder I tried to do it quickly, the more I was fumbling and slow, especially with the gloves and the mask. By the time I'd gotten her changed, Sophie had worked herself into a fury.

"Come on, little missy, you and I are going to have a feeding session," I whispered. As soon as I picked her up, her cries changed to hiccups. I went past the smooth fold-out bed—the covers hadn't been turned down—to sit in the rocker in the corner. The minute I introduced Sophie to her favorite feature, she latched on like a remora.

The abrupt silence was a blessing. *You would think she hadn't eaten in a week,* I thought, and I glanced at the nursery clock. It was after 2:00 A.M. She had slept for about five hours, God bless her.

It was the fourth time she'd stayed down five hours or more, which meant it was a welcome trend. I was the world expert on Sophie Crusoe.

As she calmed, the shuddering breaths flattened out into a regular pattern. I relaxed, too. It felt good to make Sophie happy, and I hummed to her as she fed.

But below that surface contentment (both mine and Sophie's), I was wondering, *Where the hell is Virginia?* My eyes fell on the fold-out bed again. I couldn't imagine why Virginia would have fallen asleep out in the living room, unless she remembered the fold-out to be really uncomfortable. Even if she hadn't heard the baby crying with her ears, she should have had the monitor. I was surprised the Hermans and the Cohens on either side of us hadn't heard Sophie. As if to comment on that idea, I heard a distant bark from one of the neighbor dogs.

Why had Virginia put the monitor in my room? Had she actually left the house? But why, when it was her job to take care of Sophie all night long? I was absolutely outraged. And I was scared.

What the hell was going on?

When Sophie was through, I carried her in my arms when I knocked on Phillip's door.

"Roe?" His voice was heavy with sleep. "What's wrong?"

"I can't find Virginia." I hadn't switched on a light yet, and I was still talking in the lowest voice I could manage. I don't know whom I was afraid of waking. But something was very wrong, and it was time to get all hands on deck.

"Okay," he said, sounding a lot more awake. "Okay. I'm coming." After a moment, the door opened. Phillip looked at me blearily. By the tiny glow of the hall night-light, I could see that he was wearing pajama bottoms and a T-shirt. His hair was a rumpled mess.

"You've lost Virginia?" he said, as if he couldn't get the idea through his head.

"She's lost herself," I said impatiently. "I can't find her."

Phillip looked a bit more alert. "Have you gone over the whole house?"

"No. Sophie woke me up crying, and I had to take care of

her." I was jiggling her gently, and for the moment, she was content.

"Okay," Phillip said valiantly. "Okay." He shook himself, trying to wake up. I could see him assume the mantle of the man of the house. Phillip walked briskly into the living room and switched on one of the lamps while I hung back a little. "No one here," he called.

If there had been something awful out there, I hadn't wanted Sophie to see it. I knew that was ridiculous. If Phillip was trying to be brave, I had to try, too. We had to find out where Virginia had gone; I had been angry at the woman, but now I was frightened for her. I deposited Sophie on the playmat on the floor and ripped off the mask and gloves.

We began to search the house, room by room.

Phillip looked in Robin's office. I could hear him opening the closet, which held all kinds of office supplies. I checked the hall bathroom, which was very simple. Nowhere to hide. Or be hidden.

I opened Sophie's closet. I glanced under her crib. I went into my own room and looked in the closets there, and scanned every inch of the bathroom. I went in Phillip's room, since he was such a heavy sleeper it was possible Virginia could have gone in without him knowing it. But all I learned was that Phillip needed to pick up his dirty clothes.

That was the end of that wing of the house, so I carried Sophie back to the kitchen area. I looked behind the big island, the only space I couldn't see from the living room.

Phillip was with me by that time. He was wide awake.

There wasn't much more to check. Phillip opened the pantry door and stepped inside. Nothing. Next we opened the kitchen door leading to the garage. Robin's car was crowded in by mine, because it was supposed to rain while he was gone. His car was locked. I checked with my keypad to be sure my own car was, too.

I couldn't imagine how anyone could open the automatic garage doors and then hide in my locked car—unless such a person came through the house and stole my keys—but I was compelled to verify it. Handing Sophie off to her uncle, I circled both vehicles, and I made sure they were both empty of everything but car seats and extra pacifiers. I stepped back inside the house, and I closed and locked the garage door before taking Sophie back from Phillip.

We'd been turning on lights as we moved around the house. Every corner was illuminated. We looked at each other, baffled.

"This is so weird," Phillip said. "Did you see a note? Did she maybe leave a message on your phone?"

I hadn't checked for a note. I'd never even thought of it. Now I made a quick tour of the obvious places Virginia might have left one. I fetched my cell phone from the bedroom charger and checked it.

No phone call was logged since Robin's, and I didn't have a text message. I glanced at the light on the answering machine attached to the landline, and it stared back at me without blinking.

Though I wanted to keep the baby near me, I could not carry her any longer. My arms were exhausted. Thank God, her eyes had fluttered shut.

After I put Sophie to bed (and made sure her window was locked), I made a detour to my room to collect the baby monitor. I also took a second to put on a dry nightgown and a different robe.

I think I was hoping—still—that we'd find Virginia asleep somewhere, and we'd all get to go back to bed, and everything would be okay. If I kept on my nightclothes, that would happen, right?

Phillip was pouring a glass of orange juice. He said, "Sorry, Sis. I just haven't seen a thing. Have you checked to see if her car is parked on the street?"

"What does she drive?"

"A black Impreza."

I must have looked blank.

"A small car," he said, in an annoyingly tolerant way. "Not too expensive."

I switched on the light over the front door, which just barely reached the curb. "A car's out there," I said. "I can't tell what's inside. We have to go see if . . . if she's in there."

Before I could say, "I'll do it," Phillip was out the door, walking across the grass with bare feet. He paused for a moment to look up. The sky flashed with distant lightning. There was a grumble of thunder.

Phillip had had the foresight to grab a flashlight from the coat stand by the door. Thanks to Robin's flashlight fetish, we had one or two in every room of the house. This one was Robin's favorite, one of the big lantern-style ones. Phillip swept the beam across the front yard as he moved slowly to the curb, checking the ground in front of his feet all the way. When he didn't pause, I knew he hadn't seen anything out of the ordinary. At the curb, he directed the beam into the car.

I held my breath.

Phillip turned and shook his head.

No Virginia.

As he hurried back, I realized that the only place we hadn't searched was the backyard. Since we lived in an area full of older homes, the yard was large, with a couple of big trees, a brick patio, a lot of grass, and a professionally planted bed of bushes and flowers softening the lines of the black aluminum fence, Robin's pride.

I turned off the front door light and went to the back door, just in the hall leading back to our library/office, to switch on the back lights (which pretty much illuminated the patio and cast only a dim light on the grass around it). I moved to the living room picture window and stared out. Of course, I couldn't see a thing.

With great intelligence, Phillip switched off every overhead light and lamp before he joined me at the window. We could see much better, naturally.

Sadly.

"Oh, no," I whispered. I could just discern a dark mass partly hidden by the mimosa tree growing close to the southeast corner of the yard. I couldn't make out what it was, exactly: it was as far from the light as anything could get in our yard. But whatever it was, it didn't belong in our yard.

Phillip said something sharp and to the point.

"Yes," I said, feeling incredibly weary. "I agree. I'm going outside."

I was the older, and it was time for me to shoulder the burden. Drawing myself up to my full four feet, eleven inches, I jammed the baby monitor into the pocket of my robe. So far adrenaline had carried me along, but now it had become an effort to put one foot in front of the other. I was shamefully glad when Phillip followed me out the patio door.

I looked up to see how full the moon was, but a distant bolt of lightning showed me the sky was full of heavy clouds, moving fast. As we stepped onto the grass, a slight breeze picked up locks of my tangled hair, and I had to hold it off my face. There was another ominous rumble.

"Smells like rain," Phillip said quietly.

I felt a terrible impulse to turn back; but of course, we had to keep going. If we were seeing a person, that person needed help. We had to check. Too soon, we passed the mimosa tree and looked behind it. Phillip aimed the beam of the lantern, and all too clearly we saw the woman.

Phillip said, "This is big trouble."

I had to agree.

She was wearing tight jeans, loafers, and a sweatshirt. Her body lay on its back, with her arms flung out to the side and her knees slightly bent. With a shiver of revulsion, I realized the body's posture mimicked Sophie's as she lay sprawled in sleep, her little arms thrown out, her head turned to the side, and her legs slightly akimbo.

But this woman wasn't sleeping. She was dead.

And she wasn't Virginia Mitchell.

Chapter Six

Though her face was turned away from us, and the light wasn't good, there was no mistaking the fact that this woman was a few things Virginia was not: white, full-figured, and blond.

"What the *hell*?" Phillip said very quietly, a beat before I said exactly the same thing.

Phillip's flashlight was wavering in his hand, so the beam trembled in a disconcerting way. Still, I could tell the woman's skull was not shaped like a skull should be. The flashlight grazed her hands, and I could see her fingernails were painted green. Somehow, that just tore me apart. I saw that something glinted in the grass beside her right hand, but I couldn't tell what it was, and at the moment I didn't care.

Phillip made a noise that expressed disgust and distress, all at once. He handed me the flashlight, and took two big steps to squat next to her.

"Don't touch her, Phillip!" I sounded like death was contagious. I meant that he should not lay a finger on her, that the police would take care of her, but it didn't come out that way.

"I have to make sure she's dead." Phillip sounded far more reasonable than I did.

"You're right." I felt guilty. I should be doing the checking.

Phillip laid his fingers on her neck. After maybe a minute—a very long minute—he said, "No pulse, at least none I can feel."

"Her chest isn't moving at all." I'd kept a sharp eye on her. I felt a weird impulse to put my hand on her chest, as I did Sophie's. In fact, I moved forward, despite my previous advice to Phillip. He said, "She's gone, Roe. No breathing."

He rose to his feet.

We looked at each other for a long moment. Phillip said, "I hate to confess this, and I know you won't fall for it . . . but after the trouble last year, I feel like dumping her over the fence. So she'd be in someone else's yard."

"I wish we could, too," I said, and I meant it. "But you know we can't. Of course, it would be wrong. For another thing, I bet we'd get caught."

Phillip looked regretful. "So . . . where is the babysitter?" My brother said this as if he were sure I knew the answer.

"I'm totally at a loss." I'd thought of, and rejected, a dozen possible scenarios. Maybe Virginia had gotten an emergency phone call from her mother and this woman had coincidentally happened to die in our yard. Or maybe Virginia had suddenly developed appendicitis, and this woman had tried to stop her from going to the hospital. . . .

"I can't think of any reason she'd leave. Can you?" He looked down at me. "Do you think Virginia might be dead, too?"

I shook my head drearily. "She's missing, and a body's here. I don't know what to make of it. We'd better go call the police."

As we trudged back to the door, accompanied by the grumble of thunder not quite so distant, I said, "I am way more familiar than I want to be with the law enforcement people of Lawrenceton and Sparling County."

"Me, too." My brother had had to undergo intensive debriefings with the locals and the FBI after he'd survived the kidnapping, and the experience was still fresh in his mind.

Though the baby monitor had remained silent, I quickened my steps to be closer to Sophie. While my baby had been inside our house, unguarded, while I was asleep, while Phillip slept, someone had murdered a woman just yards away. The realization and its implications were becoming clear to me.

Since Virginia, *my baby's caregiver,* had vanished, she was a prime candidate for the role of murderer.

When the dispatcher answered, I hesitated for a moment. I didn't know where to start. "I'm Aurora Teagarden, I live at 1100 McBride. There's a dead woman in my backyard," I said, since that was my most serious problem. "*And* my babysitter is missing. And . . . could you not turn on the sirens? My baby's asleep. I don't want to sound self-centered, but the body's not going anywhere."

There was a moment of silence. "All right, Roe, gotcha," said the dispatcher. "Dead woman, missing woman, baby." Though I couldn't place her voice, I was certain it was someone I'd been in calculus with, or someone whose brother I had dated, or someone who sat three rows behind me in church (or all of the above). "Someone will roll up within five minutes. Don't leave the house."

Too late for that. "Thanks," I said politely, and hung up.

Though I desperately needed to sit, I had to return to

Sophie's room to lay eyes on her . . . on her back, arms flung out, legs slightly akimbo. This time, I did put my hand gently on her chest, and I was reassured to feel its rise and fall.

I would kill anyone who tried to harm her. I would give my life for her.

And for the first time in this terrible night, tears ran down my cheeks.

I struggled to get back on an even keel. The police would be here any minute.

I had just rejoined Phillip in the living room and collapsed on a couch when the first knock came at the door. Sure enough, it was discreet. Phillip opened it to admit a uniformed patrol officer, Susan Crawford. I had sent her a card when I'd heard she was pregnant a couple of months ago.

"Where's the body?" Susan asked. She might be thicker about the middle, but she was all cop. "Why are your lights off in here?"

Phillip took her to the picture window and pointed. "We turned the lights off so we could see outside. See the body? By the mimosa tree?"

I could tell when Susan spotted it, because she took a deep breath. "Go outside to check her, or wait for the EMT?" she asked herself in a whisper. While she tried to remember procedure, the decision was taken out of her hands. The lights of the ambulance flashed across the front windows.

"Susan, there's a gate into the backyard to the left of the house," I said. "That will save you time." She dashed out of the front door to guide the EMTs to the body, her dilemma solved.

"Good thinking," Phillip said. "They won't have to come through the house. You better stay down on the couch. You don't look good, Roe."

I couldn't count the times people had told me that during the past two days. I stayed down, and covered myself with the fuzzy afghan I kept thrown across the back of the couch from September through March. Phillip sat by me, his phone in hand, his thumbs flying. He was texting away.

"Who's up at this hour?" Even as I spoke, I realized it was an absurd question. Phillip slept with his phone, so I had to assume a lot of other teens did.

"You going to call Robin now?" He was trying to sound casual, but I wasn't fooled. He thought Robin needed to be here.

"Not right now," I said. "There's no point waking him up, assuming he's even left the hotel bar. We don't really *know* anything yet."

"We know there's a dead woman in the backyard. That's pretty major."

I couldn't deny it. "Robin's catching a flight at noon tomorrow. I doubt he could get here any faster even if I called him, and he'd just worry the whole time."

Phillip didn't look convinced, but he let it go.

The whole sad procedure—with which I was already too familiar—played out in the next forty-five minutes, while the storm advanced with ominous sound effects and dark clouds scudding across the moon. I was surprised the rain had held off this long. I was sure the police were hurrying with whatever they had to accomplish, before the rain washed the yard clean.

The yard was now lit up like a runway. With the curtains open and the inside light dim, I watched a trail of people enter and leave the yard. Most of the visitors wore dark windbreakers with "LPD" in big bright yellow letters on the back. I recognized almost all of them.

Finally, everyone reacted when a man I didn't know appeared in the yard. His jacket read "CORONER." I saw a head of dark curly hair, and I caught the glint of a pair of glasses. Arnie Petrosian. I'd voted for him in the last election, but I'd never met him face-to-face.

And I'd sure never imagined he'd be in my backyard.

It was like watching a movie with the sound turned off. The coroner knelt, checked the pulse and respiration, and pulled down the eyelids, which made me squeamish.

"Yuck," said Phillip.

Petrosian rose, nodded in the general direction of all the police in the yard, and moved out of my sight as briskly as he'd arrived. That formality over, everyone flew into action. The urgency was underlined by a crack of lightning that made everyone jump, myself included. Phillip called up the weather screen on his phone, and we were able to watch the front approach minute by minute.

Soon, the body was removed in a black bag, with a patrolman at each end. The bag hung between the men, limp and formless. What had been a human being was now a limp tube of flesh and bone.

"Where will they take her?" Phillip said.

"To the GBI medical examiners in Decatur," I told him.

There was a moment of silence, and I thought Phillip might have dozed off. Just then, he glanced at the screen of his phone. "Storm's almost here," he said. "I hope they've got all their pictures and found all their clues."

The mimosa tree where we'd found the body was rippling in the wind. Even the short bushes were tossing their heads.

The night actually *could* get worse.

A quiet knock made my head snap to the front door. Phillip popped up from the couch to answer it.

"Ms. Teagarden available?" said an unfamiliar voice.

Phillip said, "She's in here. But can you keep it short? She's been really sick."

I was surprised—to the extent I could feel surprise anymore—when the coroner himself stepped into my line of vision. He stood by the couch awkwardly. I could see the deep lines around his eyes. I decided he must be close to fifty. He shook my hand very lightly, as though my bones would break if he squeezed.

"Ardos Petrosian," he said. "Call me Arnie. Ms. Teagarden?"

"Yes. Would you care to sit down?"

"Thanks, I will. You look unwell, if you don't mind me saying."

When a coroner says you look bad, that's pretty dire. "Flu," I explained.

Phillip silently handed Petrosian a little bottle of hand sanitizer that had been on the side table. It wasn't mine. Virginia's? Petrosian, opposite me, lost no time in squirting some on his hands and rubbing it in vigorously. I hoped he'd used some after touching the dead woman.

Phillip sat by my feet, I guess so he could tackle the coroner if he tried to assault me. My brother was earning stars in heaven tonight.

"The police will be in soon to talk to you about your missing person. I'd sure like to put a name to the body. You sure the dead woman is not your babysitter?"

That would have been neat and tidy.

"Definitely not. Virginia is African American, she's very slim, her hair is short, and she wasn't dressed anything like the dead woman."

Arnie Petrosian looked grim. He had a woman's body without a name, and we were missing a woman whose name we knew. The fact that they didn't match was baffling.

Petrosian took a long look around him, which I thought was odd. "I used to come here all the time when the previous owners lived here."

I didn't know what to do with that, so I simply nodded.

The coroner thanked me, though I wasn't sure what for, and took his departure.

Our lot had never been lit up like this. I thought, *You can probably see our backyard from the moon.* A huge exaggeration, of course—but still, it was plenty bright, and crammed with people searching every inch of the ground.

"Maybe they'll get done in time," Phillip said, though the last word was drowned out by a roll of thunder. "You want something to eat?"

My growing brother. "No, thanks," I said. "I wouldn't turn down a drink, though. Some fruit juice?"

The crime scene investigators and the other official people were not making any effort to keep quiet, naturally enough. This was a death investigation. The termination of a human being took priority over keeping the peace and quiet of the neighborhood. This was not much better than sirens.

I confess that my heart sank because of this petty issue. Though none of this was my fault, my neighbors were not going to be happy about this disruption on our placid street. I couldn't imagine how the Herman sisters were reacting. I knew the Cohens would be livid.

But that's not important in the grand scheme of things, I told myself sternly. When I thought of the woman sprawled on the grass, her skull broken, her life taken away, some inconvenience and a few wakeful hours seemed like nothing.

Phillip returned from the kitchen with a greasy pizza-related snack. He made another trip to get a glass of milk for himself and some apple juice for me.

I was too queasy to watch him eat. It was like watching a boa consume a goat. In seconds the little pizza snacks were gone, and so was the milk. He returned the dishes to the kitchen and came back to his spot at my feet. In less than three minutes, Phillip was asleep with his head tilted back on the couch.

I looked at him fondly. Phillip was already a man, albeit a very young one. Life had battered him, and he had come out of his ordeals stronger and kinder. Though there was over twenty years' difference in our ages, I loved my brother a lot.

Watching him sleep made my own eyelids heavy. Just when I was about to succumb, there was a quiet knock at the door.

"Come in," I called in a low voice.

Detective Trumble was middle-aged and graying, sturdily built, and no-nonsense. None of this silly TV stuff of wearing high heels and low-cut tops on the job. I doubted Cathy even owned a pair of high heels. I'd talked to her before, several times, and I'd liked her. Though the circumstances were bad today, I had to notice that Cathy looked rough. There were pouches under her eyes, and she walked like her back hurt. Trailing behind her was a familiar lanky African American with a close-cut buzz. He was wearing a suit, and he looked good in it.

"Wow!" I said. "You got promoted?" I'd gone to high school with Levon Suit. My brain tried to make a joke about a Suit wearing a suit, but finally it just gave up.

He gave me a weary smile. "Yep," he said. "Last week. And look at me now. Murder investigation."

Levon and Cathy sat down on the opposite couch, relief

crossing Cathy's face as she sat back. She must have had a very long day.

"If you all want a drink, there's some Coke in the refrigerator, or I could make some coffee." That was my best offer.

Cathy shook her head, though Levon looked as though he would have liked to take me up on it.

"I hear you have the flu and a missing babysitter. And you don't recognize the dead woman?"

"Yes to all of that." I'd been working the narrative out in chronological order while I lay on the couch: Robin's trip, my flu, the arrival of Virginia, what had happened today. Well, yesterday. I had the order of events in my head, though it was constructed from an unreliable memory since I'd been (still was) ill.

Then I heard Sophie stirring through the monitor. She was making little noises. "Cathy, I have to go feed the baby," I said. "You can come with me if you need to ask some questions. Levon, I think Phillip is waking up, if you want to ask him what he heard and saw." I'd noticed my brother's eyes flicker.

Phillip sat up straight and shot me a reproachful look.

Every bone in my body ached. Only the fact that the baby was awake got me off the couch.

In Sophie's room, with the curtains drawn tightly, the turtle night-light gave a warm glow, just enough to show Sophie's red hair as a muted halo. The shadowy room was peaceful and snug, and I was happier here. I could hear the rain beginning to patter against the window. Even if a detective was with us, even if a woman had died in my yard, I was in a little cocoon with my daughter, who didn't know death or evil.

When she was dry and powdered, I gestured to the stool that came with the rocking chair, and Cathy sat down on it gratefully. I took the chair, arranged my robe and nightgown, and Sophie latched on.

Cathy was kind (and smart) enough to keep her voice low. “Tell me what happened. Why and when you and Phillip left the house. Every detail.”

I told her about waking up to a Virginia-less house, our fruitless search, the doors we’d used, the path we’d followed, exactly what we had done.

“You have no idea where this Virginia Mitchell has gone?” Cathy asked, for the second or third time.

“If I did, I’d sure tell you,” I said, more than a little exasperated. “Mother had gotten good references for Virginia. She hired Virginia to help me when I first came home from the hospital after I had Sophie. When I was back on my feet, I told her goodbye and gave her a thank-you check. My mother actually hired her and paid her salary.”

“And you called her back again because . . . ?”

I sighed. We’d come full circle. “Because Robin had to leave for Bouchercon, and I could tell I was getting sick.” Just now, I felt I was going to keel over any second.

“Any visitors tonight?”

“No. Wait, yes. Sarah Washington, Phillip’s girlfriend.”

“I remember Sarah.”

I nodded.

“Did you get the feeling Sarah already knew Virginia?” Cathy said.

“I never saw them together. I was flat on my back in bed and barely conscious. You can ask Phillip.”

“When is Robin coming back?”

“Early this afternoon, thank God,” I said, realizing it was now well into Sunday. “I have to warn him to expect chaos.”

"And where was he? Explain again?"

"At Bouchercon," I said, for what seemed the hundredth time. I was hanging on to my temper by a thread. I spelled it for her. "It's the world mystery convention. You know Robin's a writer. He won an Anthony last night."

"So he was in front of a lot of people."

"Yes. A lot." No way could he have anything to do with this, I said silently.

Sophie had been looking around in her googly way. She had tried waving her hands and occasionally kicking. My arms were about to fall off, so I was relieved to notice she was beginning to tire. I was ready to lay her in the crib. Holding her, a warm bundle, was a real comfort to me—but I had been reminded again of how weak I was.

"I'm going to put Sophie down," I told Trumble. I rose very carefully, feeling weak in the knees. I had to step around Virginia's folding bed to lay the baby down.

The baby looked up at her slowly turning mobile. Rabbits dressed in charming clothes rotated above Sophie's head while the music played—"Peter Cottontail." It seemed terrible to stand in this room and think about murder.

"My nephew's nursery had a mobile," Cathy said quietly. "It was flying cats. I thought it was the cutest thing ever made."

"I didn't know you were an aunt," I said. "How old is he? Is this your sister's son?" Cathy had a younger sister, Carmen, who'd been ill recently. I couldn't recall any details, so I was leery of asking how she was. Maybe she had passed. I was embarrassed not to know.

"Duncan's seventeen now. Phillip probably knows him."

I thought she'd follow up with some other detail, but she

didn't. Instead, she looked away, seeing something besides this snug room. Clearly, Duncan was trouble.

When I was sure Sophie was asleep, we stepped out into the hall and I closed the door to the nursery, leaving a small gap.

Abruptly coming out of her preoccupation, Cathy said, "I'm sorry, I should have told you to keep the baby with you. We need to search the house."

"Oh, no," I said in dismay. "Why?"

"The dead woman was here. The missing woman was here."

"But the dead woman wasn't in my house!" At least, I hoped not. But now I felt even more jangled. How could I be sure of that?

"It has to be done. I hope you consent, because the sooner we start, the sooner it'll be over. If you don't consent, we'll wait for a warrant."

"Is there any way I could just go to bed? I'm running on empty, and I'm also running a temperature." I hated to sound pathetic, but truly I wasn't sure I could stand up, or sit up, any longer.

"I'll ask them to search your room first," Cathy promised. "I'll do the baby's room now, and as soon as I'm done, she can go back in the crib."

I had a moment of great resentment when I thought of someone rummaging around in our house, disturbing our baby's things. But I recalled a long-ago occasion when I had actually found something criminal hidden in a crib. I sighed heavily.

I had to lift Sophie out of her bed again, and carry her some more. All I wanted to do was collapse in a heap somewhere, and be sick in peace. Though I realized this was a whiny attitude, and that I was distinctly sorry for myself, that was how I felt. I wanted to maintain my anger, but I didn't have the energy. Cathy was only doing her job.

Of course the police need to search the house. It makes sense. And it puts the perfect cap on the evening. I sure didn't like it, though. "And after that? Phillip can go back to bed, too, after his room is searched?"

Cathy nodded. "Levon will have explained this to Phillip. And Levon will talk to Sarah and her family to confirm what Phillip told us."

"Can't that wait until tomorrow?" I said, dismayed at how unhappy Sarah's parents would be when the police knocked at their door. This might doom the relationship. I tried to tell myself this was trivial, under the circumstances, but . . . it really wasn't, to my brother.

"Oh, sure, Levon won't talk to them for a few hours," Cathy said. She opened the front door. "Okay, guys, it's a go."

Two uniformed officers nodded at me before going down the hall to start with the bedrooms. They were happy, and I could see why. It was a good thing to draw search duty inside, when the rain was drumming the ground outside.

Phillip was still, or again, sitting on the couch. Levon was nowhere in sight. "They're going to search," he said, and he had energy enough to be grouchy.

"After our rooms are done, we can go to bed."

"Let me take Sophie," Phillip offered. I could hardly wait to pass her over. After a moment, he said quietly, "Did Detective Trumble tell you there was a knife by the dead woman's hand?"

"That was the shiny thing?"

He nodded.

"She didn't tell me." I tried to think intelligently about what the presence of the knife might mean, but I found it hard to care. We sat slumped in miserable silence.

After an eternity, Phillip and I got the green light to retire.

Phillip took Sophie to her room. She stayed asleep while he put her in her crib. At this point, that seemed like a miracle.

Finally, I was in a room with a bed, and I was alone, and I was about to climb in it. I was so exhausted I was scared I wouldn't hear Sophie unless she cried right in my ear, so I put the monitor on Robin's pillow. The rain was pounding against the roof. I curled up on my side, and after saying a short prayer, I was out.

Chapter Seven

"Roe."

I heard someone talking. I groped for the monitor, unable to open my eyes.

"Roe."

The voice was insistent. And it wasn't coming from Sophie's room, but approximately a foot away from my head. With a huge effort, I dragged my eyes open. "Robin?" I couldn't believe it. He was back. "Oh, you got here so fast. I was going to call you this morning. I didn't want you to freak out last night."

"I get to choose whether I freak out or not," Robin said. His face was stern and serious. Though the last thing I wanted was to wake up to a very unhappy husband, that seemed to be the case.

"I didn't think you could get a much earlier flight back," I said, as my plan of going back to sleep retreated farther and farther into the realm of impossibility. "And you were so happy. And we were all okay."

"Roe. You don't get to make up my mind for me. I get to be scared if something happens to my wife and my daughter."

I hadn't had a moment to think about my decision at all.

Robin was right.

"I'm so glad you're here," I said. "I'm *so* glad. But all I could think was that I couldn't bear ruining your big moment."

Robin took me in his arms and held me fiercely. "Thank God you and the baby and Phillip are okay," he said, his voice ragged. "I talked to the police before I came in the house. But I want to hear the whole story."

"Wait," I said, finally and completely awake. "How come you came back early?"

"Phillip left a message on my cell, but I didn't check my messages for maybe an hour. While I threw my stuff together, I saw the phone light was blinking. Detective Trumble had called my room. But I was in too much of a hurry to return it. Maybe she was checking to make sure I was really in the hotel. I called her when I was waiting to board my flight."

Phillip was a traitor! I'd told him I wasn't going to call Robin, so my brother had taken it upon himself to brief Robin about our situation. Cathy Trumble, I could understand—I didn't know why I hadn't foreseen her calling Robin. She was doing her job. But Phillip!

"I checked on available flights on the Web. Found one on Delta. Took a cab to the airport. Called Uber when I got to Atlanta. It was raining awful hard, and he had to drive slow. I got pretty impatient." I pulled back to look at his face. I could see that he had been not only "pretty impatient," but frantic, to reach us to make sure we were okay.

It was a bit bitter to admit to myself he had reason to be upset. I had not done the right thing, and Phillip had made the right call (literally and figuratively)—which didn't mean I wouldn't be a little angry at him for a while.

"And when did your cold turn into the flu?" he said accusingly. My husband was determined to get all his grievances into the open, here and now.

"Uhhh . . . pretty soon after you left."

He rubbed his stubbly face with his hands. "Roe . . ." He sounded hurt and exasperated and baffled. A lot to pack into one word.

"You can't blame me for not calling you about that," I said, feeling on more solid ground. "There wasn't *one thing* you could have done to make me better. I had help, right? Virginia and Phillip. Angel came by, too. And Emily Scott!" (Though most of that help had been completely by chance. Again, I realized I had been wrong. This was a very unpleasant conviction, and one I wasn't used to.) "I wanted you to have your celebration. I *knew* you would win."

That brought a reminiscent smile to his face. Robin is amazingly attractive when he smiles. He's not model-handsome by any means, but he has charm oozing out of his pores. His anger was draining away, but he still looked serious. "I wish you had been honest with me," he said.

"I wish I had been, too," I said. If I had an apology to make, I liked to think I was woman enough to do it. "I am really sorry. I was wrong."

There was a long moment of silence, while I cringed inside. I think Robin could see how miserable I was. Finally, he said, "But I did enjoy the win. I've waited a while." I knew the incident was over.

"Where is the Anthony? The actual award?"

"Still packed in my carry-on bag. This year it's a little carved tombstone," he said. "I'll show it to you in a few minutes. Roe, tell me what happened. Where is Virginia? Who was the dead woman?"

With her usual strategic timing, Sophie begin to fuss. Robin was out of the room before I could count to one.

"Here's my girl," he crooned. "Wet? Daddy'll change you. Hey, I missed you, little pumpkin."

Sophie made a tiny noise, which came clearly over the monitor.

"Hear that?" Robin called, forgetting I could hear in stereo. "She's trying to say 'Daddy'!"

"I'm sure she is," I said, trying not to sound skeptical. "If you can keep her busy for a minute, I need a little time." I slipped into the bathroom, washed my face, brushed my hair, and laid some toothpaste on my teeth. When I realized I cared about the way I looked and smelled, I knew I must be getting better. By the time Robin came in with Sophie, I was ready for her. While she and I had our little communion, I explained to Robin what had happened the night before. Only the night before! It seemed like a week.

"So, what did the nanny cam show?" he asked.

"Huh?"

"When I left," he said, using his Very Patient voice, "I told you I'd bought a nanny cam and put it in Sophie's room. I didn't think about Virginia spending the night in there. I hope I didn't film anything that would embarrass her."

"Since Virginia's missing, I figure she has bigger problems than you seeing her in her panties or whatever. You need to call the police department *now*. Where is it? Maybe this can tell them exactly what happened." I was excited.

"You don't remember me telling you?" Again with the judgment, about what I considered the least relevant part of our previous conversation.

"I was beginning to feel bad by then, so I guess it didn't register." (Frankly, I suspected that Robin, who seemed to *think* very loud, simply believed he had told me. Also, this was not important at the moment.) "Where is it?" I said again. Since Sophie and I were through, I handed her to Robin for the burping routine.

"It looks just like a plug-in air freshener," he said proudly. "It sends a signal to the receiver attached to our TV." He was patting Sophie's back forcefully, and he was rewarded with a huge belch.

"Which TV?" I *really* didn't like things taking place in my house I didn't know about. That had been happening a lot lately.

"The one in the living room. Pretty timely installment, huh?"

I swallowed my irritation, because that was the truth. "Speaking of time . . . what time is it now, anyway?" Robin was between me and the clock.

"Eight A.M.," he said, with a jaw-cracking yawn. "Okay, I'll call Cathy about the camera. I guess she's the one to call? Not too many detectives on the Lawrenceton force."

"Yeah. Oh, Levon got promoted. He was with her last night."

"Was Phillip a help?" Robin asked, as he punched in the Sparling County Law Enforcement Complex (SPACOLEC) number on his phone. "Cathy Trumble, please," he told the clerk.

"Before he gets up, I want to tell you what a rock Phillip was," I said, from the bottom of my heart. "He was a tremendous help. He'll probably sleep until noon."

Robin held up a finger to let me know Cathy had picked up. "Detective Trumble? This is Robin Crusoe. I got back an hour ago. No, I didn't answer my room phone, but I finally heard your message. You got mine? I called from the airport. I was focused on getting home." Robin's expression showed he was definitely discomfited. "I'll explain that later. Listen, I called to tell you something I'm sure you'll want to know. There's a nanny cam in Sophie's room. Maybe there's something important on it." He listened, looking even more unhappy. "Okay, if you really think so. Bring it by." He hung up.

"What?" I was playing with Sophie's fingers and toes. She looked at me seriously. It was still intoxicating to realize I was *Mama*. When I had been a child, my mother had been everything to me, since my dad had not been home much even in the years before they divorced. Mother had been interested in my life. She'd been my manners coach, my yardstick of correctness, my moral compass. She had always loved me. She'd praised me when I'd earned it, and she'd expected better of me when I fell short.

Now I was this almighty figure to my own baby. It was awesome, and it was terrifying.

I glanced up at Robin, to see that he too was lost in rapt contemplation of the miracle we'd created.

He sighed heavily, and returned to planet Real Life. "Cathy wonders why I wasn't in my hotel room when she called last night. She's bringing by a photo of the dead woman for us to look at. Let's watch the recording right now. Once the police take it, we'll never see what's on it."

"Should we?" I couldn't deny I really, really wanted to see the recording. More importantly, I was relieved Robin and I were again in sync. We hadn't been married long, and I'd realized there would be rough patches. We'd just hit one of them.

"If you'll hold on to Sophie, I'll get dressed," I said. "I'll feel better when Cathy comes if I'm dressed." I pulled my nightgown over my head. Robin watched with some interest.

Maybe I'm shallow, but that made me feel better. I hesitated. I was reluctant to get dressed when I felt I wasn't really clean. "I'm going to take the quickest shower on record. Do you really think it's okay if we watch the recording before Cathy gets here?"

"It's ours," Robin said, and shrugged expansively.

When I emerged from the two-minute shower and pulled on some jeans and a T-shirt, Robin and Sophie were in her room. His nose was wrinkled. "I needed to change her again. You want to get the cam?"

I noticed the "air freshener" immediately. It really *did* look just like a plug-in. If I'd been in the habit of using them, I would never have questioned its purpose. I unplugged it while Robin laid a sleepy Sophie in her crib.

In the living room, I sat expectantly in front of the television. I hoped so strongly that the nanny cam would reveal everything, and there would be no more mystery. We'd learn what had happened to Virginia.

Chapter Eight

Robin had an instruction book in his hand, and he referred to it to start the recording.

Among the multiplicity of small machines surrounding our television—DVR, sound system, cable transmitter—the new black box was hardly noticeable.

I was surprised at how excited I was. This was almost like being at the movies, but with an elevated element of suspense.

After a minute of fiddling, Robin sat beside me. "It's motion-activated," he explained. "And it's in color."

Of course it was. I didn't even want to know how much it had cost.

I was disappointed, at first. All the actions caught by the camera were innocuous, not to say boring. I walked in and out once or twice, visibly dragging, holding my arm over my mouth and nose when I coughed or sneezed. You could see me deteriorate into a staggering wraith in a nightgown with a mask over her face. But interspersed with these glimpses, there were moments of Virginia. The first afternoon, she looked around the room, opening and shutting drawers and closets, reacquainting herself with the arrangements for changing Sophie and the location of her clothes and so on.

We saw Virginia carry Sophie to the changing table. She never turned away from Sophie. I nodded silently. Virginia put on the fresh diaper quickly and efficiently before she picked the baby up and turned Sophie to her shoulder while she patted Sophie's back. Wisely, Virginia had thrown a burp cloth over her shoulder. Sophie spit up copiously on it.

"Aw, girl!" Virginia said. I could read her lips. I could tell when Sophie produced one of her prodigious burps, because Virginia laughed. She lowered Sophie into the crib while she disposed of the used diaper and tossed the wet cloth into the clothes hamper. Virginia checked her shoulder, evidently found it was dry, and looked relieved. She checked on Sophie, saw Sophie had fallen asleep, and left the room.

Then light was coming through the shades on Sophie's window when we next saw movement. Phillip came in and took care of Sophie, talking to her and blowing on her stomach, before carrying her out of the picture. I appeared once, looking like death. Then we watched Emily and Angel come in and out, and I reminded myself to write them thank-you notes.

We had seen nothing out of the ordinary. Up to this point.

We reached last night's footage. Virginia entered the room alone, her cell phone held to her ear. It was like watching a pantomime. It was clear Virginia was agitated. Her whole posture was tense, and her movements were emphatic, exaggerated. She might as well have had I AM UPSET in a balloon over her head. She paced back and forth as she spoke. After a short and angry conversation (going by the expression on Virginia's face), she stabbed a finger on the "end call" icon on her phone. (Though we couldn't see the face of the phone, her actions were clear to read.)

After disconnecting, Virginia stood rooted to the spot. Though her face was turned away from the camera, the hunch of her shoulders read as "despairing." Or maybe "resigned."

Robin and I glanced at each other. "Wish I could have heard that conversation," he said. I nodded, and we turned back to the screen. What happened next was another surprise, though a slight one.

Phillip came into the room, clearly to ask Virginia a question. She waved a hand, as if to sweep away his words. Phillip looked at her narrowly, but after a moment, when she said nothing else, he left the room with a shake of his head. *If you don't want to talk, I'm outta here.*

When she was alone, Virginia's shoulders slumped. She turned to face the camera, and we saw she was crying. After a minute or two, she seemed to pull herself together. She left the room.

Since the camera was motion-activated, the sequences jumped forward in a disconcerting way. Virginia, her face shuttered but calm, popped in and out carrying Sophie. If she put Sophie in the crib to sleep, in the next segment we saw Virginia hurry in when Sophie's arms were waving.

In what was one of the last bits of the recording, Phillip and Sarah tiptoed in. Sarah bent over the crib, smiling, to admire Sophie. She glanced up at Phillip, and he beamed back at her. Then they tiptoed out.

There was one of the jerks that indicated a time lapse.

Then a strange woman appeared. She glanced around the room.

"Oh my God," I whispered. I glanced sideways at Robin. He was as appalled as I was.

"That's the dead woman," I said. "She was in Sophie's room. In our house."

"You know her," he said, sounding tired and sad.

Now that I could watch the woman alive and moving, a sense of familiarity tickled at me. I shook my head, trying to fix a name to the woman. As we watched, the dead woman crossed the room to the crib. She looked down at Sophie for a long moment. Though I knew perfectly well Sophie was okay, I was terrified.

There was a loud knock on the front door, and I gave a little shriek.

"Sorry, honey," I told Robin, my heart thudding. "I'll let her in?"

He nodded wordlessly. He looked very grim, an expression that did not sit on Robin's face with any ease.

Cathy Trumble looked every day of her age, and maybe a few more. She'd clearly been up for hours, maybe hadn't ever gone to bed. "Seriously, a nanny cam?" Cathy said. "You didn't know about this last night, Roe?"

"I would have told you."

"Robin, you're home very quickly," Cathy said, with no inflection. "Hard to get in touch with you last night."

"I had my phone on vibrate for the banquet duration. I didn't even think about checking my messages," Robin said. "I called Roe to tell her I'd won, and then I called my mother. I went around the bar to have my pats on the back." He smiled. "Jeff and I started talking again about collaborating. We wanted to get into the nuts and bolts of how it would work, so we went to Jeff's room where we could hear each other. So I missed your call to my room. And finally, I saw Phillip's text."

"You sure have it all worked out." Cathy looked sour.

"I had the plane ride to think about it," Robin said.

"You went straight to the airport? Your friend Jeff give you a lift?"

"I took a cab to the airport. A Yellow Cab. I checked flights from the hotel, and I found an empty seat on a Delta flight, leaving in around an hour."

"Use a credit card?"

"Sure."

It was clear to me that Cathy distrusted Robin, which was startling as saying you distrusted ice cream. I opened my mouth to say a few things (sharp and pointed things) to Cathy, but Robin held up his hand.

"Roe, she'll find out I'm telling the truth. Let's skip the argument. It's more important for her to see this." Robin took a deep breath. "Cathy, we just watched the footage."

She didn't seem surprised. "And?"

"The woman on it . . . if she's the woman who was killed, I know her."

Cathy opened a folder she'd had in her hand and took out a picture of the dead woman. It had been taken from the uninjured side of her face. Her hair was shoulder-length and unrealistically blond. She had a big jaw, which made her miss being pretty.

"Oh, *no,*" I said, recognizing her for certain. I was unable to think of anything more eloquent. *This is incredibly bad,* I thought, dismally sure our lives were about to get worse.

"That's Tracy Beal." Robin's voice was full of distaste, unhappiness. He looked the detective right in the eyes. "Cathy, it's the woman who attacked Roe in her kitchen. While the movie crew was here. You didn't recognize her?"

Cathy looked at the picture again, a little line between her eyes as she concentrated. "This woman's hair is longer and a different color," she said slowly. "And she's gained a lot of weight. But I see it's Tracy Beal, now." Cathy was clearly unhappy she hadn't caught this earlier, but she shook off the self-reproach. "It's good to know her identity. We would have found out from her fingerprints later today, but the sooner the better. What's your complete history with her, Mr. Crusoe?"

When had we gotten so formal?

"Please, sit down," I said, not because I wanted to be polite, but because I was still weak and needed to sit, myself. I collapsed gratefully in my favorite corner of my favorite couch, next to Robin. "We went over all this when she tried to kill me," I said. "And over it and over it. You know our history with this woman. How come she's out, now? How could it be possible she was *in our house*?"

"I'll look into that. But first I need to hear about your relationship with Ms. Beal," Cathy said. She wasn't going to budge.

I could tell from her face and the way she was sitting that Cathy was being such a jerk because she was ashamed. The police had screwed up, somehow. She would tell what bothered her so much . . . when she had to. I glanced sideways at Robin, knowing that he would rather talk about hemorrhoids than Tracy Beal.

"Tracy had already been sentenced to court-ordered therapy before she came on my radar. She'd stalked Dan Lonsdale and threatened his fiancée."

Cathy looked blank. "Who?"

"Another mystery writer," I explained.

"I just saw him at Bouchercon," Robin said. "But we didn't talk about Tracy. Nothing to say."

"Then what did you talk about?" Apparently, Cathy couldn't imagine a conversation that didn't touch on the stalker they had in common.

"Dan's publicist just got promoted, so he was worried she wouldn't be handling his books anymore. Dan's editor just moved to another house . . . another publishing house. I was commiserating."

Cathy looked blank. Well, she'd asked. "Let's return to how you first encountered Ms. Beal," she suggested.

"While Tracy was in therapy for stalking Dan, she was in the mental ward of a hospital. It had a library. She picked up one of my books. She liked it. She was released from therapy two months later because she showed such amazing progress. Of course she seemed better, because she didn't care about Dan anymore. She'd transferred her obsession to me." Poor Robin looked tired to death of talking about Tracy Beal, and no wonder. "It wasn't a secret I was in Los Angeles working on the script for *Whimsical Death*. When she was released, she made her way to LA somehow."

Robin would never get over his mortification at being the object of Tracy's obsession. That was one of the things I liked about him; he was really surprised when women found him attractive.

"She was your Number One Fan," Cathy said, predictably. She had watched *Misery,* along with everyone else in the free world, apparently.

"If only I had a dollar for every time someone has said that." Robin was trying to stay cool, but he hated rehashing a painful memory, and he hated it even more when people made fun of what had been a fraught situation.

"How did you meet her initially?"

"I didn't meet her at all. She started leaving messages on my Web site under the name LastFanStanding. At first, they weren't really loony. Comments about my books, some of them really perceptive." Robin sounded faintly surprised. "Talking about how excited she was to see the movie. Discussing the actors cast in the production. I've had readers who got invested before, so I wasn't too concerned, though my Web-management person got antsy." Robin slung his arm around my shoulders. I leaned against him. "Then Tracy started writing letters. To me. To my Los Angeles agency. My New York agency. They weren't signed, but the phraseology was the same as the postings on my Web site, and each message was more or less the same. She wanted to meet me in person."

"How did you respond?"

"I didn't. In fact, we called the police and reported it." He shrugged. "But my signing schedule was available to anyone. I was a little worried, but I figured if she really had to meet me, it would be better in public. She didn't show up at any of the events, or if she did she didn't introduce herself. She kept posting, though, wanting to talk to me one-on-one. And she would *not* let it rest. The situation got major, both in public and in private."

"So what happened?"

"Dawn—my Web person—banned her from the site."

"How did Tracy react?"

"She found my mother's address."

I'd never heard this part of the story. Robin gave me an apologetic look; and I understood he'd simply found it too distasteful to discuss.

"Tracy wrote my mother a horrible letter, and upset Mom . . . very much."

I couldn't imagine Corinne, whose favorite topics of conversation were her two little dogs and her grandchildren, reading such a document. "Oh, *Robin,*" I said, taking his hand. I wished he had told me before, but I understood why he hadn't.

"Mom took the letter to her local police—she lives in Florida—and they faxed it to LA. The police got really interested then, because there was some threatening language. And there were elements of that letter that matched one sent to Celia Shaw, the actress. The one who was murdered on the set of *Whimsical Death*."

"So the police got serious about Tracy," Cathy said.

"Right. They tracked her through the Web site, where she kept posting under different names. But Tracy kept moving, always a step ahead. She's not stupid. But she did finally make a mistake. She blamed Dawn for the Web site ban, not me. She researched Dawn's address, just like she'd tracked my mother. One night, she broke all the windows in Dawn's car and slashed her tires. It was on Dawn's security camera."

Cathy was learning forward. "They arrested her."

Robin managed a wry smile. "She had left her hotel room just before they got there. But they got fingerprints, and identified her from her previous stalking sentence. About that time, *Variety* ran a story about me coming here for the filming. Tracy got here ahead of the film crew and got a job with the craft service company hired for the shoot. The LAPD had shown me a picture, but it was like a driver's license headshot. I didn't have a clear idea who I was watching for."

"You know what happened after that," I said, cutting short this unpleasant trip down memory lane. When Tracy had tried to kill me, Sophie had been a tiny cluster of cells in my womb. I hadn't even known I was pregnant. The thought of Sophie never existing . . .

Tracy had been arrested and taken to jail. At her arraignment, the judge had agreed with her court-appointed lawyer that Tracy's mental condition should be evaluated. Again.

The last we'd heard, she was in a secure facility being "evaluated." I hadn't even wanted to know where she was. I'd dismissed Tracy Beal from my thoughts.

"You haven't heard from her?" Cathy asked.

"I've gotten a couple of e-mails that sounded reminiscent of her. But she was locked up. I was sure it couldn't be her." Robin did not look at me as he said this.

And he felt that concealing the flu was outrageous?

"Do you have these?" Cathy said. "You didn't delete them?"

"I saved them," Robin said.

"I'll need to see them, of course. Now I need to get in touch with Tracy's mother and sister," Cathy said, making a note on a little pad she kept in her purse. "Their contact information should be in our records."

"Have you found Virginia's cell phone?" I said abruptly.

Cathy and Robin both looked at me as if they'd forgotten I was in the room.

"No," Cathy said. "Why?"

"When you watch the film," I said, "Virginia gets a phone call that clearly upsets her. Maybe it was from Tracy?" I wanted something to tie together.

Cathy look doubtful. "It doesn't seem likely they'd met, but we'll ask about that. Naturally, we've checked Virginia's apartment. Her neighbors haven't seen her in a couple of days. Neither has her mother, who is very worried about her daughter. So she didn't go to either place she could call home after she vanished from your house."

"I'm not surprised, since her car was still here after she disappeared," I said. "You towed it? I can't imagine Virginia's disappearance and the death of Tracy are *un*related."

"Yes, we towed it, and no, those can't be unrelated," Cathy

said. "Not even you could have luck that bad." She stood up slowly. She wore her weariness like a coat on her shoulders. "All right, then. Tracy Beal. We can start tracking her movements now that she's been tentatively identified. We'll find out how she turned up in your backyard."

"Good," I said, not bothering to make my tone any less snappish. I was angry on so many levels.

Cathy looked at me in an evaluating way, if I can call it that. "Roe, do you think I'm not trying my hardest to find out who killed this woman? Do you think I'm not trying to find out where Virginia Mitchell is?"

"No," I said, flustered. "Not at all."

"Do you think this is the only case I have?"

I'd never thought about that one way or another. "I guess not?" I said.

"It isn't. We've got an elder-abuse case. I'm helping with the interviews for a teen party shooting at Dr. Clifton's, same night Tracy got killed." There was something desperate in Cathy's face, something I wasn't able to define.

"Okay," I said hesitantly. "Are you telling me this because you think we expect miracles?"

"I'm thinking you and Robin have some knowledge you're not sharing about this Tracy Beal."

"Not so," I said forcefully.

"Uh-huh." Cathy looked at me skeptically, and then she left, taking the depressing picture and the nanny cam recording with her. I walked with her to the door. We didn't speak.

Since I was already on my feet, I looked in on Sophie. Sound asleep.

When I returned to the living room, Robin was sitting with his head in his hands.

"I know this seems like I was hiding something from you," he said, not looking at me.

"It doesn't just *seem* like that. You did. You suspected Tracy was back on your trail, and you didn't tell me."

"I didn't want you to worry. After all, this is the woman who tried to kill you."

"Which is exactly why I needed to be on the alert." I grabbed hold of my temper and sat across from him. "Listen, Robin, you had a valid point; I should have told you I was really sick before you left. I shouldn't have withheld that knowledge from you. And I should have called you the moment I found the dead woman. But I feel we're about even, now. What do you say?"

He peeked between his fingers at me, looking relieved. "I say yes. Cathy thinks I've concealed something else, something crucial. I don't know why she feels that way. I can live with her disapproval, but not with yours. Come give me a hug. I'm too tired for anything else—I never thought I'd say that, I must be getting old. Roe, I missed you so much. And I was scared to death."

I expelled a deep breath. Our teeter-totter relationship was back in balance. Being newlyweds—with a baby and a body in the yard—was no walk in the park.

Chapter Nine

Robin trudged off to our room to sleep. Evidently, Phillip was still zonked out. I was a couple of degrees better than I had been the day before, but I had zero energy. This was the house of dull people.

There were many little tasks I should take care of. I should have asked Cathy when the crime scene tape could be removed from our backyard. I should definitely call my mother; it was really weird she hadn't texted me. Even though she was out of town, surely some crony of hers had let her know what had happened. Maybe there was a voice mail on my cell? No, and that was her usual choice. I could see the blinking light on the landline answering machine. I told myself I should get up to listen to those messages.

But I didn't want to talk to anyone. Anyone at all. And I didn't want to move.

I resorted to my tried and true comfort. I settled on the couch to read a Leigh Perry mystery, one I'd begun three days ago (it seemed like a year). To my chagrin, I had to backtrack to pick up the narrative.

I felt like a different person had started reading this book, and that person had a bad memory.

Whether I was sure about the characters' names or not, it was relaxing to enjoy a book . . . all by myself. I sighed when Phillip stumbled into the room thirty minutes later, rumpled and in need of a shave. He made a beeline for the refrigerator, where he poured a huge glass of orange juice. It disappeared in a few gulps. Then he began rummaging in the pantry until he found a Pop-Tart.

"Sis," he said, by way of greeting. "What's up?"

"Robin's home. I understand you called him." I gave Phillip a steely stare.

He looked guilty. "Well . . ." He couldn't think how to go on with the sentence.

"I was mad for a few minutes," I said, relenting. "But I understand why you did it. You were probably right. Did you know about the nanny cam?"

His blank expression told me the answer. "That's . . . what is that?" he said.

"It's a hidden camera meant to give parents the real picture on how their child's caregiver acts when the parents aren't around."

"You have one?" Phillip was immediately interested.

"Unbeknownst to me, yes. Robin put one in Sophie's room before he left. He *says* he told me. I was too out of it to register that . . . apparently."

Phillip was wise enough to let that pass by. "So did you watch the recording already?"

"We did, before we turned it over to Cathy Trumble."

Phillip was clearly disappointed he hadn't gotten to watch. "See anything interesting?"

I'd seen an intruder in my daughter's room, and it had scared the hell out of me. "I'll tell you about it in a minute. Listen, when did Sarah leave? When did you get to bed?"

"Sarah had to be home by eleven thirty," Phillip said. "She walked out the door at eleven twenty. She'd driven her mom's car."

I nodded. Sarah's family lived only two streets over.

"I was in bed by midnight. I read awhile before I turned out my light. At the latest, that might have been a quarter to one." Phillip shook his head. "That's all."

"I guess you and Sarah saw Virginia during the evening?"

"Not much. She sat in the living room maybe an hour. We talked to her," Phillip assured me. "She watched part of the movie. She had the monitor, so when she heard Sophie making noise, she left the room. That was about—ahhh—ten? Anyway, we didn't see her again."

"Did you see anyone else?"

"Like who?"

"Like the woman who got killed. She was in the house. It was on the nanny cam."

Phillip was aghast. "That's awful."

"She went in the baby's room. With a knife. In Sophie's room."

"I would have killed her myself if I had caught her doing that." He meant it.

I had tears in my eyes. This was a declaration of love. And I knew exactly how he felt, because I did, too. "You've been great throughout this," I said. "And before I forget it, I want to say thanks."

Phillip gave me an awkward hug. Our mutual dad and my

brother's mom were not big huggers, apparently. But Phillip was learning our ways.

"You think it would be okay if I went to the track to run?" he asked. "Josh is going. He can bring me home."

"I don't see why not." My conscience twanged, and I looked at the kitchen clock. It was too late to get to church for the service, and I was mostly relieved. I needed to go, but it would have been an ordeal.

Phillip might as well burn off some energy.

In five minutes, Phillip was out the door in track gear. "I'm running to the school," he called over his shoulder. He'd begun doing that after I'd observed that it was pretty silly to drive to a place and then run around the track. "Oh, Roe, your mom called last night, late. She said you hadn't answered your cell."

"Did you talk to her?"

"Just for a minute. She was in a big hurry, and plenty unhappy."

I could no longer ignore my conscience. I had to respond to messages. I called Mother first, but she didn't answer; if she and John were back from the reunion, she was probably at church. I left a voice mail.

Sarah Washington's mother had left a voice mail, too. I could tell Beatrice had thought out what she wanted to say very carefully. "I'm so sorry you've got troubles. I hope the police clear it up real soon. If you need anything, call me." I could hear the undertone of relief, of course; Beatrice had to be thinking, *Thank God Sarah had left by then.*

My pharmacy had called to tell me a prescription was ready for pickup. The children's librarian had called to say if I wasn't coming back to work, a friend of hers would love to apply for my job. I grimaced. I had to get off the fence about going back to work. But I was putting all this off until another day. My real life still felt far away from the current situation.

Angel had called, but she hadn't left a message. I decided to fill her in on recent events later.

Right at eleven, when it was safe to conclude we were all up and dressed (under normal circumstances), our neighbors Deborah and Jonathan Cohen came to the front door. I was not particularly glad to see them.

The Cohens were decent people, but they were sticklers about their property and the appearance of our neighborhood. (Though I had never heard the Cohens' history, I guessed it had included privation.) They were vigilant about the upkeep of all the houses and yards on McBride Street. You could expect to hear from the Cohens if your garbage can stayed out at the curb after pickup day (guilty once), or if your Halloween pumpkin was rotting on your front porch, or if your Christmas lights stayed up past January 31. In the course of a neighborly conversation, either Jonathan or Deborah would give you a strong hint about correcting your infraction.

I answered the door very quickly, since Robin was still asleep. I was literally armed with Sophie. The retired couple bent over our beautiful baby and admired her, almost as much as I thought was Sophie's due. They'd never mentioned any children. I figured it would have entered the conversation by now, if they had. Though I was not enthusiastic about talking to the Cohens this afternoon, I had no option; I had to invite them in.

Of course they accepted, since they had a message to deliver.

I put Sophie in her bouncer seat, and she made some tentative moves. She was always surprised when the seat reacted.

After they'd refused a drink, Deborah began, "You can imagine how we felt last night. We had to get out of bed, Lulu created such a ruckus! And we were awfully surprised when we saw the lights, people everywhere, the ambulance and whatnot." Lulu the dachshund was a frequent barker who could get really excited about a squirrel, or the shadow of a bird flying over the yard. I could only imagine Lulu's excitement at the flashing lights and the strange people.

"I was certainly scared too, especially with Robin out of town," I said, playing the I-was-all-by-myself card. Shamelessly. I glanced down at Sophie, and I saw that her eyelids shut for a second. Then she rallied, waving her arms and looking up at me. *Who are these people?* she was saying.

You might as well go to sleep, I told her.

Deborah and Jonathan (who were weirdly alike, short and stocky with curly gray hair and glasses) exchanged a loaded look. I knew something bad was coming. Something *else* bad. I went on the alert.

"I'm surprised you're telling me that," Jonathan said, with heavy significance. "Since when I got up in the night to go the bathroom I looked out the window and I saw someone I was sure was Robin. I thought, 'What the heck is Mr. Crusoe doing wandering around the yard at this hour of the night?' "

I could only stare at him. Finally, I got my reply together. "Jonathan, Robin was out of town at a banquet at that moment, winning an award. So whoever you saw, it wasn't my husband." I smiled, to show how unconcerned I was.

"If you say so," he said, in that aggravating passive-aggressive way people have of letting you know they think you are totally wrong.

I had no doubt Jonathan had told the police what he believed he'd seen. Tension tightened my arms and shoulders as I had a sudden rush of raw anxiety. This was why Cathy had questioned Robin so intently and in such detail . . . because of Jonathan's big mouth. And his even bigger mistake. I didn't know who he'd seen, but it hadn't been my husband. I took a deep breath to control my desire to snap at him. Or pop him one in his confident face.

"I sure hope we don't have more nights like last night," Deborah said, leaning forward with an artificial smile.

Message received.

But I was loaded for bear now.

"I certainly didn't want a woman murdered in my backyard," I said sweetly. "I didn't want my babysitter to vanish, either. I hope the police get to the bottom of this, so we don't have to be scared of *something else* happening."

Sophie was diplomatic enough to choose this moment to make a little "Ehhh" noise, which of course was adorable, but her next noise came from another area of her body and was less pleasant. Deborah and Jonathan rose to leave hastily. *Thank you, Sophie,* I thought.

Though I managed to keep my smile tacked on my face, I was glad to see the back of them. I stood in the doorway, Sophie in my arms in an odorous bundle, as I watched Jonathan and Deborah enter into a spirited discussion as they went out to the street, walked down the sidewalk, and turned in at the flagstone path to their own front door. (God forbid they should cross on the grass.) After a minute I heard barking. They'd let Lulu out.

"They were dumb for thinking they saw your daddy, huh?" I told Sophie. I could tell she agreed with me. I shut the front door behind me, and realized it was such a lovely day I ought to take Sophie outside . . . after I'd changed her diaper. Maybe we'd sit on the patio for a while. That sounded incredibly normal and relaxing, and I was ready for both.

Chapter Ten

Doing anything with an infant requires planning and several steps. I grabbed the bouncer with one hand, Sophie with the other arm, and went to the patio door. I set down the bouncer, opened the patio door, stepped outside, and reached back to get the bouncer seat. I set it safely in the shadow, and shut the door with my hip. I strapped Sophie into the bouncer. She was wearing a ruffled sun hat.

And then I collapsed into the deck chair, pretty much wiped out. Being sick had drained me of energy and strength. I felt enormous relief that Robin was home, that Sophie was no longer my sole responsibility. My world was not a surreal blur any longer. I turned the pages of the local paper languidly, until I found an article on the elder-abuse case Cathy had mentioned. I felt my mouth pucker up with distaste. It was awful. But there was nothing about the Clifton party shooting; maybe it had occurred too late to make the press run. The paper came out twice a week, now.

I dropped the pages on the ground beside me. I closed my eyes and pretended the backyard looked normal. No crime scene tape, no trampled grass. All was well; all was calm.

I fell into a pleasant stupor, near sleep but not quite. Sophie's eyes were closed and her face was relaxed. The Cohens had let Lulu inside when she'd barked at their back door, so there was almost no noise. Our street is not a high-traffic area, and the next street east (backing on ours) was lined with houses older and statelier, with expensive and well-grown hedges of boxwood or photinia circling the backyards. Those hedges provided a sound and sight barrier.

We had countered their boxwood hedges with one of our own, at least along our beautiful fence. We'd gotten tall ones for an immediate result, and they'd cost an arm and a leg. We couldn't splurge on the big plants to go all around the yard, so we were open to view from north and south, from Cohens to Herman sisters.

Speaking of whom . . . well, thinking of whom . . . I heard the distinctive squeak of the Herman screen door opening, and then the sound of it slapping shut. After a lazy moment of curiosity, I opened my eyes. I was looking straight into Chaka's. He was standing on the other side of the fence observing me intently, in absolute silence. I was startled, in an unpleasant way. But Chaka had never been anything but friendly, and I'd watched Peggy and Lena work on his training every day.

"Hi, Chaka," I said. I'd read somewhere you weren't supposed to bare your teeth at dogs, since it might be interpreted as a sign of aggression. I smiled with my lips closed. (Though I wondered if dogs even registered that you were smiling, since it was a human facial expression.)

Chaka's whippy tail began waving to and fro. Peggy had

told me that meant the dog was interested, not that it was necessarily happy with you. But the wagging did make me feel better.

After glancing at Sophie to make sure she was still asleep, I strolled over to the fence. "Hello, good dog," I said, for lack of anything better to say, and Chaka's tail moved faster.

Peggy came out of her back door. She seemed pleased when she saw I was making nice with Chaka.

"How are you today, Roe?" she called, walking over to the fence. "I hear you were really sick."

I didn't even bother to ask Peggy who'd told her that. "Well, I'm not running a fever anymore. Just a little wobbly." My illness was not more important than the fact that a woman had died not five yards away from where I stood.

"I'm glad you're better," Peggy said. Close up, I noticed that Peggy's face had many fine lines, but her fitness and vigor made her seem much younger. Today she didn't seem quite as lively as usual. None of us were.

"I'd apologize for your lost sleep, but there was nothing I could do about it," I said. "The Cohens told me Lulu barked all night. I hope you and Lena weren't too troubled?"

Peggy snorted. "Lulu barks when Deborah Cohen farts," she said.

I was so startled I couldn't stifle a laugh.

"I shouldn't be crude," she added without sounding sorry at all. "But really, that dachshund is a little yapper."

"Are all dachshunds like that?"

"No, no! They can be nice little dogs. But they're stubborn. They'll do anything you let them get away with." Peggy shook her head. "If Jonathan and Deborah just worked with Lulu, she could still be trained to be a better pet."

And again, Peggy wasn't talking about the murder. Well,

okay. "Chaka is very well behaved," I said. Not only was that the key to Peggy's (and Lena's) heart, it had the virtue of being true. "I'm sure it's because you spend a lot of time with him." Flattering, but also true.

"We had to do some retraining after we adopted him," she said. "But he's such a smart dog, it's been easy. Mostly. His breed are naturally quiet dogs, so we started out well on that score."

"I've never heard him bark before," I said. I looked down at his sleek golden-brown head. "Can I pet him?"

"He'd love it," Peggy said.

I reached over the fence and stroked Chaka's head. He felt smooth as silk, and when he looked up at me, I suddenly understood why people wanted dogs. You could certainly read "adoring" into those beautiful dark eyes and the steady gaze. Chaka was big; I hadn't realized how big until I was close to him.

"How much does he weigh?" I asked.

"About seventy-five."

"Is he typical for a . . ." I groped for the breed. "A Rhodesian ridgeback?"

"Yes, he's a healthy boy," Peggy said, smiling at the dog. "Though he was a rescue, he'd had excellent care. It wasn't a neglect case. I think his former owner had died. You see that line of hair on his back, the one that runs the opposite way to the rest of his coat? That's why they call them ridgebacks."

"So they were bred that way." I had no idea where to go with this conversation. Sophie made a couple of wakeful noises, and I got her out of her bouncer seat and carried her back to the fence, though it was quite an effort. Sophie seemed to have gained ten pounds overnight.

However, Peggy deserved to view the wonder that was Sophie. I looked from the baby to Peggy, with a smile that invited her to share my admiration.

Inexplicably, Peggy continued talking about the rescue organization where she'd gotten the dog. It was interesting (about one drop of interesting) to learn that dachshunds were bred to hunt badgers, and ridgebacks had been used to hunt lions.

To the best of my knowledge, badgers and lions were in short supply in Georgia.

Chaka extended his neck to sniff Sophie. He couldn't actually touch her, so I was okay with the sniffing.

"Now he knows she's a friend," Peggy told me. She beamed at me as though this were a great milestone in Sophie's life.

"When did you get the little statues?" I really did not want to listen to a monologue about dogs any longer.

Peggy turned to look, as if she'd forgotten what was in her garden.

She and Lena had put in a row of huge urns around their patio. The sisters kept them filled with flowers all spring and summer. In the nearest urn, a little statue of a frog on a lily pad perched in the middle of the fading flowers. In the next a pixie (maybe) was scattering something from a basket on the flowers. In the third . . . well, you get the idea. Gnome, squirrel, and so on.

Peggy shook her head ruefully. "A couple of weeks ago. They were on end-of-season sale, and Lena just fell in love with them."

Right on cue, Lena came out the back door. We went through the greeting ritual.

"I was just admiring your dog and your little statues," I said awkwardly. I didn't want to walk away just as she'd joined us, but Sophie was getting so heavy. My arms felt like rubber bands, rubber bands that had been stretched out of shape forever.

"We just love Chaka," Lena said. "Best dog we ever had. I bet Peggy's told you she wasn't in love with these statues. They sat by the back steps for a week, but then, surprise! I just came out and found them in place." She beamed at her twin.

Peggy looked embarrassed. "You liked 'em," she said.

"Glad you're back to yourself again, Chaka," Lena said to the dog. The ridgeback went down on his belly and put his head on his paws, the very picture of contrition.

"Roe says Lulu barked and barked," Peggy told her sister.

"Well, Chaka didn't care for all the flashing lights," Lena told me. "They made him anxious. He whined and went to the back door and just stood there. He was worried that someone was going to invade our yard."

"So all the strange people going in and out upset him? You, too, I guess." I was trying to draw the conversation to a close without being abrupt. I was reaching the end of my endurance. It was awful to be so weak.

"I can't say we weren't anxious, at first," Lena said. "The police came by the house this morning, really early. But after they'd explained what had happened, we were sorry you had such a scare. I understand your husband wasn't home?"

"No, he was in Nashville. Phillip was home, thank God."

"Oh, the blond boy," Lena said. "He's your . . ."

"Half brother," I supplied. "Same father."

"We knew your father," Peggy said unexpectedly. "We remember him well. Not a looker, but sex appeal coming out of his ears!" The sisters laughed simultaneously.

I found that not a little weird.

After a bit more chitchat about the inconvenience of a police investigation (!), I said good-bye to the sisters and the dog, and carried Sophie to the patio door.

"Roe," someone called, and I saw Deborah Cohen standing at their fence.

I had to return Sophie to the bouncer. My arms were trembling. I knelt to strap her in, and it was a little scary to stand up. But I took a few steps over to Deborah.

Deborah looked embarrassed, but determined. "I hope you don't mind that Jonathan told the police what he saw. It was his duty to let them know he'd seen someone going into your backyard." Her mouth was set in a determined, righteous flat line. At least she was asking me how I felt about Jonathan's action.

I bit my lip to keep back my first response, which was not printable. "But it wasn't his duty to tell them it was definitely *Robin,*" I pointed out in a glacial voice. "Because at that moment, Robin was in Nashville getting an award in front of seven hundred people." (Slight exaggeration for effect, okay?) "But now, because of your husband, the police are asking all kinds of questions trying to find out whether or not Robin could have made it here and back again, and I'm sure the gossip mill is working overtime."

And then, since I absolutely could not stand up any longer, I turned my back and went into the house. With one eye on Sophie, I was relieved to see Robin. He was awake and staggering around the kitchen, and he gave me a bleary wave.

"Honey, can you come get Sophie?"

"Sure," he said, and came out to the patio to lift her.

Phillip, red-faced and dripping sweat, came in just after Robin had put Sophie down on her play mat. He mopped his face with a towel and headed straight into the hall bathroom to shower. "I need to talk to you in a minute," he called as he shut the door.

After Robin had finished his coffee, I said, "Jonathan Cohen told the police he saw you going into our yard by the gate. Last night. That's why Cathy was asking you so many questions."

My husband stared at me. "But that's impossible. I wasn't there," he said.

"Of course you weren't. Apparently, the police have to take an eyewitness seriously, even if he's clearly mistaken."

"But . . ." Robin was outraged.

"It's so obvious you couldn't have returned, killed the woman, flown back, and conferred with Jeff, only to fly to Atlanta yet again. At least you were at the banquet and the bar with lots of witnesses for a big chunk of time. I'm sure the place was packed."

I'd only been to one previous mystery convention, but the bar had played a major role in the social aspect of the gathering.

Robin nodded. "For at least an hour. In retrospect, it was a bad time to get out of the public sight to talk to Jeff. But we were just so pumped about the plot, and how we'd work out who would do what . . ." His eyes went out of focus.

"Well," I said stoutly, "I don't know anyone who wouldn't believe Jeff. And he'd have had to be an active collaborator in a super-elaborate plot for you to have pulled it off. If you even *could* have."

"Even if I'd had Jeff cover for me, to have come home, killed a woman, and returned to Nashville only to fly back here in the middle of the night . . . I just don't think it's possible."

"No one came to Jeff's room while you were talking?" I asked wistfully.

Robin shook his head.

I brightened. "The cell phone records will show where you were, right? From the tower pinging, or whatever?" I'd read enough mysteries to know that was possible.

"Sure," Robin said. "But I had my GPS tracking device turned off. It creeps me out when I get ads tailored to my location. I think it can still be done, even if they won't be able to tell where in the hotel I was. But if I was anywhere in the hotel, I could not be here." He turned. "I have to brush my teeth before they grow moss."

"Of course he didn't think about staying in the bar," I muttered after he'd vanished. "Why would he? Just won a major award, the man of the hour, and he goes off to talk to another writer he can e-mail any day."

The flight time from Nashville to Atlanta was just forty minutes. That was sure a short flight. Damn. But still! People can't go through airports unobserved and unrecorded anymore. Robin would have had to pay cash for the surreptitious flight, to and from, and as Robin had remarked earlier, people using cash for a last-minute flight are conspicuous. Also, he'd have had to get from the airport to our house, which easily took as long as the flight itself, by some untraceable means.

And (simplest of all) Jeff was an upstanding citizen, and so was my husband. Robin was in the clear without a doubt . . . at least in my mind. I knew the police would have to (eventually) come to the same conclusion.

But I also knew how people talked. I knew the presence of two other women in our house, and the murder of one of them, would make the mere mention of Robin's possible involvement really juicy.

I'd heard the hall shower stop moments before, and I caught a glimpse of a towel-wrapped Phillip zipping into his bedroom. In a few minutes he reappeared, fully clothed.

"How was your run?" I asked. I wanted to talk about something else besides the murder.

"A few seconds better," Phillip said. "Sarah came to clock me."

I felt relieved and pleased. "Her parents really aren't put off by the . . . ?"

"Dead woman? No, I guess not." He seemed surprised, and I could tell he hadn't considered Sarah's parents' natural aversion to having their daughter visit a house where murder had occurred. "Josh and Joss were sure excited, though. They want to know if they can come see where she was." Joss was Josh's twin sister. I felt surrounded by twins.

"I'm not going to run tours," I said tartly.

Phillip was both resentful and embarrassed.

Then I realized I was a jerk. Of course they'd want to see. Human nature. I said, "But if they happen to come over here, and if you happen to take them into the backyard, it would be only natural to point the spot out. No touching the police tape. No one else, though. Seriously."

Phillip grinned. It was like the sun coming out. With my brother's blond hair, gorgeous blue eyes, and steadily increasing height, I didn't believe anyone would ever pick us out of a crowd as siblings.

I was only surprised that there weren't smitten kids lined up around the block. I had a high opinion of my little brother, though that didn't mean I didn't get exasperated with him at least once a week.

Over the months he'd lived with us, I'd learned Phillip's greatest attraction was that he was not judgmental; he was truly content to let other people live their own lives as they chose, unless they hurt someone else. And he was kind. This was refreshing to find in a person of any age.

"Okay, I'll call 'em later," Phillip said. "Are you fixing lunch today? Or should I just scrounge?"

"Sorry, honey, you'll have to scrounge. I'll cook, or at least arrange, tonight."

"No problem. Remind me to tell you about the party last night that got interrupted, Josh just told me," Phillip said. He turned to go to his room, but then he swung around. He had the guilty air of someone who'd just forgotten to relate a major point. "Roe, you might want to try to call your mom again," he said.

"Why?" I went on full alert.

"I'm sorry, I just started thinking about . . . not important. When Josh drove past your mom's street, there was an ambulance leaving. I don't know which house. But you might want to check with her."

I had a flash of exasperation, deeply tinged with fear. I was tempted to let Phillip have it for not remembering to tell me earlier, but he looked appropriately unhappy, and anyway . . . not the most important thing right now. I waved him off as I grabbed for my phone.

My true anger was with myself. In the back of my mind, I had been wondering why I hadn't heard from my mother, whether she'd come home or was still at the reunion. Why she hadn't texted or called or pounded on my door, demanding to know what was happening at my house. Though I had been somewhat relieved I hadn't had to answer her questions, I had been a little concerned. Now I was gripped with panic.

Mother answered after five rings.

"Where are you?" I asked. "There was an ambulance?"

"I'm at the hospital," she said, her voice dull. "John's had another heart attack."

Chapter Eleven

In the same listless voice, Mother continued. "He was feeling bad at the reunion. We came home early, thank God. As soon as we took our bags into the house, he collapsed."

"I'm *so very* sorry. Oh, Mother."

"Yes," she agreed. "This is really serious." My mother, always brisk and in charge of her emotions and actions, sounded hopeless.

"I have to get Sophie situated, I can't bring her to the hospital," I said, thinking out loud. "She should be up in a little while. I'll feed her and get over there."

"John David and Avery are here. When John started feeling off-kilter, they decided to come home from the reunion early, too. They were at the house."

These were John's two sons by his first marriage. Melinda, Avery's wife, was a friend of mine, though she was so busy with her kids and her community work that we didn't see each other as often as I'd like. John David was a widower.

"I'm glad they're there. Call me when you know something.

I'll come as soon as I can, Mother. I'm praying for you and John." I hung up, almost in tears. Mother had married again late in life, and she and John were very happy together. Avery and John David liked Mother a lot, John's grandkids called her Gran-Gran, and Melinda was a sweetie.

I loved John for himself, and because he made my mother happy. Not only did I want John to stay around, I also didn't want my mother to be grieving as I had when I'd lost my first husband, Martin, to a heart attack.

"Roe, what's wrong?" I hadn't heard Robin approach. He'd cleaned not just his teeth, but his whole self. He smelled of after-shave and soap.

I told him the bad news, having a hard time keeping my voice level.

Robin said, "How long until Sophie needs to be fed?"

I looked at the clock and estimated. "She should sleep another half hour, and then she'll need to nurse."

"Why don't I go to the hospital to wait with your mom? When the baby's fed, tell me, and we'll switch places."

This was another instance when Sophie's dependence on my boobs caused a lot of complications. People had told me I'd look back on the trials of early motherhood and laugh, but for now . . . I heaved a deep sigh. "Thank you," I said. "That's the best we can do."

"Where's Phillip?"

"He's in his room, probably on his laptop. He *forgot* to tell me he'd seen an ambulance on my mother's street."

"No!" Robin winced.

"Yes. But at least he told me. It's good I called her. I don't think she would have called me until she knew something." I felt my shoulders sag.

"I'll tell Phillip what's happening." Robin loped off, and I returned to my gloomy thoughts. He was back in a flash. "Okay, I'm off. While I'm gone, can you look for my keys? I was sure I put them in the bowl before I left. Maybe I missed them."

"Okay. Your extra car key is in the bottom left drawer under the microwave."

Robin grabbed the key and hurried out the door, barely taking time to pick up a jacket and a book.

I fidgeted and prayed and fidgeted after Robin left for the hospital. For once, I could hardly wait for Sophie to wake up. Phillip, passing through to assemble a cheese and cracker and soup lunch, asked me if I had any news. Phillip liked my mother well enough. But when John, who'd raised two sons, made an effort to know Phillip and include him in the family, Phillip had responded with affection.

My brother apologized all over again for dropping the ball, but then he lingered in the living room in a way that triggered an ominous feeling: obviously, Phillip had something else unpleasant to tell me.

"Spit it out," I said wearily.

"Some kids are saying online that the dead woman was Robin's old girlfriend," he blurted.

"The Internet has a lot to answer for," I said. This was the last thing in the world I wanted to hear, though I wasn't surprised. I tried to contain my anger, since Phillip was not the one who had been a rumormongering asshat.

"He didn't know her, right?" Phillip sounded hopeful.

"Ahhhh . . . the answer to that is a little complicated."

Phillip's face fell. "I was afraid of that."

"He didn't know her as a friend or 'girlfriend,' but as his stalker," I said. "And she tried to kill me last year."

His eyes widened. "The woman who stabbed your maid? That was her?"

"One and the same."

"And she's the woman who came in the house? Looked at Sophie?"

I nodded.

"That is extremely scary," Phillip said, and I could only nod again. "No wonder she got killed."

"But we didn't kill her."

Phillip nodded. "What was her name?"

"Tracy Beal. But the police may not have gotten hold of her family yet. So don't put her name on Facebook or any other social media."

"I understand," said Phillip. "And, you know, I'm sorry. About not telling you about the ambulance first. Josh told me that some guy fired a rifle into the house where the party was, Saturday night. He and Joss were there. It was pretty scary. That sidetracked me."

"Why didn't you and Sarah go?" I asked, because it was the first question that popped into my head.

"Her mom doesn't like Justine's parents. Dr. Halverson and his wife? They were giving the party. So, you know, that knocked the ambulance out of my head."

He'd apologized several times now, and I had to accept it. "I know you're sorry. I got in touch with my mother. A couple of minutes didn't make a difference. And having someone fire a gun into a house is pretty scary. I'm glad you and Sarah weren't there. Detective Trumble told me that had happened."

Phillip, looking relieved, returned to his computer. I began the search for Robin's keys, just to have something to do. He was a regular misplacer of keys. I'd put a special bowl on the island, designated the key bowl. We'd had to search much less often since we'd formed a habit of tossing our keys in that bowl every time we came in. Unfortunately, we'd also started dropping in other odds and ends, too.

I overturned the bowl and sorted through the contents, with no key results, though I did find my Starbucks gift card. Then I started checking other possible places. But my mind wasn't on the search, and I came up with zero.

I zoomed into Sophie's room at her first little sound and fed her in record time. As soon as I'd burped her, I called Robin. I loved to look at our child more than anything in the world, but today I could hardly wait to hand her off when Robin came in the door.

"How's John?" I said.

"Hanging in there. Still alive."

I was out the door in thirty seconds. I nodded to Lena, who was walking Chaka, and Jonathan, who was trimming the bushes by his front door . . . with a tape measure attached to his belt. I took off like a rocket.

For a couple of decades, Sparling County Hospital was little more than a way station where patients were stabilized and sent to bigger hospitals in Atlanta. In the last five years, it had been growing and competing. Some doctors simply didn't want the pressure of maintaining practices and bringing up their families in the inner Atlanta metroplex, which was about to swallow Lawrenceton . . . every year it got closer. Since we had the doctors, a few energetic citizens had started a vigorous campaign to raise money for some of the diagnostic machines necessary to advance our facility to a higher level. My mother was one of them. I was proud she'd worked so hard to make this happen, and I hoped the effort was now going to pay off for her husband.

I hurried to the elevators. The ICU was on the third floor. Every moment inside in the hospital raised harrowing memories for me. The smell of the hospital, the glaring overhead lights, the nurses' station, the anguished atmosphere . . . it all made me feel I was strangling. Though my heart was now with my new husband and our baby, I had loved Martin Bartell. His memory was bittersweet, but it was still part of me.

I forced myself to walk into the ICU waiting room. When Avery and John David saw me, they rose to their feet. They were both good-looking men. You could tell from Avery's demeanor that he would never stray from a narrow path; that was not a bad thing, when you considered John David's checkered past.

"How's John?" I perched on the edge of one of the chairs, so they would sit, too.

"Still alive," Avery said. "Melinda had to go home because the babysitter could only keep the kids until three."

"We appreciated Robin coming." John David was a better man since the death of his wife, Poppy. He was more serious, more determined to provide a stable life for his son. He'd been crying. His brother looked haggard. They had a close relationship with their father.

"I'm so sorry," I said helplessly. There was nothing else to say.

John David nodded in acknowledgment.

"Your mom is alone with him now," Avery said. "You can go in. It's two at a time." He looked away to hide his anguish.

My mother, disheveled for the first time in my memory, was sitting in a chair shoved in the corner. Her eyes were fixed on the man in the hospital bed. John was gray, his face empty and slack. He was hooked up to many devices that blinked and pulsed. His eyes were closed.

There was a straight-back chair pushed against the wall. I moved it closer to Mother. "Hi," I said softly.

Without looking at me, she felt around until she found my hand, and she gripped it hard. She couldn't speak. Tears began to run down her face.

I wanted to ask her what the prognosis was, what the doctors proposed to do to help John's faltering heart, but in a rare moment of clarity I understood it was best to keep silent. We held hands, and we watched John's chest move ever so slightly, and we watched the machines register the fact that he was still alive. Together, we went someplace where life was suspended, and all things waited in the balance. From far away, I heard the sounds of the hospital coming from the hall: a food cart rattling, nurses talking, families walking by, phones ringing at the desk. Somewhere not too distant, a janitor was buffing the floor.

But in this room there were only the small clicks and whirs of the machinery. Quiet people went in and out, checking on the machines, checking John. They might nod, but after a look at my mother they didn't venture to speak. It was clear she did not want to hear pleasantries or conversation.

After an hour had passed, I slowly descended to my normal mortal plane. I began to feel the prickling in my boobs that meant I was ready to feed Sophie again. I glanced at the clock set high on the wall. I could stay another hour, in case she needed me.

My mother had all she could handle. There was no question of troubling her with the unpleasant occurrences at our house. I leaned over to pat her cheek. I was too anxious about germs to kiss her. "I'll give one of the boys a turn," I said quietly.

She nodded, without looking at me. Her hand loosened on mine. I left the room as soundlessly as I could and rejoined the world.

In the waiting room, John David was asleep in his chair. Avery rose to take a turn sitting with my mother.

"If something happens, please call me," I said. "Mother may not be able to." Avery nodded.

For another interminable hour, I sat—uselessly—with the sleeping John David and an elderly woman whose lips moved in silent prayer. I was tired and weak, absorbed in my worries and my fears. I didn't even register leaving the hospital until I walked past the fountain in the middle of the circular drive and made my way across the jammed parking lot.

When I'd driven here, the dashboard display had told me the temperature was a balmy 75 degrees Fahrenheit, not unheard-of for late September in Georgia. Now the wind was making itself known, and the sky to the northeast looked dark and ominous. The air felt noticeably cooler.

Another storm. Great.

This had been one of the longest and most unpleasant days I'd ever had. The only good thing had been Robin coming home early.

If things had been normal, I'd have planned a special dinner to celebrate his Anthony and my whole family (now including all the Queenslands) would be sitting down at the table.

I was hit with a wave of self-pity.

After I climbed into my car and turned the key in the ignition, I simply sat there with my hands over my face. I had to move forward. I had to drive home and take care of my daughter. I could not retreat to a dark closet and wail.

I made myself think of good things. Or at least, relatively good things. Robin had identified the dead woman, so her family could be notified. (If there had to be a dead woman in our backyard, it was good to know her name.) No matter what our neighbor Jonathan Cohen thought he had seen, Robin had a good alibi, unless the detectives decided Jeff was not a reliable witness. I couldn't imagine any reason why that would happen. To the lay mind, it might seem fishy that Robin had forgone an evening of triumph to plan a new series in a hotel room with his buddy. But at least he hadn't been in his own room, asleep.

As I drove home through the dark streets, the great thing, the best of all, hit me in the face.

Sophie was safe. Despite the strange and dark happenings in our house, under our roof, in our yard, our daughter remained healthy and untouched.

I could only feel deeply grateful. From that relief, I found the courage to pray for John: that his doctors were skilled and discerning, that he would regain health and strength, that my mother would be able to endure this ordeal. It was amazing how much more I felt the power of prayer since I'd had Sophie. Maybe I was whistling in the dark, superstitiously drumming up something to make me feel that I was helping to keep her safe.

But I didn't think so.

Chapter Twelve

I called the hospital first thing in the morning, and the nurses told me John had made it through the night. I texted Melinda to get some details. I really wanted to talk to Mother, but she was out of reach in the ICU. I had to try to schedule some hospital time. I wondered if I could persuade Mother to go home to rest.

When I got out of the shower, Robin was sitting in one of the living room armchairs. Sophie was lying on his lap, her feet to his stomach. He was talking to her in a manic, high voice. "Oh, who is the cutest baby? Sophie is! Yes, she is! Look at her little feet!" He tickled her little feet gently. "Look at her little tummy!" He blew on her stomach. "Her starfish hands!" He clasped her tiny hands. They both seemed to be very happy.

Robin had moved my purse in his renewed search for his keys. I shoved it back into its accustomed place in the corner of the kitchen counter. Robin told Sophie, "Mama's out of the shower! The milk wagon is here! But let's see if we can play a little longer." He put his fingers in the baby's grasp and then moved them gently back and forth. Sophie gave one of her fleeting smiles.

"Look at her," Robin said. "She's just been playing and playing. Hasn't fussed at all. Even Moosie came over to say hello."

"How did that go?"

"Moosie couldn't have been more nonchalant. She strolled over, sniffed her, sat and looked at Sophie for a few minutes to see if she'd do anything interesting. When Sophie didn't, Moosie went out the cat flap."

"That cat's pretty smart about staying in our yard," I said. "I know this is a minor problem—in the big picture of our issues—but I'm a little worried about her. I suspect she's deaf."

Robin was surprised. "Maybe Dr. Lowell knows how to find out," he said hesitantly. "I don't know what a feline deafness exam might be. Why'd you think of that?"

"I don't think Moosie can hear Chaka or Lulu barking at her." I was reinterpreting several past instances when I thought our cat was being either very provocative or recklessly bold.

"Speaking of Chaka," Robin said, to my astonishment. "I wonder what rescue organization the sisters used. I had been wondering . . ."

I looked at him blankly. Obviously, he was expecting me to pick up on his idea, but honestly, I had nothing.

"If we might get a dog?" he said hopefully.

That was so far from my list of conversational topics that I just goggled at him. "A *dog*?"

"We always had at least one, when I was growing up." I'd never applied Robin's mom's love of her two little pets to the likelihood that Robin's family had always had dogs. "Do you hate the idea?" Robin was truly anxious.

"No," I said, though I wasn't sure that was true. I was

scrambling to assemble a response. "I like dogs just fine. I've never had one myself, but I'm sure I can find books on how to take care of one. I have no problem with Lulu or Chaka, except Lulu gets kind of yappy. But Peggy says that's because the Cohens haven't trained her. She says if you spend time with your dog, they can turn out fun to have around. I've noticed obedience classes on the community board at the library. Robin, how long has this been on your mind?"

"Well, since before Sophie. But we had so much on our plate that it didn't seem like the right time to bring it up."

"We're still pretty occupied with our new household member," I said, nodding toward our daughter. Her arm waving was done, and her eyes were fluttering shut and then snapping open. She didn't want to miss the party. (I was a little concerned that she was falling asleep without feeding, but I was willing to give it a try.)

Robin was still waiting hopefully.

"Okay, I am not *against* us getting a dog. But let's let Sophie grow a little bit first, since she's taking up so much of our time and energy."

A quiet knock at the door ended the dog discussion, to my relief. Since Robin had Sophie, I answered the door.

Detective Levon Suit grinned at me. "Roe, how you doing?"

"Hi," I said, off balance. I was no longer glad to see Levon. It was unpleasant to realize that our relationship had changed overnight, since he'd become a detective. But I forged ahead. "It's a little early in the morning for a visit. Can I get you something to drink? Coffee?"

"No, but thank you," Levon said, ambling by me. I looked over his shoulder to see that the sky was overcast and the air felt damp. Just great.

Robin said hello, and gestured to Sophie on his lap to explain why he wasn't standing to shake hands. Levon was tactful enough to take the opportunity to praise Sophie, and I felt somewhat warmer toward him.

"Katrina's due to pop at any moment," Levon said. "And we'll have us another one of these." Levon and Katrina had been married since high school graduation.

"That's so great! Have you picked out a name?"

"Katrina's old-fashioned about that. She thinks it's bad luck, like buying baby clothes before the birth."

I had never heard that one, and I'd thought every tired old superstition and bit of folklore had been trotted out and presented to me as gospel while I was pregnant with Sophie.

I was thinking about our bed. Though I'd slept all night, I was still tired. That weakness told me just how sick I had been. I needed to feed Sophie soon. I should call Aubrey to tell him about John, though I was almost certain he knew already. A cadre of parishioners kept Father Aubrey Scott abreast of all the happenings in his flock.

"What can we do for you, Levon?" Robin asked, thank God. He could tell I was zoned out.

"I came to tell you a few things."

Not to ask them. Great! "We're all ears," I said, and I noticed that Robin and I were actually both leaning forward slightly.

"The preliminary word is that what killed Tracy Beal was a blow to the head," Levon said. "But she didn't land on a rock when she fell. There was nothing like that in the area of her head. So the blow wasn't accidental, we figure. As you probably saw at the crime scene, she had been holding a knife. At least, it was by her right hand. But there was no blood on the blade. She hadn't used it."

That was a lot of information to absorb at one time.

"Okay," Robin said. "Thanks for telling us. Can you say if she was hit while she was standing up, or while she was on the ground?"

Good question. I leaned against Robin's shoulder, which felt very comfortable just now.

"The medical examiner says she wasn't standing upright," Levon said. "But she wasn't lying flat on the ground, either. It's a strange depression, Dr. English says. Whatever caused the dent in her skull, it hit her really hard, one big blow. And that's what—that's all—we know about her death until the ME does a thorough autopsy. Her clothes didn't turn up anything interesting."

"How come she turned up here at all? With no warning?" What little energy I retained was channeled into this grievance. Why hadn't we been alerted when Tracy had escaped?

"We were waiting on a doctor's decision about whether or not Tracy was mentally competent to stand trial. She was in the jail wing of a private psychiatric facility until four days ago. Then she escaped."

"No one told us," I said, my anger (and my voice) rising as I spoke. Sophie's eyes flew open, and Robin glanced at me meaningfully. He stood to carry Sophie to her room, jiggling her gently, and humming.

In a quieter voice I said, "Levon, she tried to kill me the last time she was out. Don't you think we should have known the minute she went missing?"

Robin returned to sit by me. We were waiting for Levon to answer, and we had the same accusing look on our faces.

"I don't blame you for feeling that way, but it was a series of delays that added up to failure. The hospital didn't realize Tracy was gone for at least five hours. Then they searched the grounds in case she had committed suicide, probably another forty-five-minute delay, and a clear violation of the protocol. Then they notified the local police. It's a small force. They were dealing with a three-car wreck in the middle of downtown at rush hour. Another delay. The staff didn't finish dealing with all the traffic consequences, site cleanup, and paperwork until late the next day. Then they found they were supposed to notify our police department, so we could contact you. They did call our department. A clerk took down the message and stuck it at the bottom of the paperwork pile on Cathy's desk. She had a backlog because—well, I think she told you we've been busy lately. She didn't work her way down to that message until after Tracy turned up dead. I'm sorry. I understand if you're upset."

Oh, yes, I was upset.

Robin was shaking his head in disbelief.

"This didn't go to the top of her pile?" Robin said, his voice very quiet. "Levon, maybe you don't understand—the woman who'd already tried to kill Roe, the woman who stabbed her maid, was *in the house with Roe and our baby*. While they *slept*. And I wasn't home to watch out for them."

Levon flinched. But maybe he felt a frank apology would be an admission of guilt. "Tracy wasn't a crazy-eyed lunatic, who couldn't think or reason," he told us. "She'd told her doctor that she'd started reading the works of another mystery writer, Michael Connelly. She didn't seem to be fixating on him in the same way. But the doctor actually told us to alert Connelly, too."

Beside me, I felt Robin stiffen. "And we know how accurate

that doctor's opinion was. Tracy wasn't dumb. She could sure understand it was to her advantage to con the doctor into believing she wasn't interested in me any longer."

"We should have had the opportunity to judge that ourselves," I said.

Though we had come to a conversational standstill, Levon made no move to leave.

"You've gotten in touch with Tracy's family?" I said, in as calm a voice as I could manage.

"Cathy talked to them. The father's been out of the picture for years. There's a mother and a sister."

In spite of all my anger at Tracy Beal, I felt relieved her family knew what had happened. Everyone should be missed by someone, or at least *claimed.*

"Where was her home?" Robin was walking around the room aimlessly. I was familiar with this restless mode; he'd wander while he talked.

"Tracy was from an army family. She'd moved too many times to count. Her mother, Sandra, lives in South Carolina. Her sister, Sharon, lives in Anders, close to here. And the sister's car is missing."

"Tracy took it?"

"That's what we're assuming. The sister was gone on a camping trip with friends."

"Wait," I said sharply. "You said Anders?"

"Yeah. Why?"

"Robin, remember those flowers, the ones without a card? They came from a florist in Anders."

"So she was in the area even before I left for Bouchercon." Robin looked as if he couldn't take much more.

I told Levon about the incident, which had seemed trivial (but odd) at the time.

Robin would have been more likely to add two and two, since he'd gotten the peculiar e-mails.

But enough of that thinking, I told myself, my teeth clenched. If we'd thought about Tracy Beal at all—and I hadn't—we'd assumed she was safely ensconced in a mental hospital with strict security. I had to concentrate on something else. I was getting angry again. That wasn't going to help the situation. "Any sign of Virginia? Maybe she's called her mother?" I was grasping at straws.

"Not yet."

I wanted to say, "Then why are you here?" But that seemed rude and abrupt. On the other hand . . .

But Robin spoke for me. "So why do you need to talk to us? Tracy is still dead, Virginia is still missing, and you don't know what happened to either one. The only new information is that Tracy got hit on the head, which Roe had seen for herself, and she probably took her sister's car. Did the sister let Tracy stay at her home in Anders? I don't believe for a minute that she didn't know Tracy had taken her car."

"Sharon swears Tracy wasn't staying at her house . . . at least with her knowledge. Of course, we've been checking all the motels around here. We were already doing that. Maybe we can pick up some other piece of information. And patrols in this area have been on the lookout for the car."

"What's your best guess?" I said.

"I think Tracy was staying in Sharon's house," Levon said without hesitation. "And I'm sure Sharon knew. But we'll never get her to admit it, and we can't prove she knew."

"You haven't found any evidence of a connection between

Virginia and Tracy?" Robin was asking every question that had occurred to me.

Levon nodded. "Sandra Beal, Sharon Beal, Marcy Mitchell, even Virginia's half brother, Carlos . . . all told us they'd never heard either woman mention the other. Since Virginia's personal belongings were gone, it seems like Virginia left this house voluntarily. At least, we hope it was voluntarily. We have no idea why she left her car. That's a little scary."

"Did Virginia have a significant other?" I said.

"She'd broken up with her boyfriend three months ago. He denies having heard from her. Marcy, that's her mother, says Virginia had dated a couple of other guys, nothing serious. So much from that end of the investigation. No one heard anything in this neighborhood. No one noticed a strange car. No one saw anything except your neighbor, Mr. Cohen."

"And he wasn't right about who he saw." I was still angry with Jonathan, along with almost everyone else. Robin patted my hand.

"It seems he wasn't," Levon agreed. "Robin, we've got people canvassing the Nashville airport, and everything checks out. And your friend Jeff is ready to knock some heads together, just because we're asking him to confirm your story."

Way to go, Jeff.

"It's too bad you can't find her phone," I said. "I guess it left when she did. She was really mad when she was talking on it, that has to be significant."

"Have you remembered anything? Something she said?"

"I wish I could help you. But I didn't hear any of her conversations. Or if I did, I was too sick to remember it."

Levon got up to leave. "I'm sorry," he said awkwardly. "I know how I'd feel if I saw a stranger in my child's room."

I reminded myself this whole situation was not his fault. "How old is Jeremy?" I asked, pulling the name of Levon's son out of the grab bag in my head.

"He just turned two." Levon grinned. "He's pretty great. This second baby's going to be a boy, too. That's what Katrina says, and she's always right."

"A great talent to have," I said, steering the conversation away from the stormy issues. "If people believed Katrina, they could save money on ultrasounds."

Just as Levon reached the door—just when I believed this interview was over—he turned to ask us some more questions. "I forgot to ask you if Virginia ever talked to you about her personal life?"

Robin and I looked at each other and we shook our heads.

"Roe, you haven't remembered anything new about Virginia's first time here?"

"I was a brand-new mom with a brand-new baby. A big adjustment physically and mentally. I can't remember us ever chatting."

"If you remember who told your mother about Virginia, let us know."

Robin said, "Levon, I hope you won't question Aida about this now. John's had another heart attack and he's in the hospital. It's a very bad time."

Levon looked uncomfortable. "I understand that. But I need to get any information as soon as I can."

I nodded. "I'll let Mother know." *When I'm good and ready. When Mother can think about something else besides her husband.*

Finally, *finally,* Levon left, after making sure we did not have any other scrap of information. We breathed simultaneous sighs of relief when the door closed behind him.

"Virginia's such a mystery. I didn't know anyone was, these days." I didn't even bother to sit down with a book, or start something in the kitchen, because Little Miss's unexpected nap was over. I sighed. "Back to being Elsie the cow," I said.

"I'm going to Google Virginia." Robin went back to his office. He called, "Roe! Did you put my sweater in the wash?"

"No," I called back. "I'm going to feed Sophie and fold some laundry. I'll check to see if Virginia threw it in the wash, though I don't know why she'd go in your office."

In seconds we had scattered, relieved to do something that felt normal.

I happily entered my "mom cocoon" with my daughter. We shared the better part of an hour, between feeding and playing. I took her into the bedroom with me while I folded laundry (no sweater), settling her in the middle of our bed and putting firm pillows on each side of her in case she suddenly decided to learn how to roll over. I sang to her while I worked, and I talked to her, and I thought about how very lucky I was.

Except for Tracy being murdered in my backyard.

And my babysitter going missing.

And my stepfather having a heart attack.

Chapter Thirteen

I called my mother the first thing Tuesday morning. John's condition was stable, and that was good. That day I took two more turns sitting with Mother at his bedside, one in late afternoon and one at ten at night. Mother was silent and stoic, but there were constant tears in her eyes. For the first time she looked old, though she was not yet sixty.

Melinda, Avery's wife, came into the ICU as I was leaving. She'd been pulling babysitting duty, so she hadn't gotten to the hospital often. "I got both my own kids down," she said. "John David came by to pick up Chase. Avery fell into bed. I figured I'd come be with your mom."

I hugged her. "Mother just won't talk," I said. "She just sits and waits."

"John's a great father-in-law and a wonderful grandfather," Melinda said sadly. "I don't want to lose him. I want the kids to know him. And he's been so happy with your mother. They haven't had long enough together."

"That's all true, and more. We just have to wait and see. I *hate* waiting and seeing."

Melinda managed a smile. "Me, too. Too much of life is spent doing that. How's Sophie?"

"Well and happy and enjoying being the center of the universe," I said. "And Marcy and Charles?"

"Marcy said a new word the other day. Unfortunately, it was a bad one. Now we have to figure out where she learned it. Charles is walking. He wanted to go with Marcy when she left the room. He just stood up and started across the floor."

"Your kids are so cute," I said, because it was true and because mothers have to support each other.

"I haven't had a chance to tell you I'm sorry for all your trouble." Melinda had suddenly recalled that my family had other problems in addition to John's bad health. "Is it true Robin had met the dead woman?"

"So had I. She was Robin's stalker. You remember, the woman who attacked me in my first house? Tracy Beal? She was supposed to be in a psychiatric hospital, but she escaped." I felt as though I'd told this story many times.

"Oh my God! You're lucky she was killed, instead of her killing you!"

Hearing this out loud made me feel weak in the knees. I patted Melinda on the shoulder and made myself march out the front door. The circular drive was choked with cars, some dropping off visitors, some picking up patients. I stood in the center for a moment, watching the water splash in the fountain. I hoped the sound would bring me peace. But it didn't.

I glanced behind me at all the blank windows, all three floors, and knew that behind them lay suffering and grief and pain. I had to remind myself that there was healing, too.

When I reached my car, I was grateful to collapse inside. I was a mess. I had to stiffen my backbone. I could not heal John, I could not resurrect Tracy, I could not find Virginia. All I could do was soldier on. I had to drive home, and I had to . . . all I could think of was going to bed. It had been a long and exhausting day. I still wasn't up to my previous energy level.

I fell asleep maybe a second before my head hit the pillow. I know Sophie woke up twice in the night, and I know I fed her, but I was on mom autopilot. When my eyes opened the next morning, I smelled something divine . . . coffee and pastry. My heart lifted. Robin had gotten up early to go to Peerless Doughnuts in downtown Lawrenceton.

My appetite came to life with a roar.

I staggered to the kitchen in my robe to find Robin at the counter, a box of assorted goodness in front of him. "Phillip get off to school?" I asked as I poured a cup of coffee. "I just missed him, I guess."

"Yep," Robin said absently. Going by the crumbs, he'd already demolished a blueberry-cake doughnut. He was hovering over the brown-and-white-striped box, taking his time with his next choice.

I ate a bear claw. And then a chocolate croissant. Though I'd regret it later (just a little bit), the sugar and fat put me in the happiest place I'd been in a week.

Robin looked content, too. We'd been reading the newspaper as we ate, and I'd swapped sections with him silently.

"When all else fails, eat something bad for you," he said, when he judged I'd had enough coffee to be ready to talk.

"Thanks for thinking of Peerless. You are truly a great husband."

He looked grim. "I'm the husband who brought down a

stalker on you when I wasn't even around to defend you," he said. "I was the one who hired Virginia to come help you."

"Don't be ridiculous. You didn't break Tracy out of the hospital. And you couldn't anticipate Virginia would vanish. She was so solid the first time she was here! If you'd asked me, I'd have said she'd be the last person to skip out on a job."

"Skip out? I just hope she's alive."

I stared at him with my mouth hanging open. My brain had heard "missing" and simply categorized Virginia as "lost." Like Robin's still-missing keys, or Sophie's stuffed lamb. It had never fully registered with me that Virginia might well be dead. *I'm an idiot,* I thought. But after a second of considering the awful possibility, I said, "I can't see why someone would kill Tracy and leave her body, yet haul Virginia's away. If you've got one dead woman, what's another one?"

"Valid point. You think she's still alive?"

I nodded. "That's what I want to believe. And we don't have any evidence to the contrary."

Robin's face didn't lighten. "I wish we knew something, anything, for sure. Tell me how John is doing." We hadn't talked much after my second stint at the hospital. I had run out of conversation.

I shook my head. "The same. Mother won't talk about it or leave the hospital. Every night I keep the phone by the bed in case she calls me with bad news."

I was losing the happy buzz of the bear claw and the croissant. Since I'd been thinking about his keys, maybe there was an update. "You find your key ring yet?"

"Nope. I searched my car this morning. By the way, Sam just called on the landline," Robin said. He put the newspaper down on the counter and looked at me directly.

Apparently, we were about to get even more serious. "This early? What did he have to say?"

"He wants you to call him back."

Sam Clerrick, the library director, had been my boss for years. Sam was not tremendously likable, or witty, or exciting. He didn't much enjoy talking to actual people. But he was an efficient director and a fair boss. I had exceeded the maternity leave the county policy allowed, by many weeks. I was guiltily aware I had an obligation to give Sam a return date, since he was not obliged to hold my job for me any longer and I was fortunate he hadn't fired me. I didn't want to decide right now . . . but I'd procrastinated long enough. I covered my face with my hands and groaned.

My husband regarded me without much sympathy. "Roe, you've had your mind made up for weeks, and you know it. Don't make another crisis out of this."

"I was there for so long." Even to my own ears, I sounded whiny. "I'll miss everyone." The staff, the patrons. . . .

"But you also want to be home with Sophie, and we can afford that. The income from your investments is more than your salary's ever been. I'm doing well. You can't stay at home with Sophie *and* go in to work at the library."

I stared down at my empty cup. There was no advice written in the bottom. "You're right," I said. "I can't sit on the fence any longer." Before I could think of a reason to put it off yet again, I called Sam. My friend Lizanne answered the phone. "You've reached the library," she said in her sweet voice. "Office of Sam Clerrick."

"Lizanne," I said. "How are you?"

"Hi, Roe. I'm fine, the kids are fine, and the divorce is final," Lizanne said. "We need to have lunch if you can detach your little barnacle for an hour." (Sophie was the little barnacle. In fact, she was attached to me at the moment. I was multitasking.)

"So you and Bubba are both free as birds, huh?"

"Bubba has already been on the wing," she said dryly. "I saw him out with Teresa Stanton."

"Shut your mouth!" I said. Teresa, a terrifying and impeccably groomed woman, was the ex-wife of another lawyer, Bryan Pascoe. "Keeping it in the legal family, huh?"

Lizanne laughed, but then she grew serious. "How's your stepdad? I've been so sad about him. He's such a sweetie."

"I haven't talked to Mother this morning," I said. "She's at the hospital all the time, and Avery, John David, and Melinda are taking turns. I go when I can get a couple of hours free."

"John David calls me when he can. I feel so bad for him. First he loses his wife, now maybe his dad. Being a single father isn't any easier than being a single mom." Lizanne knew all about that. Bubba had not exactly been a hands-on father even when they'd been together.

Lizanne had just told me in a delicate way that she was dating John David Queensland. This was new information. Two separate circles were intersecting, like a diagram. I drew breath to ask her how long this had been going on, but Lizanne said, "I see Sam's free now, Roe. I'll put you through."

My conversation with Sam was terse and unsentimental. If anything, Sam was put out at the prospect of having to interview and hire another librarian.

And that was that. I was unemployed. After I hung up, I waited for the regret to flood me.

To my surprise, I felt fine. It wasn't likely we would have another baby; I wanted to watch Sophie grow and change, day by day. I didn't want to drop her off at a babysitter's house or a child-care center every day. I didn't want to be exhausted when I picked her up. I didn't want to resent Robin because he worked from home and could see more of Sophie than I did.

I blessed Jane Engle (my fairy godmother) yet again, for giving me the financial freedom to make this choice.

I felt at loose ends, though I was following the same general routine I had since I'd had the baby. Somehow, it felt different now that it was the way things were going to be. Robin kissed me and went to work in his office, carrying a good sweater from his closet to replace the saggy baggy one he wore while he wrote. After I finished with Sophie, I put the doughnuts away. (They wouldn't survive the day; Phillip would descend on them when he got home.) I took the monitor with me into the bathroom while I showered and Sophie was playing in her crib . . . if you can call watching rotating rabbits "playing."

Just as I finished drying my hair, Avery called. "Dad's a little better," he said. He sounded exhausted. "I persuaded your mom to go home to get in bed for a while. If she can sleep and shower and eat, she'll feel better. John David had to go to work, and I have to check in at my office. Melinda's got the kids. I wondered . . ."

"I'll be there in half an hour," I said.

"Thanks, Roe."

I finished dressing and went to talk to Robin, Sophie in my arms.

"I know it's your work time, and I'm sorry to ask you . . . but today, I have to go sit with John. Everyone else is zonked out. If no one makes it back to take over, you might have to bring Sophie to the hospital, so I can nurse her in the waiting room." I had a shawl for just such occasions, folded tightly in Sophie's diaper bag. I thought of Robin's absentmindedness (no keys had turned up, and no sweater).

"I think I'll take the diaper bag with me," I said. I felt like a camel when I carried both the bag and my purse, so leaving one at home would halve my burden. The green-and-white-striped bag, with its designer logo, looked a lot nicer than my purse, I had to admit. I tucked my driver's license in one of the diaper bag's many outer pockets.

"Sure," Robin said. "I'll put her in her bouncy thing right by my desk. We'll do great, won't we, Madame President?" I followed him to his office to watch him strap Sophie in.

Sophie had begun to conquer the bouncer seat. Sure enough, now she began flinging her arms and legs to make it move up and down. Our baby had learned something!

She was beyond cute. I swooped down to give her a kiss on her soft cheek, and stretched up to give Robin one on his wonderful mouth, and then I was out the door, bag slung over my shoulders. My hair resembled a bunch of streamers going in all different directions, but today that didn't seem important. I was wearing my green-framed glasses, which hardly seemed appropriate for the ICU . . . but they did match the bag.

This morning, the hospital parking lot was not as crowded as it would be later in the day. As I approached the main door, my shoulders grew tight. The minute I walked through the automatic doors I would find myself back in a fog of unhappy memories. I gritted my teeth and forced a smile to my lips.

The elevator doors whooshed open at the ICU floor, and I waved at the nurse at the duty station as I walked by. They all knew us by now. The door to John's room was ajar. I stood by the bed for a minute or two, searching his face, hoping something had changed. Maybe his color was a little better? I sighed, and took the more comfortable chair. I'd left my crossword puzzle book and a magazine here on the previous visit. I'd tucked a paperback into the diaper bag. I was all fixed for a couple of hours or more.

Nurse Deedee Powers (chiefly responsible for John on this shift) had written her name on the dry-erase board in John's room. Every shift, the primary nurse wiped out the previous name and entered her own. I found it reassuring to know who was in charge. I stepped out to get an update from Deedee. By now, we were on a first-name basis.

"The doctor's already been by," Deedee told me. "He talked to your mom and Avery." She was not callous, but she was brisk. This was her everyday work environment: caring for people very ill or close to death, talking to their relatives or loved ones, carrying out the doctor's orders.

John's ICU room was as quiet—but busy—as ever. Cleaners and nurses and lab workers, the food-tray deliveryman, all came in and out of the room. The pink-smocked volunteer lady with the cart of books and newspapers stuck her head in and whispered, "Do you need something to read?" I raised my book in answer, and she nodded and vanished. Other patients' visitors passed the doorway regularly. Their faces, too, had become familiar. There was the very old man who walked with a cane, and a familiar-looking woman in her sixties who looked more worn down every day. This morning, the weary-looking woman whose child was two doors down was crying as she walked by.

I shuddered. There was too much pain here. I had to block it out. Thank God I had a good book.

I was the lucky recipient of John's allocated lunch tray, which of course he couldn't eat. The corn bread was dry. The banana pudding was okay. The grapes were a little rubbery, but still had a good flavor. The meat, which might have been beef, and the vegetables (overcooked to the maximum) were better left untouched.

At least I no longer felt guilty about my extravagant breakfast.

I finished my book. I was getting stiff, so I walked around the ICU for a few circuits. I paused at each big window to look out at the parking lot at the front, or at the quieter employee lot and utility buildings at the back. Then I resumed my watch in John's room. I began to work on a crossword puzzle, glancing up at John's silent figure from time to time. When I got bored with that (when I got stuck), I closed my eyes and tried to meditate, but I have never been good at letting go of myself. Before very long I abandoned the meditation and started flipping through the magazine I'd left. I didn't have to remember a plot if I was studying red-carpet dresses worn by women I didn't know.

Even celebrity gossip palled. I laid the magazine on the wheeled table beside my chair. I simply looked at John.

I recalled introducing him to my mother. She'd been dubious at first. John had some interests she didn't share. But John's pleasant manners and intelligence had gradually won her over; plus (truth be told) John was a good-looking man.

I smiled as I thought of this. And since I was watching John, I saw his eyelids flicker.

I leaped to my feet, knocking all my reading material to the floor. "John!" I said, trying to keep my voice low and even. But I couldn't suppress my excitement.

The muscles in his cheeks and lips moved as if he were trying to form a word. I was sure he heard me and knew who I was.

He whispered, "Roe."

Then Nurse Deedee hurried in and blocked him from my

sight. Some reading on his monitor had changed. When she moved to the side, I could see his eyes had closed again, but there were muscles moving under the skin.

My mother would never forgive me if I didn't tell her about this development. John had spoken! I wanted to stay in the room, because John might talk to me again, but I couldn't phone from ICU.

Deedee made the decision for me. She "asked" me to leave while she did something personal for John.

I raced out of the ICU, cell phone in hand, and took the elevator to the lobby. I punched my mother's speed dial. I could tell she was awake—either again, or she'd never slept. "Mother! His eyes opened! Just for a minute! He said my name!" I told her.

"I'm on my way."

I returned to John's room, feeling nothing but excitement and happiness. This development was more than I'd ever hoped for. Deedee had left. John and I were alone again.

I stood by the bed watching him. His eyes flickered open once or twice, and he always looked directly at my face.

After ten minutes had passed, Mother appeared at the other side of John's bed. She wasn't there, and then she was. She looked like hell, but there was some hope on her face. She took his hand. "Honey," she said, her voice steady. "I'm here." John heard her and knew her. His fingers moved slightly in hers, and he smiled for a moment.

When I glanced at my watch, I realized it was time for me to return to Sophie. If Mother was sitting with John now, maybe I could go home, feed her there, and avoid the awkwardness of public breast-feeding. But I didn't want to leave Mother alone, since I didn't know what would happen if and when John returned to full consciousness. I assumed he would be in a lot of pain, and possibly very anxious.

I was relieved to see John David waving at me from the nurse's station. Problem solved.

I hugged Mother and whispered, "I have to leave, call me if anything changes." I turned away to gather up my belongings, and reached down for my diaper bag.

It wasn't there.

I simply couldn't believe it. I looked around the room, sure I'd see it any moment. Perhaps it had gotten in the way of one of the staff, who'd set it in another place?

It wasn't in the room.

I glanced at the nurses' station to see that John David was getting increasingly anxious to see his father. I could hardly make a big to-do about a diaper bag at this moment. It just wouldn't be right. So I left John's room with my head up, and my book and other items tucked under my arm.

"He's waking up," I told John David, smiling for all I was worth.

Before I could say boo to a goose, John David was standing by my mother at John's bedside. His face was full of hope.

It seemed to me that having people gathering around you, really hoping you lived, was the greatest testament to your life.

And abruptly, I was back to the mundane. I stopped by the nurses' station. "Deedee," I said, "I hate to tell you this, but my bag was just stolen from John's room, while I was downstairs telephoning."

She looked up at me with no comprehension, just at first. Then she was dismayed. "Out of a patient's room," she said, disgusted. "I'm really sorry. I hope you didn't have much in it?"

"My driver's license," I said. "Thank God I'd put my car

keys in my pocket. The bag was actually for my daughter's stuff, because I thought Robin would be bringing her here." I described it to Deedee in case someone found the discarded bag somewhere in the building. "Who should I tell about this?"

"Officer Rodenheiser. His office is on the second floor," Nurse Tallchief said, with a significant smile.

"He's really nice," Nurse Stanley added, grinning.

Deedee shook her head. "They're just trying to tell you he's quite a man. He'll be back on active duty soon, and we're sure going to miss him."

I got directions to track down Officer Rodenheiser, necessary because this hospital was confusing even for a Lawrenceton native. I only took one wrong turn (at Pediatrics) before I found the correct doorway.

It was easy to see why the nurses were so enthusiastic. Brad Rodenheiser was tall and blond. He clearly got some exercise. Quite a bit of exercise. His eyes were blue and steady. Well, *wow*. When he got up, I noticed he had a brace on his knee. That's why he'd been off active duty.

Brad Rodenheiser wasn't all about the good looks. He struck me as a capable policeman. Within a couple of minutes, he'd called up a form on his computer and started filling it in.

"I gather this happens often?" I said.

"All the time," he rumbled. "Date of birth?"

I gave him the information he needed.

"I'm afraid the chance of getting your bag back intact is very slim. But I'm sure you've figured that out." Officer Rodenheiser handed me a copy of my report. I started to put it away, then remembered I had nothing to put it in. "People take personal belongings from the patients' rooms, they steal medical supplies off the carts, they grab scrubs out of the dressing rooms. Even food, if you can believe it. At least the drugs are locked up and heavily monitored."

The hospital was a den of iniquity, not the place of respite and calm I'd thought it. It was disillusioning, but not a shock.

"The diaper bag was a gift. We're really fond of the people who gave it to us. I can fall back on another one, but this is kind of special." I almost felt like apologizing that my loss was so trivial.

All the way home I thought about the theft. In the grand scheme of things, it was not a big deal at all. But I was upset in a hurt way, and I was upset in an angry way. Two sides of the same reaction. I strode (if a person of my height can stride) into the house not knowing which stance to take, and I made the bad choice of trying both of them.

Robin was sitting in the living room with Sophie, who was just beginning to fuss. "Look," he told Sophie brightly. "There's Mama! Yahoo! Food!"

"Robin," I said tragically, "my bag got stolen."

His eyes went first to my huge leather bag, sitting slumped in a corner of the kitchen counter. He almost told me it was *right there,* before he thought twice. "Your bag," he said cautiously.

"The diaper bag," I said. "The striped green one with the designer emblem on it."

"The diaper bag got stolen," he repeated, as if verifying my information.

Luckily, I was able to restrain myself. "Yes," I said through gritted teeth. "From the hospital room. Just now. At least I had my keys in my pocket."

Robin could tell I wasn't going to take the baby from him until I got a reaction, so he hurried to supply one. "And no one saw anything?" His voice was an appropriate blend of disbelief and outrage. "Someone came in the room when John was by himself?"

"Apparently," I said, and described my trip downstairs to call Mother.

"So John's awake," Robin said. "That's great. But the bag getting stolen . . . um . . . incredible. I'm sure you called the police. What did they say?"

I was getting myself under control by then. "There was a policeman right there in the hospital. He told me things go missing all the time, and he wrote down a description of the bag," I said. "Maybe the thief will drop it in a garbage can at the hospital or somewhere outside, when he's been through it."

"That would be great," Robin agreed, feeling it was safe to hand Sophie to me now. "Though you know . . . well, I'm sure that was the *very best* bag, but we got another one, from Jeff's wife. It's on the shelf in Sophie's closet."

"I remember," I said, and realized I sounded ridiculous and petty. Time to shut up. I sat down with Sophie and pulled up my T-shirt, unsnapping the nursing bra. It was the most unexciting piece of lingerie I'd ever worn in my life, and I am not someone who collects pretty lingerie.

If I had to be honest—I didn't, but I was going to—the green and white bag had seemed a little pretentious to me. A designer label on a baby bag? And the fact that it really didn't look like a diaper bag had not been a recommendation, in my eyes. Why shouldn't it look like what it was?

Robin was still looking for ways to be helpful. "While you're feeding Sophie, walk through the scene in your mind. Maybe you can picture who was outside the room when you left with your phone."

"I was pretty excited and intent on getting to a place where

I could call Mother, but it can't hurt to try." While Sophie partook of refreshment, I closed my eyes and tried to re-create the scene. I stepped out of John's room. There was the orderly who usually bathed and shaved John, a little guy with a lot of tattoos. There were the nurses going in and out of the circular desk area. Most of them were familiar to me by sight. There'd been one I hadn't seen before, a stout woman with iron-gray hair and a serious overbite. But she'd been talking to a woman I did know, so she must have checked out okay with the other nurses. And she had all the requisite accouterments: aqua scrubs, heavy sneakers, a lanyard around her neck with an ID tag, a chart in her hand. If she wasn't the real thing, she was a master of camouflage.

There'd been a doctor sitting at the little desk in a cubbyhole designed for doctors to enter their notes and instructions in privacy. Dark-skinned and clean-shaven, that's all I'd been able to see. He'd been bent over his work like he knew what he was doing. Had he had on a lanyard or a name tag? His back had been to me. I couldn't have seen one. Aside from that, there was a woman walking away from the room. I listed all the passersby to Robin, who was still hovering. "That woman was maybe in her forties. She had short brown hair. Wearing a skirt and blouse. I'll bet she was a relative, but none of the people I saw looked like purse thieves." I scanned my brain a bit more. "Nope, that's all I got."

"It's amazing you can remember that much," Robin said, obviously surprised that his suggestion had proved so fruitful. "Shouldn't the hospital have security cameras?"

"They do." I told Robin about Officer Brad Rodenheiser's office, trying not to sound too wistful. "The cameras are mostly pointed at the entrances and exits. So there might be some record of someone leaving with my bag." I felt more cheerful. "Thanks, honey. Good idea."

"I'm brimming with them," he said, smiling. "I'll call the hospital, if that's okay with you."

"Ahhh . . . actually, I have his card. You can call that number."

Robin gave me a narrow-eyed look, but took the card and called the number. Robin had to leave a message, but within ten minutes Brad Rodenheiser called back.

"I'm Robin Crusoe. My wife's bag was stolen there just an hour or so ago? She talked to you." Pause. "Yes, the short woman with all the hair and the pink glasses." Pause. "Yes, it was a diaper bag, not an actual purse, but it was a valued gift. Plus, you know, it's *hers*." Pause. "I'm absolutely certain you have more serious crimes to investigate," Robin agreed. "But if this person stole from my wife in the ICU unit, he'll steal more. Maybe already has. We were wondering if she could watch some security recordings? Oh, you were just about to . . ." Pause. "That's great. Please let us know."

He ended the call. "Roe, he says no one has turned it in at the hospital. He was just about to review the security footage to see if someone was caught on camera leaving with your bag. If he sees something interesting he'll call you in to look at it." Robin seemed a little miffed at being anticipated by the policeman.

"That's the best we could hope for. I guess." I told Sophie, "Get used to it, little one. You have to be tough in this world."

I was surprised when Robin's phone rang fifteen minutes later.

"You're not going to believe this, but he has someone on camera," Robin said. "Let's go."

The second Sophie finished and we'd changed her diaper, we were on our way back to the hospital with the slightly less-wonderful baby bag, hastily stocked, on my shoulder.

I wasn't able to take Robin directly to the little office (I took a wrong turn at Radiology), but I only had to repeat a little part of the route. The door was open. Officer Rodenheiser was seated at the console . . . and Detective Cathy Trumble stood behind him. She wore her usual tailored pants (this time a navy blue), a blue and green floral blouse, and a green jacket, which almost covered the badge and gun she clipped to her belt. Dressed for business as usual.

I was not glad to see her.

"Brad here called me," she said by way of greeting. "He remembered you were involved in the Tracy Beal case."

"It happened on our property," I said. "That's the extent of our involvement."

Cathy ignored my protest. "I've reviewed the footage very quickly," she said. "Brad pointed out this one, and I agree this is the most interesting." She pointed from her position behind the seated Officer Rodenheiser.

We scooted behind the console so we could watch. There were two computer screens, each showing four separate areas in the building. The pictures were black-and-white, but the definition was good. Cathy pointed to the upper right-hand quarter of the left screen.

We were watching a series of people walking in and out of the main entrance. A couple involved in an intense discussion came in. A very old man with a cane made his way out very slowly, followed by a woman in jeans and a plaid shirt pushing a child in a wheelchair. A man in a suit and tie walked into the lobby briskly, obviously deep in his own thoughts. Then two nurses in animated conversation left, followed right on their heels by a tall dark man in scrubs with a bag over his shoulder—a striped bag.

I clutched Robin's arm. "That may be the man I saw in the ICU unit," I said. "He was sitting in the carrel where the doctors write their notes, or whatever it is they do."

"What did he look like?" Cathy was poised to pounce.

"Like the footage. I only saw his back."

"Well, that's something. We know the person who took your bag is about an inch over six feet, African American male, and he owns a set of scrubs."

"And he knows how to blend in," Robin offered.

"Why would he want my diaper bag?" I was not thinking very swiftly today.

"It was the only bag you had." I didn't get Cathy's implication.

"I'm sure he thought it was your purse," Robin said.

"No one else in the ICU is missing a bag?" I had a strong feeling I already knew the answer.

"No," Cathy said. "Only your bag was taken. What was in it?"

"Diapers. Because it's *a diaper bag*," I said, exasperated. "Baby wipes. A shawl to cover me if I have to feed Sophie in public. A spit-up rag. An extra sleeper. A plastic toy. Maybe a bib. And today, worse luck, I put my license in the outer pocket because I didn't want to carry my purse as well."

"What was he after?" Cathy asked . . . apparently herself, because she was looking into space. Then she fixed her eyes on me. "Come down to the station," she said abruptly.

Chapter Fourteen

"Why?" I was taken aback.

"There's some pictures you could look at. See if you could spot your fake doctor."

I took a deep breath. "I don't know how else to say this, Cathy. I didn't see his face. I saw his back. I'm not going to accuse someone on the basis of his back."

Robin held Sophie pressed against his shoulder. She was asleep. That was one good thing. "Up to you," he said. He wasn't any happier than I was, but he let the decision be mine.

"Cathy," I protested. "You know I can't identify him." Knowing that, why did she want me to go through this charade? I could only figure she believed one of the pictures would spark a memory.

Brad Rodenheiser looked from Cathy, to me, to Robin. He seemed highly entertained. Watching people come and go on four screens and/or answering an occasional call from some location in the hospital must offer limited entertainment.

I was tired of being questioned, tired of being at the beck

and call of the police, and most of all, unhappy that the problem still existed. I wanted the murderer to be caught. I wanted to see Virginia, know she was safe.

I realized that in the grand scheme of things, I had little to complain about. After all, Sophie and I were safe. Gossip might nip at Robin's heels, but he could not be considered a serious suspect in Tracy's murder.

"All right," I said abruptly. No matter what Cathy's scheme might be, I had to do everything I could to resolve the situation. "Robin, can you take Sophie home? Phillip texted me a minute ago, so I know he's there. Then you can come to the law enforcement complex to bring me home. This shouldn't take long." I gave Cathy a pointed look.

"You sure you want to do this?" Robin said, doubt heavy in his voice.

I wasn't sure, not at all, but if doing what Cathy wanted would get us closer to the truth, I would oblige. "See you in a few."

Robin bent to kiss me, and I patted Sophie's bottom very gently. Then they left, with the backup diaper bag. I watched them go, already regretting my decision. While I thought my own thoughts, Cathy watched the man walk out of the hospital over and over.

Cathy left the room to make a phone call, she said, and while I waited for her I had an unexpected conversation with Brad Rodenheiser.

"She's a little thorny now," he said, nodding his head at the doorway Cathy had gone through.

"What's wrong with her? She's so different," I said in as low a voice as I could manage.

He looked a little surprised. "You don't know about her sister?"

"No." I was at sea.

"Annette's in the psych ward here, had a breakdown."

But then Cathy came back in, looked at us suspiciously, and snapped, "I think we're ready to go now."

"Sure," I said, and trotted out of the hospital in her wake after thanking Officer Rodenheiser.

"He was just doing his job," Cathy said over her shoulder as we made our way to the main entrance. "You don't have to thank him for that."

I didn't respond because I simply didn't need to justify myself to Cathy Trumble. When had she turned from a friendly acquaintance to a cranky, secretive grouch? I could not understand what had happened to make her change so drastically. There was no way I was going to ask her, not while she was so touchy. Having a sick sister simply didn't seem likely to have effected this personality alteration.

It felt very strange to walk outside with empty hands. I didn't think I'd done it in years. I was always carrying something—a purse, grocery bags, books, a diaper bag, a baby. I found it liberating.

We walked around the fountain. Its central statue was supposed to represent the first female doctor in Lawrenceton, which accounted for its location close to the entrance. There were the usual rows of parking, and around the perimeter was a fringe of side-by-side parking spaces that encircled the whole lot. Cathy's car was parked in one of those spaces, nosed into a stand of scrub and trees. Directly behind the trees were long-established smaller homes. Since the garages of these bungalows were one-car, the streets were often crowded with vehicles.

It was midafternoon now. A lot of people were still at work.

Cathy's car was not a black-and-white patrol unit, but an

unmarked blue SUV, conspicuously clean. I went to the passenger's side, waiting to hear the thunk of the lock going up. When it didn't happen, I peered across the hood at Cathy. She was staring back the way we'd come.

Of course, I turned to look, too. A very old man with a cane was making his slow way toward us, holding a green-and-white-striped bag in his free hand. He looked vaguely familiar, and I thought I'd seen him in the ICU.

The bag did not have its pleasing cylindrical shape any longer. It was clearly empty.

"Young lady," he said, when he got close enough, "is this yours?"

Cathy muttered some words I'd never heard out loud. I hoped the old gentleman hadn't heard them.

"Yes, sir," I said, delighted. "Where did you find it?"

"It was down on the ground by my car. I saw the name Teagarden in it, and I knew that must be you, because you are the spitting image of your grandmother. I seen you in the ICU. Didn't cost me nothing to come over here and ask."

"People tell me I'm like my grandmother pretty often," I said, smiling. "I'm Aurora."

"Carter Redding," he said, extending his blue-veined hand to mine to hand over the bag.

Cathy snatched it as he was handing it over. "I'll have to print that zipper," she said.

"Can you just check that outside pocket to see if my driver's license is still there?"

"That's not the most important thing here," Cathy said.

Mr. Redding gave her an indignant look before he turned back to me. "Was it stole from you?" he said.

"Yes, sir, it was, while I was visiting my mother's husband in the ICU," I said.

"My daughter's up there," he said. "She's got the cancer."

I opened my mouth to tell him I was sorry, but several things happened in an instant.

I heard two loud cracks. I was looking around in bewilderment when Carter Redding grabbed my elbow and said "Get down!" in a no-nonsense voice.

Cathy pulled her gun.

She crouched at the rear bumper of the SUV, and pointed down with an emphatic finger. "Stay there, behind the engine block," she ordered us. "Don't move."

I was baffled, but I was obedient.

She pulled her radio off her belt. "Shots fired, shots fired. North side of the hospital parking lot. Code SOS, Brad."

"Instituting Code SOS," replied Brad Rodenheiser calmly.

. . . and I was still thinking, *What?*

I heard multiple voices raised in panic. I realized I was huddling with my hands protecting my head—a foolish posture if there ever was one.

There was another shot, followed instantly by a shrill scream of pain.

"Someone's down," said Mr. Redding grimly.

And finally I understood.

I was too frightened to speak. I spared a second to think how glad I was that Robin and Sophie had gone home. Mr. Redding was shaking like a leaf, but he was keeping himself together.

If it hadn't been for Mr. Redding, I might still have been standing up and looking around in confusion. "Thanks," I said, but my voice came out in a gasp.

"Been a long time, but you don't forget that sound," he said. Obviously, crouching was painful for the elderly man, and the shock had not been good for him. His breathing was harsh.

"I need to get back in to my daughter," Mr. Redding said, and began to pull up on the door handle of the SUV, struggling to stand. His cane lay on the ground, forgotten.

"No sir," Cathy said. "The hospital is locked down now, no one in or out. Your daughter's much safer than we are."

I tried to regain control of myself.

Cathy had clipped her radio to her belt. She held her gun with both hands. I couldn't see anyone else moving. A car alarm went off. The persistent honk was maddening. When it stopped, I let out a deep breath. After that, the parking lot, which had been full of people coming and going minutes earlier, fell still.

There was another *crack!* It seemed to echo in the silence.

Then a woman began screaming, screaming as if she would never stop. Mr. Redding's color had worsened. He did not seem to be completely in the here and now. "I have to get back to Kathleen," he mumbled.

"Mr. Redding, we're going to stay here for now," I said, in as low a voice as I could manage. I don't know who I thought would hear me—the big bad wolf?—but I felt the strong conviction I should stay as small and still as possible. This must be how a rabbit felt when it heard a fox in the woods. Or a wolf.

Now, sporadically, voices were coming over the radio. Cathy, looking to her right around the back of the SUV, was trying to answer the incoming law.

"On scene," said a new voice calmly. "Moving west to intercept. Status?"

Cathy responded, "Shots came from close to the entrance.

I'm behind my car with two citizens. Possible victims, screaming heard, location unknown."

The wail of sirens grew closer.

From where I crouched I could only see a little to the northeast. I caught movement from the corner of my eye. Susan Crawford, in uniform, was duckwalking from car to car, a little awkwardly because she was pregnant. She had her radio in her left hand, her handgun in her right. She did not hesitate. She didn't acknowledge our presence, but I was sure she knew we were there. After peering from behind a Ford Fiesta, she moved right behind a midsize red car, maybe a Nissan. I saw her lips move, and over Cathy's radio I heard Susan say, "I see him. Suspect's behind the Dr. Brennan statue. White male, teens, blond, blue shirt, brown pants, maybe five foot eight. Moving into position."

"Backup almost there," said a calm female voice over the radio.

"Victim bleeding on the ground. I have a clear shot," Susan said. "I'm taking it." In one smooth movement, she aimed and she fired. *Bam. Bam.* There came a howl from closer to the hospital entrance. Susan leaned left to evaluate the damage she'd done.

Crack.

Susan sprawled backward, her gun and radio skittering away from her hands. Her shoulder began turning red. I was so shocked I could not draw breath for a long moment.

"Officer down, officer down," Cathy said into the radio. She no longer sounded calm.

"I'm going to help her," I said, gathering myself to rise.

"You are *not,*" Cathy told me. "You are not moving *at all.* You're no doctor. You're no nurse. You're fodder."

It was the most crushing telling-off I'd ever received. And I knew she was right.

But looking at Susan lying on the pavement, bleeding, reaching her right hand across her chest to stanch the blood spreading in a creeping circle from her left shoulder . . . it gave me the worst feeling of helplessness I've ever had. I wanted to start screaming myself. Mr. Redding was staring at Susan, his mouth wide open, his color gray.

"Officer is down east of a red Nissan," Cathy added. "Approach from the east, keep low."

"One shooter's down," said Brad Rodenheiser. "I can see him from my window. Crawling west, leaving a blood trail."

Susan had stopped him.

"Can anyone verify the location of another shooter?" It was a new voice. "I'm almost there. Safe to approach?"

Another new voice. "Coming east from the perimeter of the parking lot," a man said. "No more signs of another shooter. No more signs."

"Stop and check everyone trying to exit that parking lot," said an older man.

"Searching civilians."

I figured out the incoming officers were stopping the fleeing civilians in case one of them was another shooter. This was horrible. I had tears welling out of my eyes. "I'm so scared," I whispered.

"Young lady, you've never been to war," Mr. Redding said, and then he fainted.

"Cathy," I said. She turned a little and took in the scene. She spoke into her radio again. All I could do was straighten Mr. Redding out and unbutton his collar and remove his tie.

"Parking lot secure," said a disembodied voice.

"Shooter in custody," said a voice I'd heard before. "Repeat. He is in custody. Gunshot to the abdomen. Waiting for lock-down to be reversed."

"Ten-four," dispatch radioed.

There was a pause. Then that first voice said, "Cathy, you need to come in ASAP."

Cathy turned completely white. She reholstered her gun in slow motion, and as an EMT crew swarmed over Susan (thank God) Cathy began walking away. I started to ask her what we should do, but I didn't. It seemed best to keep quiet.

Then another team of EMTs crowded around Carter Redding, and I told them the little I knew about him and what had happened. Mr. Redding was unresponsive, and they put him on a gurney and began pushing it through the phalanxes of cars to reach help.

And there I was, alone in a parking lot swarming with police and civilians now trying to reach their cars to get the hell out of this place.

I was so glad I had my phone. I called Robin and started crying. "Please come get me," I said. "Please come get me." He asked me questions, but I could not seem to get enough breath to answer him. I saw a familiar face and headed for it. Officer Rodenheiser looked ten years older than he had an hour before.

"Did you see what happened?" he asked.

I shook my head. I had to gasp for enough breath to answer him. "I was with Cathy. I saw Susan get shot. And Mr. Redding passed out." I had a hard time making sense. I finally managed to give him a narrative that satisfied him.

"The kid with the gun was Cathy's nephew?" I asked, finally.

Brad nodded. "We'd suspected it was Duncan who fired into that house party last Saturday night, but we couldn't build a case against him. Duncan's mom, Annette, is Cathy's sister. Dr. Clifton is the one who put Duncan's mom in the hospital."

"But . . . why would the boy start shooting?"

"Cathy thinks Duncan believes Dr. Clifton was lying about Annette's strange behavior, which was what landed her in the psych ward." Brad Rodenheiser shrugged. "I guess Duncan practiced with the rifle between the party and this afternoon. Clifton's in surgery."

There was no upside to this, no redeeming quality. Everyone lost.

There were a lot of people to pity, today. I stood alone and shocked while Brad made some notes and prepared to interview other witnesses.

"Roe, Roe!" It was Robin, being held back behind a thrown-up barricade at the main entrance to the hospital parking lot.

I had never been happier to see someone in my life. "Can I go home?" I said. I would have pleaded, if necessary.

"Yes. We may have to talk to you again," Brad said. "Good-bye, Ms. Teagarden."

"Officer Rodenheiser," I said, bobbing my head. After that curious formality, I hurried over to my husband. Maybe I should have gone back inside to check on my mother and John, but what Cathy had told Mr. Redding was true: the people inside the building had been the safest people in town.

Chapter Fifteen

By that night, the town had exploded with news trucks and reporters and curiosity seekers.

I was glad to be at home with my family. I was not going to talk about the shooting to anyone. I was very upset about Susan Crawford. I saw her fall, over and over again.

The next morning, I ran down my list of acquaintances to find someone close enough to Susan's family to have reliable information.

The wife of the brother of Susan's baby daddy worked at my mother's real estate agency. Mother had sold the majority of the firm to a group of her agents, though she kept a small percentage of the profit. And from time to time she dropped in, just to remind them she was still around and watching.

The new receptionist buzzed Brenda instantly. Brenda said hello with that pleased anticipation that told you you were going to make her day.

"Brenda, this is Aurora," I said.

"I'm glad to hear from you. How is John doing?"

"He's better, thank you. Hanging in there. I called to ask about Susan."

"She had to have an operation yesterday," Brenda said. She sighed heavily. "But she's going to be okay, and the baby's going to be okay, at least . . . we think. She'll be off work for quite a while. Her shoulder's pretty messed up."

"Is she very . . . shaken?" I couldn't find exactly the right word.

"She hasn't been talking much because of the pain meds. I think every law enforcement person in the county has stopped by or sent flowers or a card." Brenda paused. "I couldn't ever do that job. I admire her."

"Me, too," I said. "Please let me know if there's anything I can do. I saw . . . I saw it." I felt tears welling into my eyes at the remembrance. Yes, *I* was shaken up plenty.

"Oh my God," Brenda said. "Oh, Roe! I'll tell Susan you asked about her."

"Thanks." I felt better after I hung up.

The papers and the TV were raking into Duncan Carson's life, leaving no stone unturned. His "mentally ill" mother and his absentee father were presented as negligent parents who "let" Duncan live in a world of fantasy and violence. Naturally, a lot was made of the fact that the shooter's aunt was a police detective and had actually been on the scene.

Cathy did not talk to the press.

At least momentarily, the public focus veered off the death of Tracy Beal and the disappearance of Virginia Mitchell to explore the hospital shooting. Though public attention may have wavered, the police did not. Levon Suit called me that afternoon and asked me to come down to the police station with Robin.

"Why?" I was very reluctant to go anywhere close to SPA-COLEC, with the media scrutiny so intense.

"There's someone I want you to see," he said.

"And you're not telling me who that someone is? I don't know why I should oblige you, frankly."

Robin, who had been vacuuming his office, drifted into the family room and waited for the end of the conversation.

"Roe, we want this situation to end as much as you do," Levon said. "Cathy's got to focus on her family for a couple of days, but she's still monitoring the case. I'm trying to keep the momentum going."

What momentum? I would have liked to know what he considered forward progress.

Solely because Levon Suit had been my friend for many years, I very reluctantly agreed to do as he'd asked.

"Come at five, please," he said. "Both of you."

"If Phillip is home to keep the baby," I said.

Phillip, who now almost envied the kids who had been at the party last Saturday night, got home in time to watch Sophie, who had just filled up. Robin was not happy about this meeting, or whatever it was. "Maybe we should get a lawyer," he said, as we climbed in the car.

I tried to explain that Levon had framed the whole request in terms of Cathy's personal disaster, but Robin didn't think that made any difference. To me, it did, but to Robin, Levon was playing emotional dirty pool.

We were glad to see that the press seemed to be away from SPACOLEC. Maybe they were having a happy hour. I cheered up, and so did Robin. We scooted in the front door of the station and asked for Levon. He came out to greet us, and led us back into the detectives' area. We paused by his desk while Levon talked to another officer, who'd been standing before a door with a small rectangular window embedded with wire mesh. An interrogation room.

"Here you go," Levon said, beckoning. He opened the door with a flourish and gestured for me to walk in first. I looked at the man sitting at the scarred table.

He was younger than me by at least ten years, and he had a lot of curly black hair and a noble mustache. He stood politely, and I saw he was dressed in a nice shirt and khakis. He was looking at me with as much curiosity as I'd shown him.

Robin came in right on my heels. Levon had stepped to one side, and he was looking from one face to the other.

"Hello," I said, at a loss.

"Carlos Rivera, ma'am," the stranger said.

"Nice to meet you. I'm Aurora Teagarden, and this is my husband, Robin Crusoe." The other shoe dropped. "Oh, are you Virginia's half brother?"

"Yeah, that's me. You the lady she was working for?"

Robin reached around me to shake Carlos Rivera's hand, and they nodded at each other in a manly way.

"I know you must be so worried. Your poor mother!" I shook my head in commiseration.

"She's very upset." He looked down at the gray metal table. "We both are."

I sat down opposite him, so he could resume his seat. "How could you be any other way? We think so highly of Virginia. I'm praying she shows up soon, safe and sound, and explains what happened."

"You don't think she's dead?" He seemed hopeful.

"I'll believe the best until I find out different."

Now I understood why I was here. Levon had wanted to

verify that Robin and I had never met Carlos, and that he had never seen us.

I met Levon's eyes. He looked down.

It was impossible to separate Levon's job from his behavior. I couldn't be his friend and, at the same time, his suspect.

Our old friendship was simply dissolving, and I couldn't think of any way to save it.

That was the sum total of our conversation with Carlos Rivera. Robin and I left as soon as we could.

"I'd like to punch Levon," Robin said as he drove home.

"I would be glad for you to do that," I said. "Please let me watch." That might not be fair or right, but it was how I felt.

"At least I was *there,*" he said bitterly.

Oh, no. We weren't going there again.

But as it turned out, we were.

"You got shot at, and I wasn't there," Robin said. "Another thing I wasn't around for."

As we pulled into the driveway and he turned off the engine I tried to think what to say to him. He started to open his door, but I put a hand out to stop him. "Robin, how can we ever know what will happen next? You'll have your share of times, I'm sure, when I'm not around and something big hits the fan. I will *never* blame you for not being omniscient. Please don't blame yourself. It doesn't make any sense at all."

He leaned over to kiss the top of my head. "You're sounding wise. I'll try to work my head around this. But I'm still mad at everyone, including myself."

"I know," I said, smiling. "I love you."

Robin managed to give me one of his wonderful smiles in return, and he put his arm around me as we went to the front door.

Phillip was holding Sophie, and she was tuning up for a howl. He was glad to hand her over.

Again, Sophie stayed awake after her feeding, though I'd been sure she'd be exhausted after the crying jag. We put her on the floor under her play gym, and sat there watching her with endless fascination. We may have taken a few pictures.

Robin maintained that Sophie looked like his mother, Corinne. And Sophie did have the reddish fuzz that signaled "Crusoe."

I really liked Robin's mother, but I figured Sophie looked more like—well, like me, frankly. Since Corinne was nine inches taller than me, we'd certainly find out which one of us was the blueprint . . . sooner or later.

For a while, we had a pleasant respite from worrying about John, the dead woman, the missing Virginia, and the thief.

"Being a mother is making me selfish," I told Robin. "I do get concerned about other people, and I get sorrowful when they suffer, but basically, as long as our family unit is okay . . ."

"I know what you mean. I don't think it's being selfish, exactly. If it is, I'm guilty, too. I think it's just that our priorities have changed."

I nodded, feeling obscurely better now that I knew that Robin shared my altered worldview.

"What do you think about having another one of these?" Robin said, laying a finger on Sophie's head. He was smiling, but he was serious. We watched as Sophie, in a white and pink flowered sleeper, waved her little fists and made "eh" sounds in a wholly adorable way. Even more adorable now that her eyelids were fluttering shut. She kept opening her eyes again, but she wouldn't be able to keep that up for long.

"I can't believe we had *her*," I said, trying to buy some time.

Since a doctor had assured me I couldn't get pregnant—a false diagnosis that had changed the course of my life significantly—as far as I was concerned, Sophie was a miracle. I could tell that Robin was waiting for my answer. "It might be too soon after my delivery to ask me that. Having Sophie was . . . an eye-opening experience."

"I could tell." Robin looked a little queasy at the memory. "And I know it's awful soon to even think about it. But you're thirty-seven and I'm forty. If we want another baby, we can't wait long."

"Are you really so anxious to have another child?" I had lost my peaceful mood, and I was beginning to tense up. "First you want a puppy. Now you want a baby. When will it end?"

I tried to sound like I was joking, but I don't think I even came close.

Robin could tell I was unhappy, but he forged ahead. He must have had this bottled up for a while. "She's just so great," he said earnestly. "Maybe two would be even greater? So Sophie wouldn't be an only child."

"I was an only child. I think I turned out all right." True, I had a half brother, but we had never shared a household.

"I guess since I have two sisters, I thought Sophie would maybe feel a lack?"

I gave him a narrow-eyed look to indicate I thought that was a crock.

"By the way," Robin said, "a quick change of subject."

"Okay." And none too soon.

"Mom knows traveling with a little one is a huge pain, so she wondered if we could have Thanksgiving here. She enjoyed it so much last year, she said to tell you."

"*We* being?"

He looked very anxious. "The whole family. My sisters, their husbands, the kids, Mom."

Nine people, plus us, plus Phillip. I took a deep breath. "Sure, we can do that. Maybe I'll get the meal catered, I'm not promising everything will be made from scratch. But I'll be glad to be hostess. We'll have to plan it like a campaign. A list of jobs for each day leading up to the holiday."

"Great!" Robin looked so delighted that I felt guilty. His entire family had come to our wedding, but they couldn't stay long since it was inconveniently (and hastily) scheduled to take place between Thanksgiving and Christmas. Corinne had returned a couple of months ago, after Sophie's birth. She'd stayed three days, getting to know her new granddaughter, and she'd been a tremendous help.

Apparently, the "second child" discussion had been tabled. I was relieved. I had to admit Sophie was so spectacular the world could sure use another one like her; but the prospect of birthing and raising a second baby made me tired, just thinking about it.

Sophie conked out after three more minutes.

I sat on a stool at the breakfast bar/island considering our dinner options. I was going to have to cook. That meant a trip to the grocery. I pulled over a pad and pen and planned three days' worth of meals, and the list grew and grew.

Robin volunteered to make the grocery run. "The least I can do is walk around the store," he said.

"I like your attitude," I said. All the cooking I did these days was easy. My hours in the kitchen had waned as my new job as Elsie, the milk provider, had waxed. (Incidentally, now I couldn't eat onions or lima beans: Sophie got gassy if I did. I thought that was weird.)

Robin collected our cloth grocery bags for the store, and some clothes to take to the dry cleaner's, and I armed him with my list.

After he'd left, I thought longingly of lying down for a while with a book. I didn't have to clean, since tomorrow would be the maids' day, another treat I'd given myself. (I was really into treating myself, post-Sophie.) I couldn't cook until Robin returned. Yes, I could read!

My cell phone rang. I looked at the caller ID.

"Mother," I said. "What news?"

"Roe, he's better," she said instantly. "He's fully awake. The doctor seems very optimistic now."

My shoulders sagged with relief. "I'm so glad," I said. "Any idea how much longer he'll be in the hospital?"

"At least another day. More tests. More observation."

The hospital was the best place for John right now. My mother would run herself ragged taking care of him when he came home. Aida Brattle Teagarden Queensland had high standards for everything, and maintaining a husband was included under that banner.

"Please let me know what I can do," I said. "Cook or run errands, whatever."

"Thanks. By the way, John David tells me he saw Carter Redding in the ER after that awful thing in the parking lot. Carter said he was sheltering with you and Cathy Trumble. Is that true? Are you okay?" I wasn't getting the full Aida laser-focus questioning only because John had higher priority right now.

"You don't need to worry about me," I said. "I was safe the whole time."

"Thank goodness," Mother said. "I don't think I could take more bad news. You'll have to tell me all about it soon."

"You didn't hear the shots?"

"No. The nurses just told me I couldn't leave, but I wasn't going to, anyway, and I stayed in John's room until they told me the situation was over. They didn't tell me what had happened. I was actually in the hospital, but I never knew a thing." She sounded a bit bemused . . . but not really concerned.

I wanted to keep it that way. "I'm fine," I said stoutly. "If you can, find out how Mr. Redding is doing. He didn't look so good when they took him into the hospital, and he was really brave during the whole incident."

"He told John David it was like being back in the war."

"I hope he's okay."

"I'll try to find out, honey."

"Thanks, Mother. Tell John I said hello."

"I'll do that." The joy was back in her voice.

Now I felt too restless to read. I roamed around the living room, picking up discarded newspapers and putting them in the recycle bin, throwing away outdated magazines, reshelving some books in the library in Robin's office. As my mother would have put it, I was "piddling."

I was completely taken aback when Phillip emerged from his room with Sarah in tow.

They didn't seem self-conscious or embarrassed, and I tried to be the same. I called myself an old stick-in-the-mud, and several other names. *It was just that I didn't know she was here,* I told myself. I hoped that was true.

"Hey, I'm running over to Sarah's," Phillip said. "I'll be back by suppertime. Seven?"

I glanced at the clock. "Sounds about right."

"I'm glad you're okay," Sarah said. "I heard about what happened in the parking lot."

"Do either of you know Duncan?" I had a possible source of information right here at hand, and I hadn't even thought about it.

"I do," Sarah said. "Not well. I didn't like the people he was friends with. You know how that is."

"Sure," I said, wondering if I really did remember how that was. "So, did people talk about him? Was he very strange or something?"

She hesitated, looking at Phillip as though communicating with him.

"There was that thing," he said, maddeningly.

"Sure. Duncan was at the last big party I went to, two or three weeks ago. He didn't usually come, even when he was welcome to. But he was there with a couple of . . . boys I don't like, because they're posers. Like they're *so dangerous*." She looked mildly contemptuous. "Well, after Duncan turned out so crazy, maybe they really are." She shrugged. "Anyway, this other guy showed up, an older guy. Maybe in his twenties. None of us had ever seen him before. And Duncan left with him. I didn't see the older guy again, but Duncan came back all smirky, and you could just tell he'd done something he thought was really radical. He told a couple of friends of mine that he'd bought a rifle. Duncan said he was going to give it to his dad for Christmas. So the next weekend, when the shooting happened at Carly's, we were all kind of wondering. But no one really believed it was Duncan, because he'd always acted so . . . so meek."

"Carly is Dr. Clifton's daughter?" I was trying to put this all together in my head. I wondered if Dr. Clifton was going to recover fully. He was a consulting psychiatrist at the hospital and he had a busy private practice, I'd heard.

"So now I can't ever go back to Carly's."

"Oh?" I was trying to keep up.

"But it's okay, because I don't really like her anyway. She can be okay, but she's mean to people she thinks aren't popular."

That I could relate to. Even back when dinosaurs had walked the earth (when I had been in high school) there had been girls—and boys—like that, aplenty.

"So you think it was Duncan who fired into the house?" Brad Rodenheiser had thought it was likely.

She nodded vigorously. "I didn't think about it then, but after Tuesday, well, it seems likely, huh? Carly's party gets shot up, and then Carly's dad gets shot?"

Yes, it did seem likely. Really likely.

I debated whether or not to say anything to Phillip and Sarah about letting me know when they were together in the house, about leaving Phillip's door open, about . . . but then I thought, *I either trust them or I don't.* I took a deep breath and said, "Good to see you, Sarah. Tell your mom I said hi." She nodded amiably.

"Back in a while," Phillip said, and they were gone.

In five minutes or less, the carport door opened. Robin came in with his hands full of bags.

I jumped up to help him put the groceries away. It took quite a while, since our cupboards had been pretty bare. Then I got out what I needed for supper, and I began pounding chicken breasts thin while the butter melted in the microwave. I asked Robin to turn on the oven, but he didn't seem to hear me.

I turned around to see that Robin was rummaging through the "miscellaneous" drawer, a messy catchall for things I couldn't place logically elsewhere. After watching this in silence for a long moment, I realized this was my cue to say, "What are you looking for?"

"I still haven't found my keys. I've been using my spare car key since I got back." He sounded very irritated.

I said mildly, "I looked for them the day John went to the hospital. Obviously, I didn't find them. I know a lot of places they aren't." With everything that had happened, the keys had been low on my list of things to worry about.

"Why don't you check your purse?" Robin was very careful not to delve into my purse without asking. He'd had two sisters. "It's the only thing I haven't searched."

Since I had chronically interrupted sleep patterns these days, I had done a number of strange things, like put the peanut butter in the refrigerator. Maybe I had had a brain fart and mistaken Robin's keys for my own. Repressing a sigh, I prepared for this major operation.

My outsize bag was sure to have all kinds of crumbs and lint inside. (I don't put food in my purse, but there are always crumbs, just another mystery in my life.) I spread a sheet of newspaper on the island, and turned my purse upside down. A shower of debris rained down on the newspaper: loose change, old tissues, shopping lists, grocery receipts, a credit card case, a billfold, a change purse. Lipstick, ChapStick, a compact. An ancient mint. Two pens. A case containing my dark glasses (bright blue frame). Crumbs, of course.

And Virginia's telephone.

Chapter Sixteen

Robin and I stood on opposite sides of the island, staring down at the pile of detritus crowned with a bright turquoise telephone decorated with rhinestones.

"You got a new phone?" Robin said. He looked at it askance.

"That's not mine," I said.

Phillip came in the front door at just that moment. "Hey, when's supper?" he asked, surprised at the absence of any visible preparation.

When I didn't answer, he came over to see what we were staring at.

"Where'd you get Virginia's phone?" He cocked his head, waiting for my (no doubt) simple explanation.

I shook my head. "I have no idea." We three regarded the bright phone as if it had been a snake. After a moment, I said, "I guess I'd better take it to the law enforcement complex. I can put it in a plastic bag or something. I am just . . . tired of having people come in and out of this house." I didn't add *especially*

Levon. I felt guilty—he was doing his job—but that was how I felt right now.

"This puts the theft of your diaper bag in a whole different light," Robin said, thoughtfully.

"Wait, what?" Of course I'd told Phillip about being in the parking lot of the hospital, but the regaining of a diaper bag had seemed like a small item in the bigger picture.

"Why don't I take the telephone there?" Robin said. "You've already started supper. You can brief me, if you want to. But I figure you'd rather not go. And Sophie is going to wake up sooner or later, and she'll want her mom."

"Well, she'll want my boobs, anyway," I said absently. I looked up at my husband. He was letting me know he might not return for a while, but he was willing.

The relief I felt when he offered told me I should take him up on it.

"Hey, should I go, too?" Phillip was smart enough to pick up the subtext. "And should we check out the phone before we take it in?"

Clearly, that would be very wrong, but I confess I felt a moment of temptation. I suppressed it nobly. "We can't," I said. "That's a police thing. Robin, do you want Phillip with you?"

"Thanks, Phillip, but if—if they decide I need to stay there for some long interview—Roe will need you to help her, and you couldn't do anything but sit in the waiting room at the station, if you came with me."

"Okay," Phillip said. "But I'm willing."

"Noted," Robin said. "Thanks. I'll just bag it up and take it to SPACOLEC." I handed him a plastic bag from a kitchen drawer. I found a set of tongs, and with careful precision I lowered the phone into the bag. Probably ridiculous to take such precautions after Virginia's phone had been bouncing around in my purse, but we had to try.

"Oh, wait!" I'd had a thought. I was not a mystery reader for nothing. "Don't they use paper bags now? Or . . . ?"

Robin said, "They bag people's hands. But I don't know about telephones. It's already in there. Let's go with it."

"Fine with me."

It wasn't far to the law enforcement complex, but I didn't know how many people he'd have to talk to.

Before Robin could return, I had a call from Levon. He had a list of questions, of course. He opened with, "How did you get the phone? Why was it in your purse?"

"I have no idea," and "I don't know," didn't satisfy him.

"What's your best guess, Roe?" Levon was clearly exasperated.

Robin came in the garage door. I pantomimed whom I was talking to. He shook his head, rolled his eyes, and pointed to the chicken. In return, I pointed to the bowls of melted butter and mixed Parmesan cheese and breadcrumbs. The oven had preheated.

"My best guess," I said, aware my voice was weary and limp. I was ambling around the room as I talked, and I passed by the mirror near the front door. I rolled my eyes at my reflection; "death warmed over" was an apt description. I resolved to avoid mirrors for a while. "I always put my purse in the same place on the kitchen counter. I don't remember exactly what kind of purse Virginia carried, but the first time she worked here, she stowed her bag right there beside mine, I remember that. I almost picked up hers by mistake once."

"So do you think she popped her phone into your purse to

draw it to our attention? Or did she believe she was putting her phone into her own bag?"

"You asked me to guess. That's all I've got." I hung up.

I'd always been a friend of law enforcement, even though I'd met police who hadn't liked me one bit. Anyone working in this field had a dangerous and demanding job. Just at the moment, I was frustrated and angry, convinced Levon wasn't really listening to me. "Aaaaargh," I said out loud. Nothing I could do about it now. Time to pull my socks up.

Robin had coated the chicken and put it in the oven, bless him. I assembled a green salad. Then I chopped up fruit, and I preheated the lower oven for garlic bread. Dinner was on its way to being ready. The pasta and sauce (from a jar, sadly) could be left until the last minute.

This was the quickest I had moved in a week. I felt virtuous and efficient. I also felt tired—but I was better, physically. A couple more nights of regular sleep, and I'd be back on my feet. Since I'd done all the prep work I could do for the moment, I sank down on the couch and picked up my book, wriggling into a comfortable position.

I registered nothing more until I woke as Sophie was just beginning to complain. I shook my head, trying to clear it.

"Roe, you want me to get her?" Phillip called, in no very happy voice, and I saw Robin was hurrying down the hall from his office.

"If you'll change her diaper, I'll be there in a minute," I said. I stumbled into the kitchen to peek at the chicken, took it out of the oven, turned up the heat on the pasta pot, drank a large glass of water, and went to the baby's room. Robin was jiggling her and walking with her. I looked at them from the doorway, marveling again that I had *my own family.* This seemed incredible to me, still.

"Baby," I crooned. "Mama's here." Sophie knew my presence meant food, and she was anxious for it. I sat in the rocking chair and prepared myself. *This is like being on a treadmill,* I reflected. But I loved her so much that it was worth it.

After a few minutes, my mind began to wander. I thought about the night of the murder, picturing everything that had happened. It had worked so well when Robin had suggested I picture everyone in the ICU; maybe it would be helpful, again.

This felt oddly like a board game set out for last Saturday night.

My token would be in the square representing our bedroom, and it would not move. Sarah's would have gone down the sidewalk. Phillip's was stationary, as was Sophie's. I assumed Virginia had been roaming the house, with the nursery monitor in one hand and her telephone in the other, so I pictured her token zigzagging around in an unpredictable way. But then Tracy had arrived on the scene, somehow, steered by some unfathomable purpose. Her token (red) would suddenly appear over the edge of the board.

I moved these tokens around in my head. Had Virginia been in the house when Tracy came in? Surely they would have had a noisy confrontation, if that had been the case. I was working on the assumption the two had never met, that Virginia would raise an alarm if she encountered a stranger in our house. That was what I believed, based on nothing but gut feeling.

How had Tracy gotten in the house? I should have asked myself that question days ago. Obviously, one of the doors had been unlocked. Had Virginia simply been careless, or had she been complicit? Had Tracy known she could get in? Surely she hadn't been coming by the house, testing the doors . . . that idea made my skin crawl.

Robin came in, moving quietly. He sat on the stool of the rocking chair, and whispered, "How did Tracy get in?"

And that was another reason we were married. "Exactly!" I said, but in a hushed voice. I told Robin what I'd been thinking.

"If she'd been lurking for a few nights, I'd think we'd have seen her, or one of our neighbors would have," he said. "The Herman sisters are always out late at night with Chaka. I've seen them when I was up with Sophie."

When Sophie wasn't ready to go back to sleep after she fed, Robin liked to wander around with her in his arms, gently jiggling her (and singing to her when he thought I wasn't listening).

"So maybe this was the first time she'd tried to get in. Assuming she took her sister's car, where is it now?"

"I don't think the police have found the car," Robin said slowly. "We would have heard?"

"At the very least, the Cohens would have heard and come over to tell us all about it."

Robin nodded. "So we need to find out how she came to be in our backyard at all."

Chapter Seventeen

As if the universe had heard us, but slowly, the landline rang early the next morning just after Phillip had left for school. Robin, showered and dressed, picked up the phone in our bedroom. He came into Sophie's room with the phone to his ear, conveying his astonishment by waggling his eyebrows.

"Mrs. Beal," he said, looking at me significantly.

I pantomimed amazement. Why would Tracy's mom be calling us?

"Yes, I'm Robin Crusoe." He listened. "Yes, I'm sure this whole thing has been a shock to you. Us, too."

What an unexpected turn of events.

Moving carefully, I rose to place Sophie in her crib. Robin and I left her to her sleep. He was still talking as we went across the hall. Though I was intensely curious, I needed to shower. I had some errands to run, but mostly I wanted to get out of the house for a while.

Though I take short showers, I was slightly surprised to find Robin still talking to Mrs. Beal when I turned off the water.

"No ma'am, we didn't hear anything. I was out of town, and my wife was sick in bed with the flu. That's why we had a baby-sitter here. Yes, she's still missing. I don't have any idea why Virginia would harm Tracy. I'm not sure she did. We won't know what actually happened until Virginia shows up."

Robin listened, the corners of his mouth turning down. He rolled his eyes at me. "Well, Mrs. Beal—okay, Sandra—I don't know why Tracy had strong feelings for me. And I'm sorry that made her behave like . . . ah, got her into so much trouble. I'm hoping the police can get to the bottom of her death." He listened. "Since we're talking, may I ask you a question?"

Evidently Tracy's mom agreed. Robin continued, "I know Tracy left the hospital when she wasn't supposed to. I understand she took her sister's car?" He listened for a minute or two. "Um-hum. Um-hum. Well, we'd just wondered if the police had found the car. They haven't? Well, I agree, that's really strange. Yes, I'm sure Sharon's missing her car."

Robin did some more listening, made sounds of agreement or sympathy here and there, and finally hung up with obvious relief.

"So?" I was anxious to hear a summary.

"As you can tell, Sandra Beal is prone to oversharing. I learned that she's divorced, that Tracy was her second daughter, that Mrs. Beal can't understand this whole thing. She didn't know Tracy had escaped from the hospital until hours after it happened. And of course, Sharon didn't know Tracy had walked off the hospital grounds. Sharon was camping. Sharon didn't get home for two more days. Then she reported her car missing." He thought for a minute, reviewing the conversation. "Oh. Tracy knew where Sharon kept a spare set of keys. Because they were sisters."

"What kind of car is it?"

"A silver Nissan Sentra. Bought at the year-end closeout, so Sharon got a *really good deal* on it." Robin shuddered, just a little.

"Sandra told all this to you, the man her daughter was stalking." I shook my head. "I'm amazed."

"The woman's so stunned by having a daughter as disturbed as Tracy, she was glad to have someone to talk to. Sandra doesn't seem very smart, frankly, and she hasn't been able to track down her ex to tell him about Tracy. She's very unhappy all the way around."

"I'll try to feel sorry for her." Just at the moment, I was out of pity.

Robin grinned at me. "Don't apologize to me for any lack of feeling. I have sympathy for the woman, but I was counting the seconds until I could get off the phone. And someone at SPACOLEC gave Sandra Beal my phone number," he added grimly. "Our landline is unlisted. I'm still wondering who gave it to the reporters who called."

"That's really disturbing. Sounds like after talking to Sandra, you could kind of feel where Tracy had gotten the wobbly mind."

He eased down on the bed beside me as I pulled my sweater over my head. "I sure don't think most mothers would have wanted to tell me so much. Or to talk to me at all."

I nodded in agreement as I began to brush my hair. "I wonder why the police haven't found the car. Could Tracy have hidden it somewhere? Why would she do that? I'd think she'd park it as close as possible, for a quick getaway. In case one of us raised the alarm."

"We can't know what she imagined would happen."

I tried to figure that out but gave up very quickly. It made me shiver all over.

I remembered the first time I'd seen Tracy, wearing a catering company shirt, arranging food on the craft service table for the *Whimsical Death* crew. She'd even seemed pleasant.

"I wish I'd known who she was right away." Robin's thoughts had been paralleling my own. "But I'd never seen her, or a picture of her. Just gotten the letters. To me, my publisher, my agent, my publicist . . . Celia . . . and my mother. That one really made me take alarm," Robin said.

"How did Corinne handle that?" I couldn't imagine her reaction to something so outlandish.

"I had a hard time explaining the situation to her," Robin said. He looked very grim. "She'd never encountered a woman like Tracy. Someone mentally ill and fixated on her son . . . of course, that shook her up."

"I'm sorry that your mom had to go through that. She's so nice." I was sincere. "When you actually met Tracy on the set . . . you didn't get any vibe from her? Any creepy feeling?"

"Maybe it's hindsight, but I did sort of register she watched me all the time. Didn't you tell me when she met you, her reaction was almost excessively excited?"

I nodded. "It struck me as strange, but you know . . . people are. Especially true-crime buffs."

I'd figured in the book about the murders in Lawrenceton, simply because I was part of the Real Murders Club, and I'd been able to tell the police that each murder was staged like a famous homicide. Tracy had thought of me, perhaps, as someone who'd sparked Robin's interest in true crime. If Tracy had known that Robin and I would become a couple, maybe she would have leaped across the craft service table with a knife.

She'd done the leaping and stabbing later, in my home.

When Tracy had tried to kill me in my own kitchen, I had grabbed her ankles and toppled her to the floor. In the process, she'd fallen on her knife. Her injury had been serious, but she had recovered.

Now, when I thought of the image of Tracy standing in the same room where my helpless child lay sleeping, I wished that I had killed her that day in my kitchen.

It was not the first time I'd thought that.

The maids rang the doorbell then, and I let them in.

"I'm calling a security company," Robin said suddenly, and rose to his feet. When he'd made a decision, Robin moved quickly. By the time I'd had a quick discussion with our mother-daughter cleaning team, the telephone book spread on the kitchen counter was open to "Security," and Robin was having a conversation. "Then we'll see you later today," he said, and after a second of listening, he hung up. He nodded at me, satisfied with his progress. "Spartan Shield Security is coming around two o'clock," he said.

"That was quick."

"He had a cancellation," Robin said.

Sounded like a standard face-saving strategy. "How'd you pick that one?" I said.

"I remembered the Finstermeyers got their system from Spartan." Robin went off to his office, whistling. He'd made a solid move toward protecting his woman and his baby. He felt strong.

I smiled as I sat down at the counter to plan my day.

At least I could do so with a pleasant sense of relief.

It'll be good to have an alarm system, I thought, as I put my library books in my cloth bag. Swapping day was always fun. It was so pleasant to come home with books I'd selected, like the prospect of diving into a cool pool on a hot day. I'd topped off Sophie, so to speak, so I could stay away longer. I needed some "me" time. I put the monitor on Robin's desk and waved almost cheerily.

The maids were working on the kitchen and it was beginning to look orderly and shining. They certainly didn't need my supervision.

I'd wondered if my first trip to the library as a civilian would be a little awkward, but I had no way of anticipating how very awkward it would be.

Perry Allison was at the desk, busy with a line of patrons. Perry gave me a little wave, but he also looked as though he wanted to tell me something pretty urgently. He couldn't leave his post with patrons standing there, so after I set my books in the return bin, I went over to the "New Books" shelves, ready to browse. Just as I began looking (would the new Karin Slaughter be in?), the media specialist, Janie Spellman, strode around the end of a set of shelves and almost collided with me.

This would not have been notable—Janie was always in a hurry—but she made it an incident by flinching away from me as if I had cooties. Killer cooties.

"Why are you here?" she gasped.

"To check out books," I replied. I could feel my eyes narrowing. I had what Robin called my "about to be mad" face on.

"But weren't you arrested?"

I was genuinely confused. "I got robbed. Why would I be arrested?"

"For that woman."

I spread my hands, to tell her she'd have to give me more information.

"Since that woman . . . ah, died in your house."

I was exasperated and I didn't try to hide it. But I kept my voice low, because I was *in the library*. "Janie, could you have worked with me even a week, and not known I would not kill someone? Can you possibly imagine that I would bash in someone's skull? Also, the body wasn't in our house, but in our backyard. Believe me, we'd like to know who killed Tracy just as much as everyone else. Maybe even more."

Janie seemed flustered by my counterattack, so she simply didn't acknowledge it. She did a little sidestep to get around me with no touching (murder cooties!) and then she zoomed over to the door to the employees' break room.

I was disgusted to discover I was so angry there were tears in my eyes. It makes me even angrier when I feel the prickle of tears. It sends the wrong signal.

I dabbed my eyes surreptitiously, kept my back straight, and finished picking out my books. I felt that every eye was on me, weighing my guilt or complicity in the death of Tracy Beal and the disappearance of Virginia Mitchell. I knew I'd been an innocent bystander, and I knew Robin had been in another state. Now I realized the gossip mill was grinding overtime.

My dignity was intact when I put my books on the checkout desk. Perry said, "Don't pay any attention to Janie. She's a drama bitch, and she's never been your fan."

"Why?" I asked, because I couldn't stop. "I never did anything to her." I winced when I heard myself whining like a child.

"Robin," Perry said, looking at me as if I should have known.

"What about Robin?"

"She wanted him. Famous novelist? Right up her alley."

"But he was already dating me when she began work here. I don't believe he ever even looked in her direction."

"I think she's starring in her own movie," Perry said. "Everyone looks at the heroine."

"Huh. Well, sorry, Janie, but Robin is mine forever." The idea of Janie being motivated by envy was (I'm ashamed to say) a real boost to my spirits.

I was smiling when I got in my car, but I wasn't a few minutes later when I picked up Robin's suit at the dry cleaner's. Mrs. Sung served me with great speed, as if she wanted me out of there. When I got cash from the ATM at my downtown bank, the drive-in teller was looking out her window with her eyes wide. I took the scenic route home, because it felt so good to be somewhere besides our house and the hospital.

The shooting had not diverted public attention as much as I had hoped. I should have figured we'd come in for our share of suspicion.

My childhood friend Amina was sitting in the park behind our little civic center. The moment I saw her, a memory I'd been groping for snapped into focus. I pulled into the parking area and walked over to Amina's bench. She looked up when she saw me approaching, and pointed proudly to her daughter, who was going down the slide all by herself. Megan, now three, was adorable, with Amina's clear complexion, shiny hair, and big smile. I was Megan's godmother—and Amina's friend—though my relationship with Amina had hit some speed bumps.

I wasn't sure my schoolmate was willing to put in the work to relaunch our friendship. It was time to find out.

"Hi!" I called. Amina gave me a reserved sort of smile, but Megan waved with enthusiasm. "Miss Roe! Look at me!" After she went down the slide, she swung herself along the low monkey bars, three in a row.

I was duly impressed. "You're strong, Megan," I said.

"There's Susie!" Megan ran over to play with her newly arrived friend at the sandpit. Susie's mom sat down by the girls. I joined Amina on the bench, and for a moment I simply enjoyed the sun and the quiet.

But I had to open the conversation, to begin to work my way around to my goal. "How are you doing, Amina? What's the progress on the divorce?"

"Hugh's hired a lawyer from his firm, one who specializes in divorce litigation," Amina said, her voice bitter.

What else did you expect? "Did you think he'd do anything different?" I said, as gently as I could.

"I hoped we could sign forms online and get it over with, for a couple of hundred bucks," she said. "After all, I agreed to share custody of Megan with him, and I thought the alimony I asked for was reasonable."

I was doubtful that a couple could get a quick online divorce if there were children or alimony involved, but what did I know? "I guess lawyers are allergic to filing cheap online forms," I said. "What are you going to do?"

"I've talked to Bryan Pascoe," Amina said.

"He's got a great reputation. He's who I'd go to."

"He said he was a friend of yours."

"That's stretching it a little, but we're friendly." Bryan was sharp as a tack and very aggressive. He was exactly who Amina needed.

"Megan, do not pick up that stick!" Amina yelled, so suddenly I jumped.

Megan looked guilty and dropped the offending stick immediately. Susie's mother looked up from her cell phone. "Sorry," she called. "I'm putting it in my purse! Phones are an addiction!"

Amina waved back in acknowledgment. "Got to watch out for sticks," she said quietly. "Or . . ."

"You'll put an eye out," we said simultaneously, and we laughed. That had been the standard opinion when we'd been young.

"Do you think you'll stay here in Lawrenceton?"

"I haven't decided," Amina said heavily. She looked depressed. "I have help with Megan here. My mom just loves her to death, and now that Mom's sold the shop she and Dad have a lot of time to spend with Megan. She's got 'em wound around her little finger." Amina's smile looked both fond and proud.

"Sure she does," I murmured.

Amina resumed her train of thought. "If I moved to Atlanta, I could get a good job at another legal firm. My former boss said he would give me a great recommendation. But that would be too far for my parents to commute to babysit every day. I'd have to put Megan in a day care, and that's really expensive."

"Could you find a job locally?" I had no idea what the job market in Lawrenceton was like. I'd held the library job since I'd graduated from college, a long, long, time ago.

"There's an executive secretary job open at Pan-Am Agra and I'm really qualified for it," Amina said. "And there's day care there. As you know, of course." Amina looked self-conscious. My first husband had instituted the day care. "I'm just not sure I want to become a small-town girl again."

I had nothing to say to that. If the choice had been mine, I would stay local in a second, especially with day care provided at my place of work. But that was me, and as I'd learned when I was pregnant, Amina and I were nothing alike any longer, if we'd ever been.

I began carefully framing my next question, which had been my purpose when I'd seen Amina. But she forestalled me.

"They find that Virginia Mitchell?" she said, so abruptly that I jumped a little.

"Not yet." So we were on-topic, unexpectedly, courtesy of Amina. "Your mom recommended Virginia to my mother, and I couldn't remember how your mom had met her."

"Virginia specializes in new moms now, but she used to sit for the elderly, too," Amina said. "For a while, Virginia sat full-time with Mimi Day."

Patricia Day (called "Mimi" by her descendants) had been a very exciting grandmother. She'd cursed in front of us children, she'd worn dangly earrings, and she'd smoked like a chimney. Volatile but funny, she'd been an exclamation point in my traditional childhood. I'd never met anyone like Mimi, who'd been married three times. I was sad when a stroke laid the grand old lady in bed forever.

"I was a new widow then," I said. "I guess that's why I didn't remember the details." I'd dropped in to Miss Patricia's house a couple of times, but the visits were hazy. I'd been too grieved to take on any more sorrow.

"Right," Amina said, and was silent for a moment to acknowledge my hard time. "Well, I couldn't come too often, but I do remember Virginia. She was good with my grandmother, put up with all her bad language and temper. The boyfriend was the big problem."

"Your grandmother had a boyfriend?" I was startled. Sure, Miss Patricia had been a firecracker, but I'd hardly have thought . . .

Amina laughed long and hard. "No, no! Virginia's boyfriend!"

"He came by the house? Or called her too much?"

"He went to jail. It was a big drama."

I could sure understand that. "For what?"

"Burglary, I think. From a toolshed, but it was expensive stuff. A circular saw, a jackhammer, things like that."

As far as I knew, my father had never lifted a finger to do a home repair, but I knew Amina's father had. So I took her word for it that tools could be worth stealing.

"And that was while Virginia was actually working for your grandmother?"

"You bet. It was the most interesting thing that had happened to Mimi in a year. She ate it up."

"So what was Virginia's reaction?"

"She was really upset, of course. She went to bail him out, so she called my mother to sit with Mimi. I don't know what happened after that."

"She came back to work, though?"

"Yes. But after another month, Mimi died. So Virginia was out of a job. But my mom thought the world of the woman, and she gave her a good reference any time she was asked."

"Virginia's mother told the police Virginia'd broken up with her boyfriend three months before," I said. "I guess he's out of jail?"

Amina shrugged. "I have no idea. He had an old 'movie' name . . . maybe Harrison Ford? Like the *Star Wars* guy? Something like that."

I nodded, wondering how close she'd gotten to the correct name. I made myself remain five more minutes, talking about this and that, until I glanced at my watch and told Amina it was time to feed Sophie. "Come by to see her," I said, and Amina looked pleased.

"Megan loves babies," she said. "Maybe we will."

Chapter Eighteen

When I got home the maids had left. It was time to take care of Sophie. When that was done, I told Robin everything Amina had said. "Do you think the police know all this?" I asked him. "Because they haven't said a word about the boyfriend except to say Mrs. Mitchell said they weren't together anymore. Moms don't always know." I tried not to think about what that might mean for my future with Sophie.

Robin didn't get as excited as I'd thought he would. "The boyfriend may still be in jail," he pointed out. "Or they may have truly broken up after the arrest. The police said so, right? That she'd dated some new men?"

I was sure I'd learned a vital clue. I was reluctant to hear anything different. I turned to fill my glass with water. I had to remember to keep pouring the fluids in, since so much fluid was going out of me.

"It would be great if we could know exactly what had happened, and where this guy is now," Robin said. "I wish Amina had been more certain about his name. But since the police have Virginia's phone, they'll know if Virginia was still talking to this man. By the way, I had a strange phone call from the program chair at the Uppity Women club."

My face flamed. "Strange? How so?" I was an Uppity Woman, though my life hadn't permitted me to attend the last few meetings. Up until this moment, I'd been proud to be part of a group of openly active, smart, and assertive women, a revolutionary basis for a club when it had been founded.

I could only think of one reason the program chair would call: to cancel Robin's talk. I had to fight the impulse to track down the women involved and *beat them up*. I was snarling inside with rage at the very idea. When I was sure my voice would be normal, I said, "Why did she call?"

"She called to emphasize the fact that I was *very* welcome to come to the club to speak. As if I'd heard otherwise."

Enormously relieved, I downed a large glass of water and took Sophie back to her changing table. Her face was so innocent, so guileless. I felt like a traitor for thinking about anything but her. "Sophie, your mom and dad are between a rock and a hard place," I told her. "But don't worry, we're going to come out of it okay."

With Sophie settled on the kitchen island in her infant seat, Robin and I ate tuna salad and three-bean salad for lunch, with a sleeve of Ritz crackers lying on the counter between us. Robin abandoned thinking about Virginia Mitchell's (possible) boyfriend to descend deep into book-thought, so he didn't say much while we ate. That left me free to read the newspaper. After we'd finished, Robin cleaned away the leftovers and shot off to his office. I put Sophie to bed, and then I returned to wipe off the island.

I picked up one of my library books with a sense of happy

anticipation. The novel was so immediately intriguing I was startled when the doorbell rang. Who now?

Then I remembered that the Spartan Shield representative was supposed to give us an estimate for an alarm system plan. "Robin, the security people are here," I called as I went to the door. I felt this was his project, so he should be on hand to answer questions.

Robin was obviously excited and interested about this new toy, and he was halfway to the door when I opened it.

"Mr. Petrosian!" I was dumbfounded to recognize the coroner, now wearing a khaki shirt with a golden shield on the left side of the chest and "Arnie" embroidered on the right.

Robin looked from Arnie to me.

"Robin, Mr. Petrosian is also the coroner," I explained. "He was here the other night."

There was an interesting moment while Robin absorbed this startling fact.

"Please call me Arnie," Petrosian said. He stepped forward with a smile and a handshake for both of us. "Being the coroner is only a part-time job. Installing security systems is what I do for a living."

"I guess it ties in together," I said.

Robin said, "Arnie, tell me what you think we need. Under the circumstances, I know we don't have to explain why we want the system."

"First I'm going to have a look at your house, your grounds, your windows and doors, and then we'll sit down to talk about what you really need," Arnie said briskly. "Anybody else in the house? I don't want to walk in and scare someone."

"The baby," I said. "She's asleep in her room, the last one on the right down the hall."

"I won't wake your little girl, I promise," Arnie said, with a gleaming white smile as he began making a circuit of the doors and windows. We seemed to have an abundance of both; I'd never remarked on that before.

Robin and I sat side by side on the couch, glancing at each other from time to time. Though I was holding my book and he was fiddling with his phone, we were both more interested in what the coroner/security expert was doing. I don't know what Robin was thinking about, but I was hoping that I felt safer after Arnie had done his magic. I was also hoping that Robin wouldn't waste any more time feeling guilty. That was nonsensical.

Arnie carried a clipboard with a form on it, and from time to time he made notations. He also tested the lock on one of the windows, and I was dismayed to see that the actual lock mechanism was loose. I could only be surprised intruders hadn't been strolling in and out.

Arnie hummed while he worked, a tune I couldn't identify. It wasn't irritating; in fact, it was pleasant.

He made a circuit, ending up in the living room again. He walked into the kitchen and went to the door. "The garage door, right?" he said, as he opened it. I dug my elbow into Robin's ribs. Robin glared at me. I mouthed, *How did he know that?*

Startled, Robin looked at Arnie, who'd opened the door to step into the garage.

It could be he's a master of floor plans, I thought. Or it could be that somehow he'd noticed that detail when he'd been here after Tracy was murdered. But I couldn't recall that door being called to his attention in any way. Wait, he'd said something about knowing the previous owners.

After a few minutes, Arnie was seated opposite us, ready to get down to business. I had made the ritual offer of a glass of water, or a cup of coffee, and just as politely he had turned those down. Arnie began explaining all the security options—motion-sensor cameras outside, alarms on the windows and on the doors—and if we wanted, we could opt to look on our computers to see who was at the door. Robin brightened, since any new gadget was shiny to him, but I gave him a dampening look. Did we really need that?

I wanted the entire yard, front and back, lit up, after my experience of the week before. But lights that would stay on all night were out of the question, since they'd be a pain for our neighbors and for ourselves. Instead, we got motion-sensor lights.

"Could our cat set them off?" I asked. Sometimes, when I was up with Sophie, I heard the sound of the cat passing through its little door at very odd hours. Arnie assured me he could set the sensitivity of the lights to go off only if the moving object was larger than Moosie.

"How long have you had a security company?" Robin asked. I recognized an indirect approach when I heard one.

"Must be ten years now." Arnie's head was bent over the form while he figured out our cost, and I saw that his intensely black hair was threaded with some silver.

"Did you know the previous owners of this house? Laurie and David Martinez?"

Arnie looked up, his pen poised above the form. "He worked at Pan-Am Agra. Laurie was a nurse at Dr. Graham's office." He looked down again. "When my wife got sick, Dr. Graham was her doctor. We saw Laurie all the time. After Halina passed, we got to be friends."

Did Arnie mean he and David and Laurie were friends? Or was his friendship strictly confined to Laurie? At least such a friendship explained why Arnie knew the layout of the house so well.

After some more discussion about our options, Robin signed a contract with our coroner/Spartan Shield Security expert. We were excited about the transformation of our home into an impregnable fortress.

"I'll be over tomorrow with my assistant, and we'll get you all fixed up," Arnie said, standing. "I think I have all the components I'll need, but I'll check as soon as I get home."

When Phillip breezed in, I told him about the Spartan Shield security system. "They'll be here tomorrow afternoon," I said. "With all their stuff."

"That's great! I want to watch them install the sensors." Phillip tossed his head to throw back his hair. (It looked uneven and messy to me, but Phillip could wear his hair like he wanted. I pick my battles.)

"They're supposed to get here at two thirty, but I'm sure you'll be home in time to watch at least part of the work. Oh, by the way . . ." I warned Phillip that our security expert was none other than the coroner.

He was indignant. "How can he have two jobs?"

"The coroner is elected, and the job doesn't pay enough for anyone to live on," I said. "Most coroners have another full-time job. Like funeral director. But the job can be anything, like a salesperson at Lowe's or a beauty parlor operator."

"That's just not right," Phillip said.

"I agree, but that's the way it works in Georgia. And a lot of states."

Phillip shook his head. "People," he said, disillusioned.

At least he hadn't said, "Grown-ups."

When my brother had gone to his room, presumably starting

his homework, I admitted to myself that this was only one of many things about the adult world that Phillip would think were "not right."

The next day, I took advantage of Sophie's naptime to visit John at home. His doctor had let him go the day before, in the afternoon. On the way, I stopped off at Mother's favorite deli/bakery and bought assorted salads, some containers of soup, and some rye bread, John's favorite.

Mother was pleased. Though she scolded me, I could tell she was relieved to have some ready-to-eat food in the refrigerator. I hugged her because she looked depressed and ill, as if she was the one who'd been stricken. Mother held me for a moment without speaking, and I knew she was struggling not to cry.

I can't tell you how unusual that was.

"John's in the den," she said, and stepped back, her weak moment over. I followed her into the den to find John lying on the couch, staring at the ceiling: the television wasn't on, and he didn't have a book nearby. This was as unusual for John as depression and emotional displays were for my mother.

This was not the joyful celebration of homecoming that I had expected. I perched on the ottoman, midway between them.

Mother resumed her seat in her favorite armchair and picked up some needlework. Mother hadn't done needlework since—well, since forever. Though I was looking at it upside down, the piece appeared to be an alphabet sampler. Obviously, she was employing it as an excuse to sit and watch John.

I could understand why.

John looked bad. His complexion was pasty, his face slack, and he was not lying there like someone who was going to jump up eventually. He seemed to be on the couch to stay.

"Hi, Stepdad," I said, doing my best to sound cheerful. "I know you're glad to be out of that hospital."

"I have to go back to the doctor tomorrow," he said listlessly.

To mask my anxiety, I rattled on about the baby and her magnificence and quitting my job and getting the security system. Anything to fill in the awful silence. Mother gave up any pretense of working on the square, and dropped it in her lap. She tried to respond, but couldn't muster much energy. Since she thought Sophie was the world's most important citizen, this was really a bad sign.

I had a brainstorm. I knew what would really interest John! I gave my mother a narrow-eyed look to indicate I was about to do something she wasn't going to like.

"John, you were at your family reunion when Phillip and I found the body in our backyard," I said.

"What?" John looked startled, and I realized he didn't know anything about events on McBride Street. "Whose body?"

I told John the entire story of the night Tracy had been killed: the inexplicable absence of Virginia Mitchell, my illness, Phillip's steadfast help, the horror of the body, the threatening storm. The shooting, and my subsequent discovery of Virginia's cell phone.

John *did* look much better when I'd finished, and it wasn't my imagination. He was engaged and his mind was working. "So I was lying there in the hospital while people were getting shot outside," he said. "I'm having a hard time believing that happened here in Lawrenceton. What's happened to the boy? Duncan?"

"I don't know. I assume he's in the hospital—probably not ours—under police guard. Susan got him in the abdomen."

"Hmmm. Have the police told you anything about Virginia's phone records?"

"No, and I don't think they're likely to." I'd tried to come up with some reason I simply had to know who Virginia had been talking to, but there was no argument that would persuade Levon I had any right to have that information. I did tell John my theory of how the phone had come to be in my purse. "What do you think?" I asked.

John said, "Aida, can you put another pillow under my head? I'm having a hard time seeing Roe."

Mother shot from her chair and got a larger pillow. John eased himself up while she positioned the pillow so he could look at me directly. Mother sat down again, hiding a smile.

"Either she wanted it to be found, or she put it in your purse by accident," John said. "Of course, the man who took your diaper bag thought it was your purse, and he was sure the phone was in it, not yet discovered. So his name is in that telephone."

"I never put that all together," I said. "Motherhood's made me stupid. I'll bet you're right."

"After all, how many purse thefts do we have in Lawrenceton in a year?" John continued.

"Not many," my mother said. "I'd know."

Mother has close ties to the Chamber of Commerce, and she'd be among the first to hear about any negative statistics.

We discussed the crimes—the murder, the disappearance, the shootings—for another thirty minutes. Then John said, "Looks like I'd better come to your house to see the scene."

"Whenever you feel you're up to it." I glanced at Mother, who was giving me a very significant look. "If the doctor says it's okay," I added hastily. "By the way, I brought you something to read." I reached into the reusable grocery bag to retrieve *New Developments, Old Crimes: How Today's Forensics Can Shed Light on Murders of the Past*.

"Haven't read that one," John said, sounding *very* pleased.

I knew he hadn't been reading much of the literature that interested us both, since my mother took a very dim view of our mutual interest in crimes of the past. And since Sophie's birth, I'd stuck to conventional mysteries. But I'd figured John needed a solid distraction. I was delighted at his pleasure.

My job here is done, I thought, and I rose to say good-bye. I'd had the vague conviction that if John didn't react to my stories, I would have been sure he wasn't going to recover.

Robin was glad I'd returned, because he was trying to keep a plot twist for the new book fixed in his head. The second I took Sophie from her bouncer seat, he made a beeline for his office.

For about half a minute, I wondered why I'd been so determined to stay home with Sophie. I had a moment of wishing I had *hours* free from the necessity of being tethered to my baby's needs. But I reminded myself that (a) this was only one phase of Sophie's life, that (b) we would all feel better when our sleep was regular (I'd gotten up with her twice the night before, though that was getting increasingly rare), and that (c) someday Sophie would accept another food source.

I bundled her into the stroller and set out for a walk. It was a mild day, sunny and clear, but there was a tang in the air that warned me we'd all have to bundle up soon. The nights were already cooler. I felt dismayed at the prospect of maneuvering Sophie into still more layers of clothing—but that was in the future, and I was going to enjoy our excursion.

I talked to Peggy Herman (and Chaka, who sniffed Sophie again, with interest). From his yard, Jonathan called hello. Lulu was with him. She barked at me so vigorously I thought she might have a fit.

Sophie seemed to enjoy the change of scenery. When we got home, she fell fast asleep. Robin didn't emerge from his office for lunch, which sometimes happened. So I ate all by myself, with a book propped up in front of me, and I enjoyed every minute of it.

Chapter Nineteen

Robin was fast enough to abandon his work when the Spartan Shield team—consisting of Arnie Petrosian and an assistant—arrived with several boxes and bags and tools. Robin was ready for some stimulation outside of his own head.

I had very little interest in the physical process of making our house secure. As long as the result worked, that was good enough for me. I played with Sophie when she got up, fed her out on the patio discreetly draped, and went in to greet Phillip when he came home from school. He brought Sarah, Joss, and Josh with him.

After they'd all said hello and admired Sophie, Phillip ushered them outside to see the site of the murder. This was not my favorite choice for an activity, but I knew it was only natural, so I didn't comment. They were back within ten minutes—because after all, what was there to see but a yard? No clues, no bloodstains, no corpse, only a (possibly deaf) cat up in the mimosa tree.

Phillip poured drinks and actually prepared a snack for his

guests. I tried to (very casually) glance sideways as he put items on a tray on the island, but I was very interested to see what he'd served.

I identified Triscuits, Ritz crackers, and a block of sharp cheddar on a cutting board with a couple of knives. He added the bowl of grapes I'd washed earlier. As a final flourish he put a stack of napkins beside the bowl. Not bad.

I sat on the floor with the baby, singing "The Itsy Bitsy Spider" and other babyhood hits. No singer me, but Sophie had never seemed to care, and I kept my voice very low. I didn't want to embarrass my brother.

The kids observed the security-installation team with great interest. Josh and Joss remembered that Spartan Shield had installed their own security measures, and they said hello and had a bit of conversation with Arnie.

Neither twin seemed to know the assistant, who wore an ill-fitting khaki shirt matching his boss's.

"You didn't come to our house when we got our system," Joss said, when the assistant was within talking distance. "You new with the company?"

He gave her a fleeting smile before he turned away. Over his shoulder, he said, "No, just back at work."

Phillip and his friends lost interest when it became clear the installation would take more than an hour or two. They all decided to go to Sarah's house to play Ping-Pong. When Phillip was on his way out, he said, "Not a school night, Roe."

"Got you. Eleven thirty, please." I stood in loco parentis to my brother, and sometimes that was an uneasy position.

It's probably good training for when Sophie is a teen, I thought, though I could not imagine such a thing just now.

The next time the assistant walked through the living room,

I said, “Are you all through in the baby’s room? I’d like to put her down for a nap.”

“I’ll ask,” he said, in a friendly way. He went out to the truck to retrieve something. When he came back in, I could hear him asking Arnie my question.

Arnie popped out from Sophie’s bedroom to tell me he was through with her windows. I was glad to stow my sleeping daughter. I wandered back to the living room aimlessly. It was hard to settle down to anything while the two men were in the house. Even Robin had gotten bored and returned to his office.

I sifted through the mail that had accumulated over the past week, and pitched most of it. I took care of a couple of bills.

I checked my calendar (I entered appointments on my phone, but Robin and I kept an actual physical calendar on the wall). I was glad I had when I saw that the Women of the Church were meeting in two days to plan the annual holiday bake and handcraft sale. This was our big charity fund-raiser, and it was an all-hands-on-deck event.

I decided to take Sophie to the meeting in her carrier. Robin had missed enough work. I was looking forward to getting out of the house again, seeing fresh faces. I felt my smile fade when I had a very unpleasant thought. What if people were creepy to me? Surely, at a church gathering, people would be reminded of their Christian duty to love their neighbors? No matter how unsettling that neighbor’s circumstances?

By golly, I was for sure going, now.

I immediately began to second-guess myself. But my mother would have gone, if this had all happened to her. And maybe, if John was a lot better, Mother even might come tomorrow. My mother would singe the ladies’ eyebrows with one glance, if they didn’t make me feel welcome. I smiled, just thinking about it.

Not that I needed, at my age, to hide behind my mother.

At that moment I heard Lulu start yapping hysterically, followed by a deep "Woof!" Someone in the Hermans' yard was shouting. I was out the patio door before I was conscious of moving.

Chaka had jumped the fence and was in our backyard. He was at the foot of the mimosa tree looking up with fierce intensity. Lulu, deciding Chaka should not be *even closer* to Lulu's sacred territory, was giving it all she had by way of negative reinforcement.

I was surprised—shocked—to see Chaka in our yard. With some vague idea of rescuing Moosie, I started across the yard. I wasn't running, but I was certainly walking very briskly.

"Roe!" Peggy called. "Slow down! Be calm!" I resented this until I understood she was warning me Chaka might become more agitated. I froze. I admit, I was scared. The dog had never been anything but quiet, well-behaved, and friendly.

I heard our patio door opening behind me. Robin appeared at my side. (I assumed he had walked slowly, because I wasn't going to look away from the large dog to verify that.)

"Hey, boy," Robin said, in an easy voice. "What you got up in the tree?" Chaka turned his head to look at Robin. He wasn't growling (Chaka, not Robin), and I thought that was a good sign.

"Moosie," I said, very quietly.

"I'm coming around to your yard," Peggy said, and I wondered why she didn't jump the fence like Chaka must have done. From our bedroom window, I'd watched Peggy vault over once when Chaka's ball had landed in our yard. She'd retrieved it handily.

Robin strolled up to Chaka, still talking in that relaxed voice about what a good dog Chaka was. Though I was skeptical at the moment, I realized it was true that Chaka, though focused on Moosie, didn't seem especially hostile. He gave Robin a glance when Robin reached his side, as if to say, "You see what the problem is?"

Robin looked up in the mimosa tree, which had begun to shed its beautiful ferny leaves. "I see her," he told Chaka. "But I don't think she can hear you, big guy."

Peggy must have made record time running out her front door and to the far side of our house to enter through the gate. In a firm voice, she said, "Chaka. Stand down."

Chaka glanced at Peggy and whined.

Peggy repeated her command, this time sternly.

Chaka sat.

Peggy took a deep breath before she said, "Chaka, come."

Slowly, his head down, Chaka went to Peggy and sat before her, exactly like a child who's been caught raiding the cookie jar.

Oh, thank God, I thought. I don't know what I had feared would happen, exactly; but I was glad it hadn't.

"Chaka, heel." Peggy walked to our gate. The dog followed her without hesitation.

Robin and I looked at each other with vast relief. At least one crisis had been quickly resolved.

Now that Chaka had left the yard, Robin began talking to Moosie, who was peering down at us, obviously anxious. I didn't think Moosie could hear Robin talking, but she could see that Robin was extending a friendly hand to her. She began creeping down the branches, darting looks over to the Herman yard. Since Lulu had not stopped barking and was running up and down the fence, for a second I envied Moosie, who couldn't hear the noise.

At long last, I heard one of the Cohens emerge. Deborah spoke sharply to Lulu, whose agitation about Chaka had gradually abated. Now that the terrible menace in our backyard had vanished, Lulu consented to go inside, having successfully defended her territory.

No voices, no barking, no agitation. The quiet was a relief. Moosie continued down the tree, until she was close enough for Robin to touch her. He scratched her head. The cat began to purr, and she didn't stop even when Robin lifted her off the branch and held her to his chest. He began carrying the little cat to our patio door. I was about to follow him when Peggy appeared in her own yard. She waved me over. Reluctantly, I joined her at the fence.

I didn't know what to say, so I didn't say anything. Peggy looked . . . I couldn't decide. Protective? Abashed? She opened by saying the right thing. "I'm so glad Moosie wasn't hurt."

I nodded.

"Ridgebacks are very protective."

"Moosie is a threat?" I sounded skeptical, which I was.

"In Chaka's mind. He doesn't have any issue with your cat until Moosie gets close to our fence."

I thought of several things to say, and I picked carefully. "The fence is ours, too," I said. "I understand that Chaka doesn't know that. But we can't risk Moosie being killed when she goes outside."

"Absolutely," Peggy said, nodding with vigor. "We've been working on Chaka's training ever since we got him."

"He's always been a very good dog." I had to give her that. She looked grateful.

Lena had joined Peggy. She looked miserable. Until now, I had never understood how much the dog meant to them, though

I should have. After all, the Cohens had bought Lulu a little British coat last Christmas. And they made her wear it when they walked her in bad weather. Though the Hermans didn't express their affection in such an elaborate way, they adored Chaka just as much.

"We'll keep up working with him," Lena assured me. The edge of desperation in her voice made me very uncomfortable. They were both looking at me as though they feared I'd call Animal Control any minute.

After all, what had Chaka actually done? He hadn't barked (aside from that one deep woof), and he hadn't lunged up the tree, and he hadn't growled at Moosie . . . or at me. I began to relax. But there was a point to be made.

"What I'm worried about is when Sophie is bigger, and walking, and she wants to go in the backyard to play," I said. "How will the dog see Sophie? As another threat? You understand, we can't have that." That was plain as plain can be.

"That gives us a long time to keep working with him," Lena said, her shoulders losing their tension. "In his year with us, this is the only time he's done something like this."

Peggy met my eyes, relief all over her face. "Thanks, Roe."

I nodded. As I turned to go inside, I wondered if I'd made the right decision. Chaka may have literally crossed the line only once . . . but with Sophie, once would be too much.

I yelled "Robin!" the minute I shut the door behind me.

"I'm in here," he called, in a very hushed tone.

I followed the sound of his voice to his office, wondering what else could possibly be wrong. At first glance, everything looked fine. Moosie was curled up on Robin's armchair. Robin was behind his desk, holding the baby monitor, which was blessedly silent. I said, "What happened?"

"When I came in, I went to the kitchen for a drink, and the helper guy was in there. I could swear he was up to something."

I had to sit down, and luckily there was another armchair available. "Like what?" I said.

"He was over in the corner of the counter, where you drop your purse. I think he was looking in the drawers over there."

I was bewildered. "What can we do? Tell Arnie? Confront the guy? Call the police?"

Robin shook his head. "I don't know. I hate to call the police. I don't think he actually took anything. It's not against the law to open a drawer."

I nodded. I was doing a lot of that today.

"And if we confront him, what good would that do? He'd just say, 'I did no such thing,' or 'I saw a roach run under her purse and I was trying to kill it for her.' "

"Right again. And . . . ewwww."

"But we can't do *nothing*." Robin looked gloomy.

"So telling Arnie is our best option."

Something finally went right. Just then, Arnie came in the room with his invoice. "Tracked you down," he said cheerfully. "We're nearly done, Mr. Crusoe. One window isn't secure yet, because I don't have all the parts I need. I'll have to come back tomorrow morning, but it should only take me about five minutes."

"Great," Robin said. "Then you'll have the system working. We have to talk to you about something."

"Okay," Arnie said slowly. "What's on your mind?"

I don't know how I expected Arnie to react to what Robin told him. Whatever I might have predicted, Arnie surprised me.

The coroner/security expert stood with his head bowed for a long moment. Then he took a deep breath and looked Robin square in the eye. "The guy's been my employee for a long time," he said. "He's been in some trouble before, and I should have fired him then. But he's a great worker, and I like him a lot. I'll have to let him go, now. I'm sorry this caused you concern."

Arnie had made a bad choice, but it seemed clear he was trying to rectify it. My eyes met Robin's, and I gave a tiny shrug.

"Okay, Arnie," Robin said. "I want the guy to leave now. It scares me that he was even inside. Please be sure he doesn't have any access to the house."

"Oh, absolutely not," Arnie said hastily. "He won't know what code you're using for your system, and it'll be up and running early tomorrow morning. I'll get him to sit out in the truck while we settle up." He laid the invoice down in front of Robin, and left the room hurriedly, his head bent as though he were thinking furiously.

"Somehow I don't feel much better," I said.

"What? He gave us an explanation, and offered to correct the situation."

"His words were convincing, but his tone wasn't."

"We can't give him the third degree over his tone." Robin wasn't being a smart-ass, he was being practical.

"When Sophie gets up, let's put her in the car seat and take a ride. I'd like us to be out of the house and doing something fun."

"Okay by me," Robin said. "I don't know how much work I'm going to get done anyway."

We talked about his book for a little while, and he told me what the holdup was in his thought process. I had already learned Robin didn't want me to offer a solution. He just wanted me to listen. I could certainly do that. I was always interested in how his mind worked.

In a few minutes, I heard Sophie howl. She'd had the worst bowel movement in the history of baby bowel movements. It was amazing how something so disgusting could come out of someone so cute. I must say, it seemed to have made her happy. She was making cheerful little noises and pumping her legs while I changed her, which added considerably to the mess. Finally, I got her bottom clean, the changing table clean, and then my hands. Robin was ready to put Sophie in her car seat. We stopped by my mother's so she and John could see the baby. I was sure John would get well much more quickly if he could see the magic baby. We only stayed a few minutes, so we wouldn't tire John. But while we were there, he mentioned coming over at least three times.

It was so nice being out together, and the weather was so pretty, we stopped off at the Finstermeyers' house after I noticed that both Beth and George were at home.

"Hey, Roe! Haven't actually laid eyes on you since the baby came," Beth said. George was sitting in the family room with a book in his hands, but he put it down and rose to greet us.

They both said the appropriate things about Sophie, Beth admiring Sophie's red hair, and George saying she was pretty like her mom, which made me laugh.

We accepted their invitation to sit.

"I know Phillip is over here a lot," I said. "I hope he's being a good guest?"

"The best," Beth told me, smiling. "He's a good kid, Roe."

"We like him," George said.

We talked about Josh and Phillip's chances on the track team. We didn't need to worry about Joss—Jocelyn. She was an excellent athlete at every sport she'd tried.

Robin said, "Arnie Petrosian installed our security system today."

"Arnie's a nice guy, isn't he?" George smiled. "When we decided we needed one, we knew he was having trouble making ends meet, because his bills from Halina's illness were just incredible. And then the funeral was expensive, they always are. Our church took up a donation to help him with it."

This was a very different picture of Arnie's finances than we'd gotten from Arnie.

"He said he'd been a friend of the previous owners of our house, the Martinezes?" I said. "Did they go to your church, too?"

"Yes, they did," Beth said. "In fact, Laurie hired Arnie to repaint their bathroom, and David hired him to pressure-wash the brick."

"He knows how to do a lot of handy stuff," I said, trying not to sound envious.

"Hey," said Robin mildly. "I know how to change a lightbulb."

I smiled at him. "You'll do," I said. "Do you two know his assistant? He made us pretty anxious, and we asked Arnie not to let him return to the house."

The Finstermeyers looked at each other, astonished.

Beth said, "I don't remember the guy. I remember Arnie had an assistant, but as far as picturing him . . . I'm really sorry you were worried."

George said, "If we've steered you wrong, we did it in good faith. We've been happy with our system, and Arnie needed the job. . . ."

We let them know we did not blame them, at all, for anything. When we were back in the car, Sophie looking sleepy in her car seat, I looked forward to going into our quiet house and throwing some supper together and then (maybe) reading. Or (maybe) having some adult time with Robin. Or both.

When we were home, and Sophie and all her baby paraphernalia were unloaded, I unlocked the front door and went inside. Robin, carrying the baby, was right behind me.

The minute I stepped inside I knew something was wrong. I came to an abrupt stop. "Back up, Robin," I said. "Get out of the house."

"What?"

"Someone's broken in."

He didn't say "Are you sure?" or push past me to see for himself, and that was another thing I loved about Robin. He returned to the car, got the baby front carrier out and shrugged into it, inserting Sophie in the pouch.

While he did this, I called the police. The first thing the dispatcher said was, "Get out of the house and don't go back in." I assured her we wouldn't.

We waited in the driveway. I was very anxious . . . and very angry. Our lives—and more importantly, our baby's life—had become unpredictable and laced with danger. This had to stop.

I hadn't met the patrolman who answered the call. He was a very handsome young man of Asian heritage. (Of course I only noticed his good looks in passing, since I was a married woman.)

He was quickly joined by Cathy Trumble, in her unmarked car.

I was very surprised to see Cathy back on duty. Surely she ought to be taking a leave of absence or something?

"You're the homeowners?" the patrolman said.

I nodded.

"Is there any other family member inside the house?"

"My brother lives with us, but he's gone."

"Pets?"

"They have a cat," Cathy said shortly. "Let's go in. Roe, you all get behind the car, at least. It would be better if you got farther away." Cathy looked very tense. It was only when they both drew their guns that I realized the gravity of the situation. There really was a chance the intruder was still in the house.

Not more gunfire, I thought. *Please, no.*

Robin and I retreated to the Cohens' front yard. Robin had one arm wrapped about Sophie in the carrier, and the other arm he wrapped around me. "How upset would you be if we moved somewhere else?"

I thought Robin was joking at first.

But he meant it.

Chapter Twenty

I had no ready answer for him, but sooner or later I'd have to respond. Right now I had enough trouble on my plate without making a life-changing decision . . . while the police were actually in our house with guns drawn.

The Herman sisters came out in the front yard, with Chaka on a leash, and the Cohens joined us, minus Lulu . . . though she could be heard making a racket in their house.

Deborah was clearly terrified, but Jonathan was angry. "I don't know what's going on in your house, Robin, but this should not be happening in our neighborhood. Everything was quiet until you moved in."

Robin took a deep breath. He's not a guy who loses his temper easily, but he was right on the brink. "Our house got broken into, Jonathan." (He said the name the same way he'd say "asshole.") "I don't think that we're responsible for that. And this happened in daylight. I don't suppose, with all your watching out windows and telling police you'd seen the wrong person, you happened to actually notice a criminal breaking into our house?"

I looked in the other direction, because I didn't want to see Jonathan's face. Or Deborah's. Unsurprisingly, the Cohens stomped back into their house trailing anger like crepe-paper streamers.

As Lena and Peggy joined us, Lena said, "It's hard to imagine a robbery in broad daylight on a middle-class street like this, right?"

"Yes," I said glumly. "It certainly is." I knew it could not be a mistake that this mysterious incident had happened right after the terrible events of the previous week.

"I'm so sorry," Peggy said. Chaka looked up at her, perhaps hearing the distress in her voice.

"Peggy, we weren't there and we're unhurt," Robin said. "We're okay."

It was far from okay, but we had not been attacked or injured, and that was enough. Just then Josh brought Phillip home. I could see them both gaping at the open door of the house, the two cars parked askew in front, and our little cluster in the Cohens' yard.

Phillip jumped out and hurried over to us while Josh waited in the car, peering out anxiously.

"What's up?" Phillip said. His eyes went from me to the baby to Robin, assuring himself that we were all well.

"We came home to find the house had been entered," Robin said. "Roe, is there a big mess?" He'd just thought of his office, and all our books, and the computer with his work in progress. Who wouldn't?

"Not too bad," I said, untruthfully.

By the time Cathy and the new patrolman came out of the

house, guns holstered (whew), I felt we'd been standing outside an hour. My phone told me it had been seven minutes.

"It's clear. You want to come have a look-see? Tell us if you notice anything missing," Cathy said. Clearly, Cathy was not going to talk about our shared ordeal in the hospital parking lot. And given the circumstances, I couldn't think of anything tactful to say. Time to keep my mouth shut.

Now that New Guy was closer, I saw that his nameplate read "Dan." I remembered that a Sadie Dan had been valedictorian three years ago at Lawrenceton High. Probably a sister.

Officer Dan began walking around the house, looking for signs of . . . well, I didn't know what he was looking for.

We followed Cathy into the house. As I'd seen when I'd first opened the door, the living room was a wreck. The couch cushions were on the floor, the kitchen drawers were open and their contents strewn around.

But they weren't ripped up. Whatever the searcher had been looking for, it hadn't been something he (or she) suspected would be concealed in some elaborate fashion.

Phillip went directly to his room, and returned within two minutes. "No problem in there," he said, sounding surprised and relieved.

Robin lit out for his office, with Sophie necessarily along for the ride.

He, too, was happy to report that his office had been left pristine.

But our bedroom had been tossed. I groaned. So much to put away! At least the bathroom was still orderly.

We were thunderstruck when we saw Sophie's room. It was a wreck. Robin unstrapped Sophie, handed her to me, and he and Phillip began silently righting the crib, restoring the bedding, picking up the stuffed animals and the diapers and the tiny clothes. Setting the rocking chair back on its base. I'd spent hours arranging that room while I waited for her birth. I started crying, and I wasn't ashamed of it.

Finally, I retreated to the living room to spare myself more misery. I was looking around helplessly, trying to find a place to sit with Sophie. Cathy pulled one of the armchairs upright and replaced the cushions.

"Thank you," I said, absurdly grateful. "Cathy, I don't understand this at all. Nothing's missing! At least, nothing that wasn't already missing, Robin's keys and his old sweater. And the only rooms wrecked were this one, our bedroom, and Sophie's room. Why?"

"Can you think of anything that would, I don't know, group those rooms together?" Cathy righted a chair for herself.

I thought and thought, and then it came to me; it should have been obvious immediately. "Those are the rooms Virginia was in," I said. "She didn't need to go in Robin's office or Phillip's room. By the way, did you get any useful information off her phone?" I just threw that in there to see if I could learn something.

Cathy said, "That's police business, not yours. You've got enough trouble of your own without taking on more."

That was for sure.

"Can you tell me who has a key to your house?" Cathy said this in a matter-of-fact way, but as she waited for my answer she was very serious.

"Me and Robin, Phillip of course, and my mom has a key in case of emergency," I said. "That's all."

"No maids?"

"We're always here to let them in."

"Did you have the locks changed when you moved in?"

"No." I started to add, "Why would I?" But the words never left my mouth. Arnie Petrosian might have a key, from his "friendship" with Laurie Martinez. I was racked with indecision. Would it be wrong to mention this to the police?

Officer Dan strolled in, and stood beside Cathy's chair. The next question he asked solved my dilemma.

"I see you have a brand-new security system," he said.

"How'd you know it was brand-new?"

"The manual is still stuck behind the keypad."

"Oh. Yeah, Arnie Petrosian and his assistant were here this afternoon installing it. He said he knew the Martinezes pretty well." I put a little emphasis on the last two words, hoping they'd get my drift.

"He did?" Cathy looked thoughtful.

"It was his assistant who bothered us," I said.

"How so?" Cathy was tapping on her phone.

"Robin was pretty sure he'd been going through my purse, or the kitchen drawers, while he was alone in the kitchen area."

"What was his name?" Dan was eager.

"Arnie never introduced him."

Cathy looked as if she didn't think much of my brains. "And Robin didn't call us," she said.

"He wasn't a hundred percent sure. So we talked to Arnie about him, and Arnie acted kind of weird, but he said he'd fire him. Arnie would fire the assistant," I said, to clarify.

"So tell me," Dan said. "Since you just got this system installed, why didn't you set it when you left the house this afternoon?"

"He didn't have one part or something, so it's not active yet. He said he was coming back tomorrow morning first thing."

Cathy and Dan (what was his first name?) both gave me the same look; as if I were the dumbest creature on God's green earth. I didn't think I deserved that much scorn. I'd trusted an elected official of the county, and after all, getting a home security system was a good thing.

When Cathy and Dan went to the door, I followed them. Standing in the open doorway, Cathy reminded me someone would be by to dust for prints in about half an hour. "And for God's sake, when Arnie comes back to finish, pick a code and arm the system," she added.

"We will." As they walked to their cars, I stepped outside with them. Despite all my troubles, it was a beautiful day.

A car pulled in to the curb, and my friend Angel got out. She had Lorna with her, and she extricated her toddler from the huge car seat and expertly balanced the child on one hip. Since Lorna was three years old, that was quite a load, but Angel could handle it easily.

"Woe!" Lorna said, as she and Angel neared us. (That was as close as Lorna could get to "Roe," and it had stuck.) Truly her mother's daughter, Lorna exhibited no excitement (or enthusiasm) when she recognized me.

"Yeah?" Angel said, looking at the patrol car and the unmarked car.

Cathy and Officer Dan stood still in our driveway. It was like the two officers had spotted a dangerous animal. They both looked cautious and wary.

"Break-in," I said, inaccurately.

Cathy corrected me instantly. "Not a break-in. Some unauthorized person came in with a key."

"Angel Youngblood, this is Detective Cathy Trumble, and Officer Dan."

"Cleve Dan," he said, and I felt relieved. At last, I knew his name.

"I know Ms. Youngblood," Cathy said. She didn't sound happy about it. "We met when someone tried to snatch her purse from her car while she was getting gas."

"I stopped him," Angel told me. Not that I had ever doubted it.

"She gave him a trip to the emergency room," Cathy said.

Angel tilted her head toward Lorna. "My daughter was in the car."

"I understand," I said, with enough energy to startle the officers. I had gotten in touch with my inner savage now. I was completely on Angel's page.

"Ms. Teagarden here didn't report a man her husband found going through things in their kitchen," Cleve Dan said, inviting Angel to join him in the club of people who found that ridiculous.

"She can report or not, as she wants." Angel's look would have squashed a bug. "You got a security system?" she asked me, inclining her head to the Spartan Shield sign Arnie had planted in our front flowerbed.

"It seemed like a good thing to do. But it won't be ready to arm until tomorrow."

"It's pretty interesting that someone came in the day before the system was going to go active." She made sure the two police officers heard her.

Lorna had been quiet all this time, but now she said, "Down, Mama."

"Sugar, we're just stopping off to check on our friend," Angel said. "We've got to fix supper for your dad." Angel looked from Lorna to me. "We were just on our way home with our groceries when we saw the police cars."

"Edamame?" Lorna said hopefully, and I hoped my jaw didn't drop too far. Cathy and Cleve Dan looked startled.

"Sure, honey, we'll have edamame. And some fruit. And maybe some tofu. Or pineapple, you want that?"

"Wonton noodles?" Lorna had trouble with the "noodles" but it came out recognizable.

"Sounds good." Angel smiled down at Lorna, and her face transformed. As she turned to leave, she slipped me a wink, and I grinned back at her.

Cleve Dan watched Angel until she buckled Lorna into her car seat and left.

He'd obviously never met Shelby, her husband. Not that Angel needed anyone to run interference for her. She and Shelby had done bodyguard work before coming to Lawrenceton.

When she'd gone and I had the full attention of Cathy and Cleve Dan, I told them something I'd just remembered. Overshadowed by the discovery of the telephone in my purse was the fact that we'd found it because we'd been searching for Robin's keys. "I mentioned them before, when you were asking about missing things, but the keys have only been missing since Robin went to Bouchercon. He's sure he left them here."

"And you just now remembered that?"

I had had it with the sarcastic cops. "Yes, I just now did," I snapped, and stomped into the house.

There was nothing more I wanted than to share a good gripe with Robin, but it was not to be. Sophie began crying the minute we stepped inside. I had to wait until later that night, after supper and Sophie's bath, before Robin and I got to talk. Phillip had gone to Sarah's house after taking his turn with the dishes, but not without ostentatiously checking the calendar to make sure it was his day. (After he'd questioned me three times in a row in previous weeks, I'd marked the calendar so there couldn't be any dispute.)

I told him about my conversation with Amina, which seemed a month ago instead of the day before. I had left a voice mail on Levon's work phone, since he'd wanted to know who had recommended Virginia to my mother. I hadn't heard back, but I hadn't expected to. That was a dead end.

Robin decided to take my keys to get another set made, first thing in the morning. "I called about getting the locks changed, but the locksmith can't come for two weeks. I'll need keys in the meantime. I'm giving up on my original set," he said. "Maybe a year from now we'll find it in the lint trap of the dryer."

"Or the bottom of the fruit basket." I got up to check the basket while I was thinking of it. Of course, the keys weren't there.

We picked out a code for the security system, which turned out to be a longer discussion than I'd imagined. The number had to be one we'd both remember, and it couldn't be super obvious, like Sophie's birthday. But we finally came to an agreement.

"Tomorrow night, the Shield will protect us," I said, quoting the brochure Arnie had left. "Will you feel safer?"

"To an extent. But we're changing the locks, too. I'm taking care of my family in any way I can."

I gave Robin a fervent hug. He returned it with the same feeling.

We speculated for about five minutes on who might have broken in (excuse me, unlocked and strolled into) our house, and why. But then we abandoned that fruitless discussion to do something much more agreeable.

I think anyone would admit that we had had a trying day. But at the end of it, I felt content and safe with Robin.

Chapter Twenty-one

After Phillip had left the next morning to go work out with Josh, we had a visitor. Another visitor. Arnie Petrosian had shown up at 8:30, before I was even dressed, to put the final touch on our security system.

I heard Robin tell him, "We had an intruder yesterday."

There was a brief silence. "No!" Arnie said. "Was anything taken?"

"Not that we've been able to find. But the police think he had a key."

"You're going to have your locks changed, as soon as possible, right? I know a good locksmith."

"Thanks, but I've already put in a few calls." Their voices faded as they entered Phillip's room, the one needing the component Arnie hadn't had yesterday. Arnie was as good as his word. He was through in five minutes, and I heard the two men talking as Robin walked Arnie out.

I got dressed and brushed my hair and teeth as quickly as I

could, because I just knew we were going to have more callers. Our house was as busy as an airport these days.

Aubrey Scott, our priest, arrived at nine o'clock. He'd called earlier "to make sure you're at home," which gave us a much-needed heads-up. We'd put everything back together the evening before with Phillip's help—and Sarah's—but there were still odds and ends to replace. I worked on that while Robin abandoned his computer to tidy the kitchen.

Aubrey was our friend, our priest, and a great guy. He (probably) wouldn't have cared at all if I'd come to the door in my bathrobe and the breakfast dishes had been strewn on the counter.

But I cared. Robin did, too.

As we swapped greetings, I really looked at Aubrey for the first time in a while. He was more serious than he had been before the awful events of the year before, and there was something luminous in his face that hinted Aubrey had undergone a spiritual earthquake. I thought he might bless us, which would be very non-Episcopalian first thing in the morning, but he just said, "Hi."

After the mandatory offering of a drink, we invited Aubrey to have a seat. Our priest was always busy, so I knew he hadn't come to engage in idle chitchat.

"You don't know how much I appreciate Emily's help when I was so sick," I said. (I didn't add how surprised I'd been that she'd given it.)

"You won Emily's heart by coming to our daughter's rescue when she was abducted," Aubrey said simply. "Emily and I have both gone through some changes, as a result of that ordeal."

I felt very awkward. There's a reason Episcopalians are called the "Frozen Chosen." To gain a little time, I took my glasses off (the blue ones) and polished them with the hem of my

T-shirt. "I'm glad all the kids are okay," I said. They might have buried emotional problems from the ordeal, but they'd all recovered physically. "I hope Liza is happy? Emily said she's much better placed, now." If I remembered correctly. I'd been in and out of that conversation.

"She is. The new school and a new group of friends have been the best thing in the world for her. I don't know if the private school exactly prepares Liza for the real world . . . but I know she met the real world last year, and she doesn't need another dose this soon."

"Of course," I said. I wondered why Aubrey was here. He could simply be showing that he recognized we'd had a crisis. That would be welcome. But I felt he was working his way toward something. I could not have been more surprised when he came out with it.

"Do you have any idea when the funeral will be?" Aubrey looked at us with gentle inquiry on his face.

"Funeral?" I drew a blank.

"For Tracy Beal. The woman who was killed in your yard," Aubrey added, in case we might have forgotten.

I didn't dare look at Robin.

"We would be the last to know," Robin said slowly, not bothering to conceal his astonishment. "Tracy Beal was a stalker. She was going to be tried for making a serious attempt to kill Roe. She came in our house uninvited, in the night. Into the room of our daughter."

Aubrey was clearly troubled. "I understand your . . . dislike of this woman," he said. "But try to find it in your hearts to forgive her. Or at least, to have compassion for her mental illness. I realize wanting to feel those things doesn't guarantee it'll happen overnight, but it's a goal to work towards."

I glanced up at Robin. We both nodded cautiously. We weren't buying into this, but we could let Aubrey know we'd registered his advice.

I was sure he was about to leave, but Aubrey had more surprises to pull out of his ministerial hat. "Roe, I wonder if you'd go with me to see the mother of Virginia Mitchell."

"Why?" I couldn't think of a single reason this would appeal to me.

"She's frightened for her daughter's safety."

"You know this how?"

"I called Mrs. Mitchell to tell her we were praying for the safe return of her daughter."

Robin's eyes met mine and he shrugged, leaving it up to me. He didn't look happy, though.

"How far away does she live?" I said, playing for time.

"About a twenty- or thirty-minute drive away, if it's not rush hour," Aubrey said.

I hesitated, dreading the additional wear and tear on my emotions such a visit was sure to cause. But this was my priest asking. I hadn't thought of what Virginia's mother must be enduring, and I felt bad about that. But it was more a dull, dutiful guilt than a sharply felt pang.

"All right, Aubrey," I said, with no enthusiasm whatsoever. "We'll have to coordinate it with Sophie. If we leave right after I feed her, we'll need to be back in two hours."

Aubrey looked pleased. Not at all to my surprise, he said he was ready to go anytime I was. "This morning would be okay," I said. "I think she'll be up in half an hour, at the most." *The sooner to get it over with,* I thought.

Sophie woke up grouchy. I could tell from Robin's face he'd been hoping to get a little work in today, since he'd missed so many hours this past week. I suggested, hesitantly, that I might take her with me.

Aubrey didn't look unwilling, though he also didn't look enthusiastic, but Robin balked. "Roe, you won't want a crying baby on deck for a conversation that's sure to be uncomfortable," he pointed out.

So after I'd given Sophie my all (in the way of milk, at least), Aubrey and I drove away. I was preoccupied. Sophie was still acting mad at the world. I was brooding about her unprecedented mood, and about dumping her on Robin. Could she have had gas? Maybe she'd started cutting a tooth (though surely it was too early for that)? Oh, gosh, maybe she'd caught the flu. But she hadn't felt hot.

There were too many possibilities to count.

I kept telling myself that Robin had promised he'd call if she didn't calm down. Up until this morning, she'd been a reasonable baby. Now I knew how lucky we'd been.

I made myself have a conversation with Aubrey as he maneuvered through the traffic. We talked about John, and how soon he might be able to come back to church. We talked about the very strong-willed lady who was the head of the Christmas bake and craft sale, and wondered who'd cry this year when she bore down.

Aubrey had heard that John David was dating Lizanne, and he wished them well. Maybe the same elements that had made John David's marriage to the volatile (now deceased) Poppy so unstable would make a solid relationship with the immensely calm Lizanne Sewell?

Aubrey never said anything bad about anyone, but he was realistic about human nature.

"How does being a mother compare to what you thought it

would be?" Aubrey asked. We were at a stoplight. The kids in the next car were staring at Aubrey's collar, and seemed to be having a heated argument about what my presence in his car might mean.

"I don't know that I ever tried to imagine it," I said slowly. "I was so sure I couldn't be a mother, I didn't think about it. I can tell you that my whole view of the world changed."

"How so?"

"There are things that will be good for your baby, and things that will not be good. Just two categories. There are people who mean no harm to your baby, and people who might hurt her. Just two kinds. Then there's the moral things you have to teach, and that's a lot harder. I'm working on a policy. I bet Robin is, too."

"I don't understand?"

"Well . . . do you teach her to defend herself, or do you teach her that striking other people is wrong? Do you teach her to keep her thoughts to herself, or do you teach her to speak up for her beliefs, and maybe get hurt in consequence? If Sophie is gay, do we teach her to be open about it? Or do we warn her that some people will want to beat her or kill her for being who she is?"

Aubrey looked a little taken aback. "I haven't ever thought about the world in those either/or terms."

"Though I'm simplifying, those are the choices. You can raise your child to be strong and outspoken . . . which is brave and honest. But the consequences of being brave and honest can be dire."

Aubrey smiled in a wry way. "Or you can teach your daughter to keep her own counsel and lay low. She'll live a life that may be unhappy and untrue. But probably she'll be safe."

"Exactly. So that's the kind of thing I worry about now. Before I held Sophie for the first time, I'd never thought about any of that."

"So your biggest surprise is how much thinking you have to do—about the effect of your words on Sophie?"

"No. My biggest surprise is how primal I feel about her. I would die for her. I would kill for her. Without a doubt. Without hesitation."

"Strong statement," Aubrey said, trying to sound less startled than he was.

"You adopted Liza, but it's like she's your own," I said. "Don't you feel that way, too?"

"Well . . . no. I would defend her to the death." Aubrey spoke deliberately and carefully. "Aside from that, I let her know what my faith tells me I should do, what every Christian should do."

"And then you just see what happens?"

He nodded. "Liza has already had a lot to contend with. Emily says she told you about her first husband."

I nodded. "I had no idea. It's great that she survived it, and she's still a good person."

"Emily's a very strong woman. We're not sure how much Liza remembers, but she saw some things she shouldn't have seen. Then there was the problem with Liza's reading disability, which she overcame . . ."

I hadn't known about that.

"And then the bullying at school. I knew, at least theoretically, how cruel children can be, but I have to say at first I found their inhumanity beyond belief."

"Did you want to whop them one?"

"Yes," he said, without hesitation. "Some days. But I couldn't decide if the venom came from their parents or was . . . well, natural to them."

When I'd talked to Liza's bullies and their parents, it had

disturbed me, too. I wondered how a mother could bear to realize that her child was naturally cruel.

I couldn't even imagine.

In contrast to that black pit, visiting Virginia Mitchell's mother didn't seem so bad.

Marcy Mitchell owned a neat, small house on a street filled with similar houses. It was located in one of the older neighborhoods outside Truman, once a little town located in what had been open country between Lawrenceton and Atlanta. "Older" is a relative term in this vast conglomeration of bedroom communities. The house had been built fifteen to twenty years ago.

Maybe Truman had once had a character of its own, but now it was homogenized. We had passed a Chili's and a Napa Valley Auto Parts and a CVS Pharmacy before we turned in to the subdivision. It was full of curb-parked cars, basketball goals, tricycles discarded in the yard, and the other signals indicating Americans were going about their lives in a normal way.

Mrs. Mitchell's house was different. There was one car parked in her driveway. The one-car garage was closed. The curtains were closed, giving the house a blind look.

"She expects us?" I said dubiously. "Maybe she went to work or something."

"She said she was staying home this week, in case news came about Virginia," Aubrey said. "I told her I might drop by."

"Might drop by?" I may have sounded a little sarcastic.

Aubrey looked uncomfortable. "I told her I'd come today, and I might bring you with me."

"Aubrey, what's going on here?"

He looked even more uncomfortable. "We'll see," Aubrey said, and then he crossed the little yard to the front door.

I felt obliged to follow—he was my friend and my priest—but to say I was unhappy would be a huge understatement.

Aubrey rang the doorbell, and in just a few seconds it opened. Through the glass storm door, we looked at a woman I assumed was Marcy Mitchell. She was wearing blue jeans and a flowered blouse. Her hair had been straightened and had a glossy sheen, unlike her daughter's short and natural do. But I could see the resemblance of daughter to mother: the shape of the face and mouth, the way the eyes were set.

"Come in, please," our hostess said, opening the storm door. "You must be that preacher?"

"Yes, I'm Aubrey Scott."

"They call you Father?"

"Some people do," Aubrey said, smiling. "You can call me Aubrey, or whatever makes you comfortable. This is Aurora Teagarden, Mrs. Mitchell." He said that with a kind of heavy significance. I could practically hear a "Ta-DAH!"

"You're the lady with the baby." Since she was holding the glass door open, we had to step past her into the living room. It was dark after the bright day outside. I could barely make out the silhouette of someone else sitting in the room.

"Yes," I said, belatedly. "Sophie's two months old."

"How is Sophie?" said the person on the couch.

It was like having a bucket of cold water thrown on my face. I adjusted to the gloom and my eyes confirmed what my ears had already told me.

In front of me, very much alive and not visibly hurt, was Virginia Mitchell.

Chapter Twenty-two

I'd had some shocks in my life, but this certainly ranked as one of the most severe. I had so many things to say to Virginia—and her mother, and Aubrey—that the words clogged up in my throat, like too many people trying to get through a doorway at the same time.

Probably just as well. I was very angry.

"Aubrey," I said. "Tell me you didn't know about this."

"I give you my word I had no idea she'd be here."

He sounded shaken, too, more than a little.

I took two steps to position myself right in front of Virginia, who stood. Maybe she wasn't sure what I was going to do. I wasn't sure, either. I took a couple of deep breaths before I spoke. "I'm relieved you're alive, Virginia. And you look like you're okay. But you should have told me earlier."

"We didn't want you to call the police," Marcy Mitchell said. "Can I get you a drink? Tea? Sweet or unsweet?"

This was just *nuts*. I closed my eyes and took another

moment. When I opened them, all three were staring at me hopefully.

"You realize that my husband and I are under suspicion for having killed Tracy Beal? And possibly you?" I asked Virginia directly. Her eyes shifted away. *Not* looking at me directly.

"I'm really sorry," Virginia said, and she did sound as if she regretted it. But she didn't continue, *I'm going to explain all of that to the police as soon as I clear up a few things.*

"Tell me what happened," I said. Even to my own ears, I sounded angry.

"Please sit," Marcy said. "We'll just talk about it. Virginia's been so upset. You'll understand."

I very much doubted that.

But *okay.*

I sat in a very uncomfortable chair, clearly the one an unlucky family member got when all the others had been taken. It was a church chair, the folding metal kind. Aubrey was enveloped by an ancient recliner. Marcy perched by Virginia on the rusty-brown couch.

Marcy repeated her offer of a drink. She was determined to observe the ritual of courtesy, no matter how grotesque it seemed in this context. After Aubrey accepted a glass of unsweet, Marcy relaxed. This meeting had turned into something she could handle.

I was too furious with the Mitchells to want anything of theirs.

Once Aubrey had his damn tea, I raised my hand, palm up. "Let's hear it," I said.

"Before I even start telling you, I don't know the whole story," Virginia said. "I don't know who killed that girl."

"Um-hum. Talk."

Virginia sighed, and looked as though she wished she were miles away. "You were so sick, and Sophie was sound asleep, so I called my ex-boyfriend."

"Is his name Harrison?" Amina had said it was a movie-star name.

"Ford Harrison," Virginia said, looking at me with some surprise.

I nodded. "Okay. What happened then?"

"Ford had called me the night before to say he was sorry for the burglary, for about the millionth time. Ford got arrested a few months ago." She looked at me questioningly.

"Yeah," I said. "I heard something about that."

"I hadn't seen him in months. When he called, I told him what I thought of his behavior," she said proudly. She was no pushover, she wanted us to know. "But we talked, and we talked. The next night, I thought I'd call him back. He sounded really sorry. I just . . . missed him."

Her mother scowled. I felt I knew the whole backstory from that one expression.

But I had to hear the rest.

"I had put up bail for him," Virginia said, her back stiff, not meeting our eyes. "He did something wrong, I know, but it wasn't violent or . . . I thought he could be an all right man. Everyone makes mistakes."

"Naturally." I tried to keep the sarcasm out of my voice. I didn't succeed.

"So Saturday night we had another long talk. But I kept the monitor with me! So I could take care of Sophie. And you."

I gave a jerky nod, acknowledging her words.

"The house was kind of still and muggy. I went in and out

of the patio door a few times. I could tell a storm was blowing up. The wind and the change in the air. Getting out felt good."

"You left the patio door unlocked," I said.

"I left it unlocked." She hung her head. "And I'd run out the front door to my car to grab my phone charger, and Ford pulled up just then, so I stood outside talking to him."

"Oh, *Virginia,*" her mother whispered, shaking her head.

Virginia shot Marcy a furious look.

"Let's set that aside for the moment, shall we?" I said, making myself sound reasonable by a huge effort of will. "Please finish your story."

"I got the charger out of my car, and I came back to the doorstep. So the monitor would pick up any sound Sophie made." *See? I was responsible.*

That made me feel so much better. I bit the inside of my mouth so I wouldn't snarl at her.

"Ford was really upset about something that had just happened at a party. Maybe we were on the doorstep a little longer than I thought. That woman must have come in through the patio door then," Virginia went on.

Don't tell me again you had the damn monitor, I thought. "And?" I was clean out of patience.

"After Ford left, I went back inside. I saw this woman coming into the living room from your husband's office. She was wearing Robin's old sweater. For a minute, I thought it was you. I said, 'Aurora? What are you doing out of bed?' She kind of yelped, like I'd scared her, and she ran at me." Virginia shuddered. "She knocked me down onto the carpet and then she ran out the back door."

I could see from her face how frightened she'd been. "Wait,"

I said, what she'd told us just registering. "She was wearing Robin's sweater?"

Virginia nodded.

A minor puzzle had been solved. Now I knew where the sweater had gone. But Tracy had not been wearing it when we'd found her. One puzzle had been replaced by another. I made a go-ahead gesture.

"I guess it took me a little bit to get up, kind of check myself out, make sure I was okay. I hightailed it to Sophie's room. Really quiet, because I didn't know who else might be in the house. For all I knew, there was someone else. After I found out Sophie was okay, I prayed for a second." Virginia said this quite unselfconsciously. "Then I went in your room, and I could hear you breathing. You sounded awful, but normal-awful, you know? I could feel the heat coming from you, and I knew you had fever. I sat down on that chair in the corner of your room and I tried to get myself together. I didn't know what to do."

How could she *possibly* have not known what to do? My hands were clenched in front of me. I was holding myself down.

"I was about to call the police. But of a sudden I thought, *Oh shit, what if she comes back in?* Because the patio door and the front door were still unlocked. So I sort of crept out to the living room window. And I saw her on the ground. At least, I thought it was her." Virginia gulped. "So I went out there. I used the flashlight on my phone. I didn't go close. Even from a ways, I could see she'd been bleeding from the head. And she wasn't moving. I'd never seen a dead person who wasn't fixed up and in a coffin." Virginia began to cry, and her mother put an arm around her.

"So I called Ford," Virginia sobbed.

Sure. That was the first thing that had leapt to my mind, too.

Call Ford. "When you went to look at the body, did you notice whether or not she was still wearing the sweater?"

Virginia looked startled. "No, I never thought about it. Wasn't she?"

I said, "Not important. Then what happened?"

"I told Ford I was going to call the police, but he begged me not to. Someone might have seen him. He said they'd think he'd done it, because he had a record. He didn't want anyone to know he'd been in Lawrenceton, because . . . well, because. Also, whoever had done it, that person might still be around. Ford wanted me to get out of there. He hadn't gotten to his apartment, he was turning around to come back. He said to turn off the front light and wait outside. I put the monitor by your head so you'd wake up if Sophie cried. And I dropped my phone into my purse. Then I thought, *I can't leave the doors unlocked,* so I grabbed Robin's keys from the bowl to lock you in."

That actually made sense. The patio door could be locked from the inside, but the front door, once exited, required a key.

"Ford told me I should leave my car. That would show I didn't have anything to do with what happened. He wanted to see the body, see if he knew her. So I told him to go through the gate. He came back around and told me we needed to get out of there. But I was so flustered, and I was in such a hurry to get away . . ." Virginia came to a full stop.

Aubrey said, "What am I missing, here?"

"She took her purse but her phone wasn't in it," I said. "She'd dropped her phone in my purse."

"I didn't find out until I got to Ford's. He was really upset."

"Because the calls to him were on your phone," I said.

Virginia looked as though she would have liked to protest, but she really couldn't. "I guess so," she said.

"So tell me," I said. "Is Ford tall and thin?"

"Yes," she said, looking at me oddly.

"And he came through the gate very late at night?"

"Yes."

"Our neighbor told the police he'd seen Robin coming in the gate."

Marcy said, "I'm so sorry."

I gave her a look I thought might very well be steely. Her words were simply inadequate.

"But she's told you what happened, and she didn't have anything to do with that girl. You're going to tell the police?" Marcy said anxiously.

Even Aubrey looked astonished that she'd think anything else.

"Yes, I am," I said. "As quick as I can."

And a tall, thin man stepped in from the kitchen and said, "I can't let you do that."

The two women gasped. They seemed genuinely shocked by his appearance.

"I know you," I said. "You're Arnie's assistant." A lot of things dropped into place. "So you took our keys out of Virginia's purse and went into our house. Looking for the phone. Because you didn't know the police already had it."

Even Virginia's jaw dropped. I believed, in that moment, that she hadn't known about her boyfriend's latest actions.

"Ford, you didn't tell me you were going to . . ." She faltered to a stop.

"And I'm betting you're the guy who stole my diaper bag from the ICU room," I said remorselessly.

Marcy gave a muted shriek. "Ford! Why?"

"I had to get that phone back," he said. "I had to. I can't go back to jail again."

"Why would you?" Aubrey asked, the voice of reason. "At the most, when Virginia told you she'd found the body, all you did was help her out in a bad situation. You might get charged with not reporting a death. I can't think of anything else."

Ford looked sullen, as if we were taking his drama away from him. "I've been in jail," he said.

"You stole some *tools,*" I said. "You think that's the big time in the criminal world?"

He didn't seem to appreciate my sarcasm. "Tools aren't a big deal," he said. "But there was something the guy who owned the shed didn't report."

One part of my mind was paying attention to the conversation, while the other was wondering how could anyone have mistaken Ford Harrison for Robin. He was tall and thin, so maybe his silhouette was similar. And at night, the darker cast of his skin might not be apparent. But Ford had a little goatee, close-clipped hair, and his arms were brawny and tattooed. His face was wider than Robin's, his neck longer.

Stupid Jonathan Cohen.

"You used those keys again?" Virginia said. If I had to describe her expression, it would be "bewildered." "You tried to steal Aurora's purse? You went in her house?"

"I tried to look around while I was helping Arnie. But that Robin caught me. And the next day, the security system would be done, and they'd arm it. So I had to get back in," Ford said. Virginia's ex-boyfriend was looking angrier by the minute. Abruptly, I realized we should rein in the blaming. We didn't need to emphasize the man's stupidity.

Ford didn't seem to have a gun, or at least it wasn't visible—but he might have another weapon. Any minute he was going to make a decision as to how he'd proceed.

"Why'd you call these people, Marcy?" He glared at Virginia's mother. "You're always against me. Always telling Virgie how bad I am."

I looked down so he wouldn't see my face.

"I didn't call them," Marcy said, more calmly than I would have managed. "The minister here, he called me. He thought I'd be grieving because I didn't know where my daughter was. He wanted to help. I thought maybe if Virginia explained . . ."

"You've known all along where Virginia was?" I could not help myself. I had to know.

"He brought her straight to my house because he has roommates in his apartment and he knew they couldn't keep quiet about it. So she's been hiding here since then. It's been hard to keep the neighbors out. They all wanted to sympathize."

All those police spending all those hours looking for Virginia, when she'd been here with her mother all along. I risked looking at Aubrey directly. He wasn't overtly frightened, but he was very alert. He understood this was a bad situation. I couldn't see it ending well for all of us.

I thought, *None of them have a plan, either.* I assumed Marcy had wanted me to hear her daughter's side, so I wouldn't be angry with Virginia for abandoning us. (It hadn't worked, by the way.) Virginia had wanted to tell her story because she felt guilty, and because she knew she'd done a stupid thing by not calling the police immediately.

Ford Harrison was faced with a situation he couldn't see a way out of; I could tell from his face that the man simply didn't know what to do next.

Would he stop us if we tried to go? Would he hurt us? I couldn't even guess.

"Who do you think killed Tracy Beal?" I asked Virginia directly. "I guess you read the newspaper stories, and you know she was a stalker."

"It wasn't me," Virginia said. "And it wasn't Ford, because I watched him drive away before I saw her in the house."

"That's all I care about," I said, lying outright. "I understand why you left, and why you took Robin's keys, and even why Ford wanted to get my purse back any way he could." I hoped my nose wasn't growing longer by the second. "I just want to know who killed Tracy."

After all, how many people could have been prowling around our yard in the dark with a storm approaching? I had a sudden, simple association of ideas, but this wasn't the time to pursue it. I had to get out of this impasse first.

"Ford, are you going to let us walk out of here?" I said. I stood to go, and Aubrey stood with me. I had no idea what he was thinking, but at least he wasn't putting a spoke in my wheels. "You know this story has to be told. You know there's no way around it." I nodded at Aubrey. "We both have families. They know where we are. They'll miss us."

Ford looked baffled. He hadn't thought this through when he'd come in Virginia's mom's back door. Maybe he was realizing that if he'd stayed out of it, this moment would have been much easier for everyone, including him. Virginia had explained her boyfriend's actions much better than he could, though there seemed to be something he hadn't yet told us. Ford shook his head like a bull pestered by a fly. "You'd better not tell the cops," he said. But his threat was empty and pointless.

To make the moment absolutely excruciating, Virginia began

crying. My nerves frayed a bit more. My unsettled hormones set up a dance in my system, and my anger grew to explosive levels. I could barely hold myself in check.

I'd thought we were possibly going to leave without any further trouble, but the sound of Virginia's sobs triggered something in Ford.

"It's your fault coming here," he said with real anger in his voice, and he lunged at Aubrey, who was totally unprepared. Ford's fist drew back to punch Aubrey in the head, and I just *snapped.* Before I could think, I leaped into the air and crashed into Ford and hit him upside his head with all the force I could muster.

He staggered sideways, tripped on an ottoman, and banged his head on the arm of a rocking chair as he went down.

I fared better. I staggered forward, but I was able to catch myself before I hit the floor.

"You killed him!" shrieked Virginia, as Aubrey pulled out his phone and dialed 911.

I almost said, *I hope so.* But that wasn't true . . . well, not completely.

Chapter Twenty-three

The police had been parked outside the whole time. After studying Virginia's phone, they'd concluded that it was obvious her ex-boyfriend knew what had happened that night. He hadn't been at his apartment, so they'd staked out the Mitchell house. They didn't know Virginia was there, but they figured it was likely Ford would at least stop in.

So they were inside in seconds after Aubrey's call.

At least I got to talk to some different police.

It was a confusing hour.

Aubrey and I tried to explain why we were at Marcy Mitchell's house. I tried to explain why I had hit Ford. Marcy tried to explain why she had consented to our visit. Virginia tried to tell the police that Ford wasn't guilty of any wrongdoing. When they begged to differ, she behaved as though he was being dragged off to be burned at the stake, when in fact he was being taken to the nearest hospital to have a head X-ray.

Ford had come to right away, if he'd ever really been knocked out. He was highly indignant while he told the Truman police how I'd attacked him.

The largest cop started laughing.

"You're really going to claim she knocked you out?" Officer Dale Finch said, when he could talk. He was a big, bluff man with a weathered face and thinning sandy hair. If you'd seen an entry for "cop" in a dictionary, Finch's picture would have been right beside it.

Ford glowered down at me from his six foot plus. "She did, man."

I looked up at him from my five foot minus. It worked.

Marcy and Virginia told Officer Finch that Ford had taken the first swing. I wasn't surprised at Marcy's testimony, but Virginia agreeing . . . that startled me.

Not that I was going to object.

The small living room grew so crowded that Finch gestured Aubrey and me outside. Another officer joined us.

Finch and his partner had been asked to watch Marcy's house by the Lawrenceton police, and they were quick to call SPACOLEC to say they had Ford in custody. "And you can call off the search for Virginia Mitchell. She's sitting in her mother's house, crying," Finch added. When he'd finished the conversation, Finch wore a different face. There was no humor in it whatsoever.

"Your Detective Suit will be here in fifteen, twenty, minutes," he said.

Ford was taken to the hospital in handcuffs, Virginia trailing behind him as far as the car, still weeping. Marcy came out to ask the police if they wanted some sweet tea.

Then Robin's car pulled to the curb, and he jumped out. There was no romantic rush across the yard to draw me into his arms, because he had to extricate Sophie from her car seat. She was bawling at gale force.

I felt that strange prickling in my chest, triggered by her wail. *Just like Pavlov's dog,* I thought. Officer Finch was surprised to see a man holding a screaming infant hurrying up from the curb. The policeman held up his hand in the universal "stop" gesture.

"I have the baby," Robin said, apparently thinking that was explanation enough. "It's feeding time."

Damp spots appeared on the front of my red T-shirt.

Officer Finch turned bright red and tried to keep his eyes above my neck.

"You go sit in the car and take care of that little baby, ma'am," Finch said.

"Thanks." I didn't waste any time.

Within seconds, Robin and I were sitting in the front seat, I had a receiving blanket covering the action, and both Sophie and I were very relieved. "That feels *so* much better," I said. I now carried only one rock on my chest instead of two.

"I got worried when I didn't hear from you, and then Phillip came home and said someone had told him Virginia had been found, on Instagram. How do they do it? I knew where you were going, so I came here as fast as I could. Tell me about it."

So I did.

Robin made appropriate noises of amazement, horror, and admiration. But when I was finished, he said, "Never again. Roe, you were in danger. I blame Aubrey, you bet I do, because he brought you over here. But why the hell didn't you hit 911 the minute you saw her sitting on the couch?"

Because it had not occurred to me. I'd wanted to hear her story. After a moment of silence, I admitted that.

"Okay, I can understand that you were blindsided by the shock. But you *hit him*."

"I had to jump high to do it, too," I said, with what I felt was pardonable pride. "I hung air. Is that the right usage?"

Robin nodded, with the air of a man who was keeping a rein on himself by the narrowest of margins.

With a sigh of relief, I switched Sophie to the other breast. Her eyes closed, she resumed her favorite activity. She was still enthusiastic, but she was slowing down.

"Honey, you were in real danger." Robin was using the level, reasonable voice that indicated he was really upset. "What would have happened if he'd had a gun or a knife?"

"If he'd had a gun or a knife, he'd have threatened us with it right away," I said. "I'm not a total idiot. But I just lost it. When he was going to sock Aubrey, I thought, *He's not getting to be the boss of this situation.* And before I knew it, I jumped and I really, really hit him. It felt great. Emotionally, that is. I think my hand is going to be real sore tomorrow."

"I love you," Robin said, and I looked up from Sophie's intent little face to meet his bright blue eyes.

My little shell of bravado cracked and fell apart. "I love you, too," I said.

"If you're ever in danger again, please think twice," he said, in such an earnest voice that I almost cried. "This won't be funny, to me or Sophie, if something happens to you."

"I don't want anything to happen to me, but somehow stuff always does," I said. "I got so angry. With people blaming us somehow because Tracy died in our yard. With people thinking somehow we were implicated. And she took your sweater!"

Robin looked startled. "But clearly, I couldn't have done it."

I nodded. "I know that, and you know that, and the police

know that. But people were talking. I couldn't stand them thinking wrong things about you, I've really wanted to hit someone for days. Finally, there was someone who needed to be hit."

This time his mouth crinkled up at the corners. "But not again," he reminded me. "I suppose the rumors were triggered by Jonathan Cohen saying he saw me that night? I must be a criminal mastermind and able to warp time."

"Yes, it's ridiculous. But the person who did kill Tracy must not have been far when she was found. Think about it. Within minutes, the yard was empty except for the body. Without your sweater. And Virginia didn't see or hear anyone, at least that's what she said."

"What are the odds that we'd have two prowlers on the same night?" Robin said slowly.

"Even for someone with my luck, that's simply unbelievable."

"You're saying that the murderer must live close."

Sophie's mouth had fallen open to release me, and she was out cold. I slid her into an upright position and began patting her on the back. Almost immediately she gave one of her huge burps. Her eyes fluttered open for a second, but she could not manage to stay awake. All that wailing had worn her out.

I knew how she felt. My rush of adrenaline had receded, leaving me feeling almost supernaturally calm and drained. Well, these days, I was used to feeling drained.

"What do you think really happened?" Robin said.

"I'm working it out in my head. I'm not trying to be mysterious, but there's a thread of an idea tugging at me. Virginia sounds innocent to me. If she caught Tracy in the house and Tracy threatened her, Virginia would defend herself, I guess. But she wouldn't chase Tracy out in the yard and bash her over the head. Not her house, not her yard . . . not her baby."

"No," Robin said absently. "She wouldn't do that. And Ford, whatever else he may have done, is in the clear, too. He left—the first time—before Virginia encountered Tracy."

We looked at each other thoughtfully.

Finally, I smiled. "So Virginia wasn't murdered, Ford was the tall thin guy who went in our backyard, and it's good to know those things. I can't figure out anything else until the dust settles in my brain."

He smiled back. "Think we can go home now? I left Phillip to answer the phone, but he's pretty worried about you."

"I'll ask Officer Finch."

The Lawrenceton police force, in the form of Detective Suit and Detective Trumble, had arrived. They were on the lawn talking to Finch. Their eyes swiveled toward me as I approached.

"How's the hand, Roe?" Levon was trying to suppress a smile. He seemed quietly jubilant.

"I'd like to go home and put some ice on it. Can we leave?"

"We'll come by to talk to you tomorrow," Cathy said. She looked oddly wired—very tense, but with an undertone of the same muted elation. "We got a call from Rick Morrison, whose toolshed got broken into . . . the break-in Ford Harrison was arrested for, the one he was out on bail for." She grinned, and it was terrifying. "Turns out Ford had spotted the lock was easy to break while he was installing Rick's security system. Do you know what else was in the shed, an item Rick maintains he had completely forgotten until the shootings?"

"No," I said. My brain was not exactly working at top speed.

"A rifle," Cathy said. "Almost surely the rifle we recovered from my nephew at the scene of the hospital shootings."

I gaped at her. "No wonder Ford didn't want Virginia to call the police," I said. "That was the night of the party shooting, right? He must have suspected the rifle he'd sold to your nephew was the rifle used."

"I am going to nail his ass to the wall," Cathy said. "Tell me the truth. Did you know Virginia was here when you came here with Father Scott?"

"Absolutely not. Aubrey brought me here for some kind of mercy visit." I glanced over at my priest, who was standing in the doorway talking to Marcy Mitchell. He had certainly gotten more than he'd bargained for. "I was glad to see she was alive, but I was mad, too, because everyone was looking for her," I said. That was a condensation of my feelings about Virginia. I felt she'd done her best to shield Sophie and me under the circumstances, but then I'd veer into exasperation at her poor choice of male friend, at her letting him talk her into doing dumb things.

"Virginia tells us she doesn't know who killed the Beal woman," Levon said.

"It would sure be nice if she did," I said.

They both nodded. "Well, if I can go, Robin and I are headed home."

Aubrey intercepted me on my way to the car. Robin, who'd been buckling Sophie in her car seat, glared at Aubrey's back.

"The last rites for Tracy Beal will be tomorrow at Memorial Funeral Home, in Anders." He looked at me expectantly.

"Aubrey, you don't really expect me to go?" I was incredulous. "That would be bizarre. And inappropriate."

Aubrey looked disconcerted. Then he said, "I understand. I got carried away with my own interior quest."

I raised my eyebrows inquiringly.

"My constant attempt to forgive the people who hurt Liza.

You got the side effect of my overzealousness. I'm sorry bringing you here today turned out to be such a . . ." He stopped, at a loss for words about what the incident had become.

"Revelation," I suggested. "Ordeal. Fiasco. Take your pick. I know you had a good motive, Aubrey. But it sure backfired pretty spectacularly."

"Again, I'm really sorry—"

I rolled right over him. I felt entitled. "I know you couldn't have foreseen Virginia would be safe and sound in her mother's house, or that she would want to get everything off her conscience. It's a step forward, knowing she's safe."

Aubrey looked relieved, but I didn't want to talk to him any more. Once again, I started toward Robin's car. This time, Finch intercepted me, with Levon and Cathy trailing him. What now?

"Have you heard from the hospital?" I asked. "I guess I didn't crack Ford's skull with my mighty blow?"

"You did not cause any permanent damage," Finch told me, with a straight face. "I'm going to talk to the guys sharing his apartment, and your Lawrenceton cop buddies are coming with me."

"Will Virginia be charged with anything?" But the law enforcement personnel of Georgia had reached an end of tolerance with me.

"We'll let you know when we need to," Cathy said, her face all squinched up and disapproving.

I'd clearly been put in my place, which didn't bother me at all. At last I got to walk away without anyone stopping me. We drove out of Truman, half-expecting someone to come after us.

Robin said, very slowly, "Tracy always knew where I was going to be, before. If the e-mails I got, the strange ones, were from her, she had access to the Internet. If she had access to the

Internet, she'd know we'd gotten married. And she'd know about the Anthony nomination. She could find out from the attendees list that I would be at Bouchercon."

"Why would she sneak into our house, if she knew you were going to be gone?" When I considered possible answers, every one of them was terrifying. "Maybe . . ." I faltered. "Maybe she thought she'd clear the deck while you were out of the picture? Get rid of your old wife to make way for the new . . . who would be her."

Robin focused extra hard on the road ahead of us. His mouth was set in a grim line. Finally he said, "Maybe she didn't know we'd had a baby." Robin glanced over at me.

"I didn't put a birth announcement in the paper. I figured anyone who cared about us would know about Sophie." I couldn't think of anything else to say. There were too many things we didn't know about Tracy's visit. We were lost in our own thoughts until Robin parked in our driveway.

Phillip threw open the door of his room when we carried Sophie into the house.

"So what's happened?" he said. "Where's Virginia? She okay?"

I told him the whole story. Phillip was delighted I'd hit a man. "You go, Sis," he said, giving me a high five.

"Don't encourage her," Robin called, as he emerged from Sophie's room empty-armed.

"Okay." Phillip laughed. "So you're all right, Virginia's not hurt, and we know how she left that night, and why. Wait. Why?"

"Her boyfriend, this Ford Harrison, had been in jail for something pretty minor," I began. "And he came here to talk to Virginia, his former girlfriend. He wanted her to come back to him. When Virginia found Tracy's body, Ford believed if he came to police attention they'd somehow find out that a rifle was in with the tools he'd stolen—which they did. Not magically, but because the toolshed owner has a conscience."

"And?" Phillip was impatient. "So what?"

"They really wanted to find out who'd sold a rifle to an underage kid like Duncan."

"Wow," Phillip said. "He didn't steal it from his dad after all. This Ford guy sold it to him?"

"Apparently. So Ford absolutely didn't want to come to the attention of the cops."

Phillip shook his head. "Stupid thinking."

"I agree. He got Virginia in a world of trouble because he was selfish."

"All right," Phillip said, dismissing Virginia and her problems. "So I'm thinking I can have Sarah over tomorrow night? And maybe Josh and Holly Maxwell? And Joss and Kay Duval?"

"If their parents are all okay with them coming over here," I said. "We're not completely free of this situation. Tracy's murderer hasn't been caught. Not that I think he'll come back or anything, but still."

Phillip nodded.

"And you have to go to the store for whatever food and drinks you want, Phillip. I'm running on empty, as far as energy goes. I'm going to rummage in the refrigerator for our supper."

My brother retreated to his room to make his plans, and Robin and I repaired to the kitchen. I searched the refrigerator while Robin went through our mail and checked the messages on his phone. I felt victorious when I unearthed a chicken and rice casserole that wasn't too old. It would be perfect for tonight. Problem solved.

I went to sit at the island with Robin. I picked up my current book, but I put it down again.

"What's on your mind?" Robin put down his phone and turned to me.

"I read an article or two about stalking, after my first encounter with Tracy. That doesn't mean I'm an expert." I hesitated. "But from what I learned about different kinds of stalkers . . ." To my surprise, I began crying. "When I saw Tracy on the nanny cam . . . in Sophie's room . . . I was glad she died. I wanted to kill her myself. But you know . . . she *didn't do anything*. She could have killed me or Sophie, or both of us. I was too weak to put up much of a fight. I would have expected her to hurt us, considering the last time she confronted me. And she didn't."

Robin put his arms around me and I laid my head on his shoulder. "I've thought about that every day," he said. "Every hour."

"I *will not* be grateful to Tracy because she didn't kill us. That's crazy."

"But we have to acknowledge Tracy had had the opportunity to commit terrible acts, and she didn't take it."

I nodded against his shoulder. "I think I know why. At least, to me this is a credible reason. She couldn't harm your child. And Sophie is so much yours. The red hair."

In quick succession, Robin looked startled, appalled, and pleased. "But the light was out in the nursery," he objected. "How'd Tracy see it?"

"The turtle night-light. There's just enough light to see Sophie's hair color. I think about it every time I go in there at night."

"Then I protected Sophie after all," my husband said.

I nodded. After a moment, I said, "Aubrey told me Tracy's funeral service is tomorrow afternoon."

"Maybe after that her mother and sister can get back to their lives," Robin said, but not as if he was really thinking about it.

I wondered if there'd be many people there. I wondered if Tracy had had normal friendships. I wondered if she'd ever held down a regular job.

It was simply weird that at that moment Robin got a call from Cathy Trumble. The conversation started off amiably enough, but Robin suddenly exploded. "You want me to do *what*?" He listened. "No, absolutely not," he said. This was a voice I'd seldom heard, and it had never been directed at me.

It seemed like a good time to start heating up supper. Behind me, I heard Robin say, "I don't see how talking to reporters would make a bit of difference. I don't have any special knowledge about this. The only relationship I have to Tracy's death is that it happened in my backyard. You don't understand how this whole situation makes me feel. The idea is ridiculous." And Robin hung up. Wow. I decided to go hang out in our room for a few minutes. After all, it was time to pluck my eyebrows.

It wasn't that I was worried about being in the same room with Robin, far from it. But he had just boiled over, and he needed a minute to settle himself.

Five minutes later, Robin came in the bathroom still fuming. "Cathy wants me to have a press conference to talk about Tracy getting killed here," he said.

I'd guessed right. "Why?" I tried to sound neutral.

"She thinks that will bring someone out of the woodwork, someone who knows where Tracy was between escaping and dying here. Maybe knows of some enemy Tracy had."

"That just sounds dumb," I said. "If she wants to know who

Tracy might have turned to, she should film the funeral tomorrow. Someone might pop up there."

"Good idea," he said slowly. "I'll suggest it." He pulled his cell phone out of his pocket. As he wandered out of the room, I could hear the phone ring over at SPACOLEC. I sighed when I heard Sophie stirring. My heart sank a little. I'd hoped she'd sleep an hour longer.

As I lifted her from the crib, I reminded myself that in another month she would not need to feed nearly as often, she might even consistently sleep through the night, and I'd probably miss that unique alone time with my daughter. Maybe.

"Sophie, your daddy is so smart," I said to our daughter as I cleaned her little bottom before putting on a dry diaper. "And he listens to me, too. Marry a person who listens to you, my little bunny."

Sophie looked up at me solemnly, and I was sure she agreed.

Chapter Twenty-four

Overnight, the season changed for good. The temperature dropped, starting early on Saturday night. We turned on the heat, though it didn't run much. In happy anticipation of her first winter, I got out one of Sophie's many blankets, and gloated over the adorable white hat with mouse ears my mother had given her for just such weather.

Since I was thinking of my mother, I called her to check in. They'd stayed home from church, too. Mother didn't want John to be exposed to germs, during his recuperation.

Since John was doing so well, Mother seemed much more like herself. I remembered to tell her about our Thanksgiving plans, and she said Robin's entire family should come over the night before for a drink and (considering the many children) a buffet supper. This was a generous offer, and I said as much. "But let's just wait and see how John's feeling by then," I suggested. "Not set anything in stone."

"Subject to change, of course. But he should be just fine in two months." There was no doubt in Mother's voice.

I ended the call feeling cheerful and optimistic.

"All we have to do is find out who killed Tracy, and we'll be right as rain," I told Sophie as I changed her diaper.

"Did Sophie answer you?" Robin called from our room.

"Just about to, when you scared her off," I called back. "You have to creep up to hear her. She'll only talk if she thinks nobody else's listening."

Phillip slept until nine, when he bounded from his room to tell us he was going to run a mile and then head over to Josh's. It was a gray day, so I checked to make sure he was wearing his fluorescent yellow. (He was.) I started to ask him to let me know when he got to Josh's, but I stopped myself just in time.

"When I get home, can you take me to the store?" he asked. "To get the snacks for tonight?"

"One of us will," I promised. "You know tomorrow's a school day, so they can't stay late?"

"Define 'late.'"

"Out by ten thirty."

He nodded, with the air of someone who is humoring an ancient elder. After stretching, he was off.

Robin was trying to catch up on his work, which had been sadly neglected this week. His word count was low, he had explained, and if he didn't catch up, he'd be behind the rest of the way. Like many (though not all) writers, Robin was very particular about turning in his manuscript on time and in good shape.

When the clouds cleared away, the sun shone in a promising way. I carried Sophie outside wrapped in a blanket, wearing her mouse hat. Before I could take her and her carrier out the door, Robin took a few pictures to send to Mother (and several other people).

After all, there had never been a baby so cute.

Deborah was in her backyard covering a bush, since it might get down to freezing tonight. I had to resist an impulse to stick my tongue out at her. I took the high road, and gave her a neighborly smile, which she returned a bit stiffly. At least Lulu was not outside barking.

Chaka was making the circuit of his yard, running close to the fence. When Peggy popped out of her back door to say hello, Chaka came to her side immediately. "Good boy," she said. She looked over at me. "I hear you had an exciting day yesterday," she called, strolling over to the fence.

"Turned out to be pretty interesting," I said. I told Peggy about the visit to Mrs. Mitchell's house.

"So the girl was okay and safe," Peggy said.

"Yes. Best possible ending."

"And I heard Susan Crawford's out of the hospital. How's this little lady?" She smiled at the baby.

I told her more than she (probably) wanted to know about Sophie, and Peggy admired the mouse hat extravagantly. I'd been leaning against the fence, my elbows propped in a comfortable way, while Sophie sat in her carrier on the ground looking through the fence at Chaka.

I told Peggy I had to get in, and turned to pick up Sophie's carrier. I remembered how Chaka had cleared the fence the week before. She hadn't witnessed it.

And an idea flashed through my head. I froze with my right hand extended to the patio door. I thought of Deborah and Jonathan and Lulu, and Peggy and Lena and Chaka. And my brain connected several dots, finally.

Finally, the weight of Sophie and the carrier on my left arm broke my reverie, and I opened the door. Robin was putting ice in a glass of ginger ale. "Hey, Roe, do you think Sophie could taste chocolate milk?" he said. "Maybe we can make hot chocolate tonight, and just dip a little into a spoon or something when it cools. . . ." He turned to face me. "Honey?" he said.

"Wait," I said, putting the carrier on the coffee table and collapsing onto the couch. "I've almost got it."

I have to give my husband credit for his patience. He stayed quiet while I kept turning over my ideas one after another, testing them for credulity. While I thought, he took Sophie from me. "Who's my little mouse? Is Sophie my little mouse?" He didn't mind talking to her in a weird high voice if I was the only one around.

Normally, my heart melted to hear Robin talk to Sophie like the narrator of a children's show, but today it was business as usual.

"Okay," I said, taking a deep breath. "Here's what I think."

He waited.

I went over it with him, point by point, to see if my theory held true.

Robin poked and prodded at my explanation for Tracy's death. But he never said it was silly, or dumb, or anything but clever.

"How are we going to test this?" he said.

"I was hoping you would help me on that."

"Of course," my husband said.

Chapter Twenty-five

I had asked Levon to come by after Tracy's funeral, and he had agreed to bring a recording of the service. I got the feeling Levon was trying to build a bridge to our former friendship. That would be great, but it wasn't my primary goal at the moment.

Phillip was home, having gone to the store with Josh (and some of my money). He'd returned laden with bags, as though the six teenagers were going to be an army. I hadn't wanted to tell him what I had planned, but I realized he'd never forgive me if I didn't.

"Cool," Phillip said. "What can I do?"

That was a touchy point. Phillip had no intention of being left out, and he was too mature to treat like a child. On the other hand, it wasn't responsible to involve a teenager in proceedings of life and death without a life-or-death reason.

Robin came to my aid. "You have to get Levon over to the window," Robin said. "He can't look away."

Robin insisted on playing the role most likely to get him

hurt. "You've already had enough illness, and you're the one who's been in danger," he said. "It's my turn."

Finally, I nodded.

Levon arrived at three o'clock.

Somehow, we sat through the video of the funeral, which managed to be both sad and boring. We noticed nothing of any value. None of the attendees were familiar. But we watched it dutifully, and Levon thanked us.

Phillip, over by the picture window, said, "Yo."

"Levon," I said. "Come watch something."

"What?" he said. He was suspicious.

"Oh, come on," I said, losing my patience. "Do you have a fire to go to?"

Luckily for me, he thought that was funny, and he gave a surprised little bark of laughter. "Okay," he said. "Let's see what you got."

The extension that was Robin's office cut off our view of the Cohens' yard. But we could see the Hermans'. At around three thirty every day, Peggy let Chaka out for his afternoon run and poop. Today proved to be no exception. Chaka was doing his silent circuit around the perimeter, trotting briskly, having completed his mission. As she nearly always did, Peggy came out to toss a ball for him. Chaka abandoned his fence patrol and ran to greet her, his tail wagging. Robin was outside already, pretending to do something to the lawn chair on the patio.

"What are you up to?" Levon said. He sounded serious, all of a sudden.

I was as tense as a violin string. "Just watch," I said.

As I spoke, Robin dropped the chair with an attention-grabbing clang.

He began to run toward the Herman fence.

Peggy shrieked, "No, *no*!"

But it was too late. Chaka was over the fence in one beautiful leap, and he went straight for Robin, who was brave enough to keep his charge going. (At least he wore a long-sleeved shirt and a heavy jacket.) With a leap reminiscent of my attack on Ford Harrison, Chaka launched himself in the air, grabbed Robin by the arm, and brought him down.

This next moment was the scary one. But Chaka, true to his training, simply stood, his formidable teeth fixed in Robin's sleeve. Robin did not struggle, but lay on the ground holding very still—right under the mimosa tree.

The dog did not worry at Robin's sleeve, or snarl, or bark, or growl. He held.

Peggy vaulted over the fence herself, as I'd seen her do once before. She wasn't as effortless or graceful as her dog, but it was something I could not have done. Ever.

Robin had raised his free hand to show he was okay. Chaka ignored the gesture. Then Peggy was there, her chest heaving.

"Chaka, stand down," she ordered in a hoarse voice.

The dog obeyed immediately, releasing Robin's arm. He sat beside Peggy, ready for the next game.

Since the minute Robin had quit moving, Chaka had simply been in a holding pattern, literally.

Levon was no longer at my side. He had launched himself from the patio door, walking (not running) toward the little tableau.

"Ms. Herman," Levon said, "I'm going to tell you your rights, now." With a grim face, Levon informed Peggy of her right to remain silent.

The back door flew open and Lena ran out, stopping short as she tried to make sense of what she was seeing. "What's happening?" she asked, terrified.

Robin rose to his feet, very deliberately. He didn't want to startle the dog.

"Lena, I'm so sorry," Peggy said, and she began to cry

"What for?" Lena knew she was about to get bad news. You could tell it in her face and the hunch of her shoulders. She looked from Levon to Robin to Chaka to Peggy. Phillip, standing at my side on the patio, muttered, "Oh, Jeez."

"What's happened?" Lena demanded, when no one spoke. "Tell me."

So Peggy did. She might not have confessed to us (though I think she would have, it had clearly been weighing on her), but she felt obliged to tell her sister the truth. Peggy began to speak, haltingly at first, then more quickly.

Saturday night, the week before, Chaka had been antsy because of the approaching storm. He'd whined to go out much later than usual. Peggy, who'd been reading in bed, had gotten up to let him out. Hoping the dog would be quick about his business, Peggy stood in the open doorway, admiring the scudding clouds and the rolling thunder, when a movement caught her eye.

"Someone was in your backyard," she said, turning to me. "And she was running toward our house."

She and Lena had adopted Chaka from a Rhodesian ridgeback rescue group, who only knew that Chaka had been well trained. The Herman sisters had discovered, to their considerable surprise and dismay, that Chaka's previous work training had been as a restraint dog. Chaka came, sat, heeled, like any well-trained dog. But he also knew that when a person—or, in fact, anything—was running toward his owner, it was Chaka's job to bring down that attacker and make sure he stayed down.

"We actually thought it was a good thing," Peggy said. "It

made us feel safer. After all, if someone was attacking us . . ." She shot me a guilty look. "But we couldn't really believe someone would actually *seem* to be attacking me."

Tracy Beal had been trying to get out of our yard in the quickest possible way, to escape Virginia. But she'd been running toward his territory and his owner, so Chaka had obeyed his earliest training. He'd jumped the fence and clamped his jaws on Tracy's left arm.

Somehow, Tracy managed to stay on her feet, but the weight of the dog on her arm had forced her to crouch.

Chaka was not interested in savaging the woman he'd brought down, only in restraining her until Peggy dealt with her.

Tracy hadn't known that.

Peggy had started running to the fence. By a flash of lightning, Peggy saw that the struggling woman had raised a knife. Acting purely on instinct, Peggy seized one of Lena's new garden statues (the elf) and hurled it at Tracy Beal.

It must have been like being hit with a missile. Tracy had staggered, then gone flat on her back, her hand releasing the knife.

Since his prey wasn't resisting anymore, Chaka let go of Tracy's arm. He sat by the body, waiting for Peggy to praise him.

Peggy said she could see Tracy was dead. She told Levon, "I didn't know what to do. Chaka was innocent. I couldn't let him be killed. And it was her fault! She wasn't supposed to be in Roe's backyard. Clearly, she was up to no good."

"What did you do then?" Levon said.

Chaka looked from Peggy to Lena, perhaps hoping for a treat.

Robin held out his arm, showing me that his sleeve was marked with dog saliva.

"You pulled off the sweater she was wearing," I said.

Peggy just nodded. "I stuffed it in the bag I took to the Goodwill drop-off the next day."

Lena began crying, almost silently.

"Shit," Phillip whispered, and I could only agree.

"After that?" Levon said.

"I got the statue and threw it back into our yard. And I told Chaka to jump back over. I followed him. I took the statue inside and washed it and put it back in the urn."

She took a deep breath. "When Chaka went into Roe's yard after Moosie, I pretended I couldn't jump the fence. But I knew Roe had seen me do it before. I guess you just put it all together?" Peggy turned her gaze from Levon to me.

I could hardly bear to meet her eyes.

"Yeah," I said. "I suddenly saw the whole picture."

"And you put this together to catch me."

I nodded.

"Well, bully for you," Peggy said, with overwhelming bitterness. "I divorced my husband, my son doesn't come to visit, and what I've got are my sister and my dog. I wasn't going to let that bitch stab Chaka. A person who'd do that to a dog deserves to die."

Levon said, "I have to take you in, Ms. Herman."

"What will happen to Chaka?" Peggy asked.

"I don't know. That's not up to me, and I'm glad," Levon said. He called the station.

"You okay? If we go?" I asked Levon.

"Sure," he said. After all, he was the one with the gun.

Phillip and Robin trailed me back to the door. We watched out the window until the uniforms showed up with their siren whooping. The Cohens wouldn't like that, of course.

Levon had to pass through our house to get to his car, parked in our driveway. "I'm going to call for an ambulance for Lena," he said. "She's distraught."

"Who will take care of Chaka?" Robin said, dismayed.

"I'll come back to get him. I'll drop him off at the kennel where the Hermans have boarded him when they had to be out of town."

I was relieved. I did not want to entertain Chaka as a houseguest.

"Do you think she'll stand by her confession?" I wondered if Peggy would decide to fight.

"She might," Levon said, shrugging. "She knows she deserves to be in jail. Or maybe the shock of jail life will scare Peggy so bad she decides to recant." Levon left.

"She deserves to be there?" Phillip was outraged. "Peggy didn't set out to hurt anyone. She's not a criminal. She was trying to protect her dog. A lot of people would think she was justified."

"Not Tracy Beal's mother and sister," I said. "For starters."

Robin said, "As Levon said earlier, not my call. And I can't forget Tracy came in this house in the night intending to harm Aurora. After all, she brought a knife."

Phillip looked troubled, maybe doubtful, but after he glanced at the clock he let out a yelp and dashed for the shower. I had forgotten his friends were coming over, and it did not occur to Phillip to cancel. He'd have an amazing story to tell them.

Down the hall, Sophie began to advise us that she was lonely.

Robin said, "I'll get her."

"I won't turn that offer down," I said, and sat on the couch, arranging a throw pillow in my lap, ready to hold Sophie in the best position.

The terrible drama that had played out in our backyard

seemed almost like a dream, one that had left trouble and fear in its wake. Virginia, Ford, Marcy, Lena, Robin, Phillip, me, Peggy, even old Mr. Redding . . . we were all dislodged from the groove of our lives, from the ripple effect of that chance encounter on a dark night.

But having had that thought, I couldn't see that it changed my life in any way. It was not some deep philosophical dilemma I would ponder.

I was pretty sure I would settle back into my place in the pond of suburban life and be content. But I recognized that motherhood had changed me, for better or worse, forever.

And I was fine with that.

The next morning after Phillip had taken off for school, Arnie Petrosian showed up at our door. Like Peggy, he seemed determined to rid himself of a burden.

"I'm really sorry I brought Ford here," he said. "He was a good assistant. When the business slumped, he didn't keep asking for raises I couldn't give him. Sure, I should have fired him after the burglary at Rick Morrison's, but he hadn't been convicted yet, and I wanted to give the guy the benefit of the doubt." He'd said this all in a stream of words, so we'd had no chance to say "Hello" (or "Go away").

We looked at each other, nonplussed.

Finally, Robin said, "It's over and done, Arnie. You did bring him into our house. But after all, he had the keys Virginia left with. I think he hoped he wouldn't have to come in while we weren't here, because that was a big risk. We might return, one of our neighbors might notice, or Phillip might have walked in. I guess that's why he was rummaging around hoping to find Virginia's phone when you two were working here."

Arnie looked directly at us, and heaved a sigh of relief. "Thanks," he said. "I won't make the same mistake again. And your security system installation is free." He turned and went back to his Spartan Shield van.

"I don't know how to feel about that," I said.

"I, for one, will not vote for him in the next election," Robin told me with great dignity, and I began to laugh.

The same afternoon, Mother brought John over. He was walking slowly, but I didn't wonder if he was going to topple over at any moment. It was another gorgeous day. We all trooped into the backyard, where I gave John the crime scene tour. I felt a little squicky about it. For all I knew, Lena might be watching from her kitchen window.

"I hear they found Tracy's sister's car behind a house for sale on the street behind you," John said. "You see Lena?"

"It's like she's gone," I said. "Along with Peggy. And Chaka."

"She killed a woman to save a dog," John observed. "What do you think of that?"

"I don't know," I said. "Peggy did what her heart told her to do. I guess I'll find out how she felt about Chaka. Robin wants to get a dog."

John smiled. "You'll enjoy it," he said.

"Easier than having another baby," I muttered.

John laughed out loud. It was a good sound, and I hoped I got to hear it for years to come.

And over the baby monitor stuffed in my sweater pocket, I could hear Sophie making preliminary sounds of hunger. Back to business as usual.

Five minutes later, I was looking down at her fuzzy red head; and I began to wonder if a second one would be so very awful, after all.